RETURN TO THE LOST WORLD

First published in the UK in 2010 by Usborne Publishing Ltd., Usborne House, 83-85 Saffron Hill, London EC1N 8RT, England. www.usborne.com

Copyright © Steve Barlow and Steve Skidmore, 2010

Cover illustration by Sam Hadley.

A CIP catalogue record for this book is available from the British Library.

First published in America in 2014 AE.

PB ISBN: 9780794531751   ALB ISBN: 9781601303288

JF AMJJASOND/14 02334/4 Printed in Dongguan, Guangdong, China.

RETURN TO THE LOST WORLD

STEVE BARLOW & STEVE SKIDMORE

USBORNE

In 1933, Germany, still smarting from its defeat in the Great War, has a new leader: Adolf Hitler. Fascist governments are rising in many parts of the world, which seems once more to be heading toward global conflict. But it is also a year of marvels. Mighty ocean liners and gigantic seaplanes criss-cross the world's oceans. This is the new Scientific Age: an age of discovery, invention, adventure – and deadly danger...

1 HUNTER...

Tyrol Mountains, Austria
May 1933

The harsh cry of a peregrine falcon brought Luke Challenger's head up with a jerk. The bird was gliding high above him, dark, sleek and dangerous against the snow-whitened crags of the surrounding mountains.

With a startled "Coo!" and a clatter of wings, the pigeon that had been investigating Luke's discarded sandwich wrapper took to the air and fled across the meadow, heading for the safety of a stand of pine trees at its edge. Instantly, the falcon folded its wings and stooped, diving at breathtaking speed. Where the flightpaths of the birds intersected, there was a brief explosion of feathers. Then the falcon, flying more heavily now with the limp body of its victim clutched in its talons, rose slightly, to clear the tops of the trees, and disappeared from sight.

Luke gave an involuntary shudder.

Nick Malone's oil-smeared face peered out from a lattice of struts and tension-wires. "Someone walk on your grave?"

Luke ran a hand through his wayward blond hair. "That's what it felt like."

"Let it be a warning to you." Nick worked a lever and the elevators in the glider's wings flapped obediently. "They'll be dancing jigs and reels on it if you don't pay attention to what you're doing."

Luke's eyes gleamed and the famous spade-shaped Challenger jaw hardened into a pugnacious line. "I *am* paying attention."

Nick's only response was an impudent grin. He enjoyed needling his hot-tempered cousin. Nick's dark, curly hair, swarthy complexion and lazy smile spoke of an irrepressible good nature that irritated Luke at times, but who else would have joined him in this crazy escapade to skip school and travel halfway across a continent to enter a competition that would prove that

Luke's insane glider could fly rings around the best sailplanes in Europe? No one else was crazy enough.

A polite cough drew Luke's attention to a new arrival. A man stood gazing at his glider with an expression that combined startled wonder with tolerant amusement. "Good day, Herr Challenger."

Luke took in the man's dark, receding hair with its prominent widow's peak, the domed forehead and deep-set eyes. "Good day, Herr Messerschmitt."

"So, this is the machine Challenger Industries believes will overcome the best my country has to offer?" Willi Messerschmitt was one of Germany's top aircraft designers and a leading figure of its most famous gliding school. He would be presenting the prizes to the winners of the competition. Luke fully intended to be among them.

"This is not a Challenger Industries project, sir," he said. "I call it the *Flying Wing*. It is my own design. And my grandfather's," honesty compelled him to add. "He worked out a lot of the details…"

"So did I." Nick emerged from beneath the wing. "Nick Malone. Luke designs 'em, we build 'em, I keep 'em flying." He held out an oily hand.

Herr Messerschmitt appeared not to notice it. His gaze was fixed on Luke. "Indeed? You are very young to have created such a device."

"He designs lots of things," said Nick.

"So. But I am surprised to learn that my old friend Andrew Challenger chooses not to sponsor your invention."

Luke's eyes glinted. "My father doesn't think it will work."

"Indeed?" Messerschmitt crouched and peered under the wing. "Fascinating. Unconventional. Where is the pilot's seat?"

"No seat." Luke pointed. "I wear a harness that clips on there. When I'm in flight, I raise my legs and tuck my feet into those stirrups, which control the rudders…"

Messerschmitt raised a formidable eyebrow. "Rudders? I see no vertical control surfaces at all: this is, as you say, a flying wing. Where are the rudders?"

"Drag rudders, sir, in the wingtips. The elevators and ailerons are conventionally controlled by a joystick."

"Remarkable." Herr Messerschmitt straightened up. "An impressive achievement for one so young. How old are you, by the way? It says on your entry form that you are sixteen."

"If that's what it says," said Luke woodenly, "it must be right."

"Strange – I understood the year of your birth to be 1919, which would make you…fourteen?" Herr

Messerschmitt favored Luke with a frosty smile. "Perhaps I was misinformed."

"Perhaps you were," agreed Luke.

"I understand it was not uncommon in the recent, regrettable conflict between our great nations, for young men, both British and German, to pretend to be older than they were in order to join the armed forces."

"I believe so, sir."

"Well – I shall look forward to your display in the competition with interest." Ignoring Nick completely, Herr Messerschmitt nodded to Luke and strolled away.

"What a nice man. I wish I had a sister so I could forbid her to marry him. And what was all that 'recent regrettable conflict' nonsense?" Nick snorted. "A fine way to talk about the Great War."

Luke shrugged. "Germany lost. Since then, our government won't allow them to build real airplanes – especially warplanes: only civil aircraft, and precious few of them. I don't suppose Herr Messerschmitt likes that. I wouldn't, if I were him."

"I guess that's why they're so interested in gliders." Nick watched as Herr Messerschmitt chatted with a pilot whose glider was decorated with the Stars and Stripes. "He seemed to know a lot about you. Is he really a friend of your dad's?"

"A rival. They spy on each other all the time. I think

he was letting me know he could have me disqualified if he wanted to, for being under age."

"Why d'you suppose he hasn't?"

"Maybe he's interested in how the *Flying Wing* will perform," said Luke. His mouth twitched. "Maybe he thinks I'll kill myself."

"Don't you do that. Your dad'll have my guts for garters."

"He'll probably do that anyway, when he finds out what we've been up to. But only after he's had mine."

"Ah, if we win, it'll be worth it. And if we don't – well, it's still a ripper of an adventure."

Luke grinned at him. "That it is."

Nick twanged a last wire and wiped his hands on an oily rag. "She's ready, as far as I can tell."

"I'd hate to get to three thousand feet and find out you're wrong."

Nick gave him a lopsided grin. "When have I ever let you down?"

"Now would be a very bad time to start…"

"Challenger! *Was machen sie*?"

"Hagen!" Luke's shoulders tensed.

"Don't let him rile you, now," Nick whispered as Heinrich Hagen approached.

Hagen was the star instructor of the *Wasserkuppe*, the most famous gliding school in Germany. He had made it clear immediately upon Luke's arrival that he didn't like the English in general, and Luke in particular. He had been about to start his pilot training when the war had ended in 1918, and this disappointment had soured a personality that could never have been sunny to begin with. His head was cropped to a bristly blond stubble, more like fur than hair, and this, combined with a snub nose, prominent cheekbones and washed-out blue eyes, gave him a look of having been manufactured rather than born.

"You were talking to Herr Messerschmitt." Hagen made it sound like an accusation.

"Herr Messerschmitt was talking to me," said Luke evenly. "It would have been rude not to reply."

Hagen gave a bark of scornful laughter. "Herr Messerschmitt is a very busy man, he has no time to make idle chit-chat with little boys. What could he possibly have had to say to you?"

"You should ask him – if you know him well enough." From Hagen's sudden flush, Luke saw that this shot had hit home. "Actually, he was interested in my glider."

"You English!" Hagen's voice was low and vicious. "So arrogant! You deny Germany a proper aircraft industry and force us to fly kiddy toys." He cast a disgusted glance around the various brightly colored gliders littering the field. "And even in this, with the

Challenger fortune behind you, you seek to overmatch us. But beware, English." The German pilot's voice sank even lower. "A new day is coming. Herr Hitler is our leader now. He will build a new Germany: a strong Germany that will no longer take orders from Britain or her allies. Then Herr Messerschmitt will make me a proper aircraft with a propeller and machine guns – and on that day, little boy, I will come looking for you."

"And on that day, Challenger Industries will build me a similar aircraft," said Luke woodenly, "and what then?"

"Then we shall meet." Hagen pointed skywards. "Up there."

"I shall look forward to that day."

"It may come sooner than you think." Hagen faced Luke eyeball to eyeball for several seconds. Then he spat on the ground at Luke's feet, said, "Bah!", and stormed away across the field.

"I didn't know people actually said, 'Bah!'" commented Nick. "I've only ever seen it written in books. Well done, by the way."

"For what?"

"For keeping your temper."

Luke was genuinely surprised. "I always keep my temper."

"Ah, so you do. I must be thinking of some other

feller." The mischievous grin on Nick's mobile features disappeared and was replaced by a frown. "Seriously, watch out for Hagen. He's a nasty piece of work, and he doesn't like you one little bit."

"I'd noticed, thanks." Luke checked his watch. "Come on. The first gliders set off in five minutes. Time to get in position."

All over the meadow, pilots and ground crews were walking their gliders into their assigned places. The meadow sloped away before them, gently at first, then with increasing steepness, before ending at a cliff edge and a vertical drop of a thousand feet to the valley floor. Luke and Nick swung their glider into line and watched as the first competitors began to take off.

The gliders were a curious mixture of designs: triplanes, with their three stacked wings, like enormous kites; biplanes and monoplanes. Some of the German pilots had decorated their gliders with the swastika badge of the Nazi party. Others sported club colors or military markings, with the roundels of the RAF and the French Armée de l'Air prominent.

The competition, sponsored by the Austrian Aero Club, was a free-distance flight. The idea was to soar for as long as you could. Gliders returning to the field would have their take-off time subtracted from their landing time, and the resulting figure would show how long the glider had been in the air. Luke fully expected to fly for longer than any of the other competitors: his leather flying jacket was tight over several layers of cotton and wool; he was wearing two pairs of pants, three pairs of socks, and gloves designed for polar expeditions. It would be cold up there!

One by one, the gliders took off, their pilots running across the cropped grass until their machines reached flying speed, then hoisting themselves onto their seats for the flight. Their gliders disappeared below the lip of the meadow for a heart-stopping moment, before reappearing to climb away from the valley floor and bank to left or right seeking thermals, the rising warm air currents that would give them lift and prolong their flight.

Several competitors took off without incident. Then, as an Italian pilot made his take-off, a sudden crosswind caught his glider, lifting the left-hand wing and causing the tip of the right-hand wing to dig into the ground. The glider cartwheeled across the field, shedding spars and strips of canvas as it went. It came to rest in a heap of tangled wreckage, from which the shaken pilot crawled with some difficulty.

Nick winced and shook his head. "Poor feller. That was bad luck." He turned to Luke. "If you get a gust like that..."

"Turn into it and use it for lift, yes, I know the theory." Luke indicated the luckless Italian who had now scrambled to his feet and was sorrowfully examining the wreckage of his glider. "He doesn't seem too badly hurt, anyway."

"You'd better hope you get off as lightly if anything goes wrong."

Luke gave Nick a sour look. "Real little ray of sunshine, aren't you?" He pointed. "There goes Hagen."

Hagen's bat-like monoplane glider, swastikas prominently displayed, made a faultless take-off. Nick scowled. "Just make sure you stay in the air longer than him."

"You can count on it." Luke pulled on his flying helmet and adjusted the chinstrap. "Two more to go, then it's us."

After that, there was little time to talk. Luke and Nick walked their glider to the top end of the grass runway. As the competitor immediately before them made his take-off run, Nick clipped Luke's harness into place and gave him a cheery thumbs up. "Good luck!"

Luke nodded, his mouth suddenly dry. Then a marshal waved a flag and it was his turn.

2 ...AND HUNTED

Luke snapped his goggles into place over his eyes and gripped the joystick. He felt the familiar surge of excitement he always experienced at the start of a flight.

He began to run, with Nick and an Austrian official alongside keeping the wing above his head steady. As his speed increased, they let go and dropped back. Luke felt the joystick begin to move under his hand – the wing was almost at flying speed, he could now steady it with his controls. Luke's breath came short. Take-off was always a tricky moment – a sudden change in the wind and he could share the fate of the unfortunate Italian. Wouldn't Hagen just love that…

"Good flying, Luke!" Nick's cry sounded thin and reedy behind him. "Be sure to be back in time for supper – I'll butter you some toast!" Luke grinned and relaxed.

The slope became steeper. Luke's speed increased, he felt the sudden lift of the wing – then he was no longer running, but paddling through the air with feet that had left the ground. He was flying. Moments later, the slope disappeared below him as he crossed the cliff edge and the world fell away.

Luke swung his feet up behind him and settled them into the stirrups. He tested both and the glider yawed to left and right. He pulled gently on the stick, came out of his shallow dive and settled into level flight. He moved the stick from side to side and the wings waggled. Everything was working – now to show what the *Flying Wing* could do!

He and Nick had built it during the long vacation at Kingshome Abbey, the Challenger family home and site of the Challenger Industries research division. They had used an abandoned stable yard: since being confined to a wheelchair, Andrew Challenger, Luke's father, had no interest in horses. Luke had become expert at "salvaging" material from the research shops and forging requisition slips for anything that failed to come to hand. They'd had the help of some of Nick's friends among the firm's apprentices (who, in Nick's words, would do anything for a laugh, but, if asked, would steadfastly deny being involved with the project in any way whatsoever).

Next had come the removal to the barn near Ashleigh House, Luke and Nick's expensive private school, by a truck whose driver fondly believed he was shipping aircraft parts to a secret Challenger Industries testing facility. Luke's subsequent interest in the school's Air Cadet Force had delighted his tutor, who had long given up hope that his most difficult student would ever show enthusiasm for anything apart from science and outdoor pursuits. As a result the poor man had turned a blind eye to the fact that Luke and Nick were both flying the Cadet Force's gliders at a younger age than would normally have been allowed. He felt himself vindicated when Luke's instructor glowingly reported that his new trainee was "a natural." However, the same instructor dismissed Nick's efforts as no more than "competent." From that moment, Luke was the pilot of Team Challenger, and Nick the engineer.

Finally, there had been the long series of tests during hours stolen from study: weekends, holidays and vacations when Luke and Nick suddenly developed such a touching attachment to the school they had previously described as "the snake pit" that they could scarcely bear to leave it. There had been crashes, cover-ups ("I fell out of a tree, doctor"), redesigns and rebuilds until, at last, the trip across Europe, again on forged documents, proved once and for all that Luke's design was sound and that his father's objections ("Too expensive, too hard to fly!") were wrong.

Luke had observed that most of his fellow-competitors had turned to the north to fly toward the German border. Luke had other ideas. He flew to the southeast, heading for the heart of the Tyrol with its soaring mountains. The terrain here was harsh and unforgiving for pilots who ran out of altitude, but with the wind in the south, he judged that, as it met the mountains, the ridge-lift would provide more reliable rising air than the thermals likely to be found in gentler country. He was taking a risk, but a calculated one. In any case, spring had come late and the mountains, which had not yet shed their winter covering of snow, were incredibly beautiful.

As he expected, Luke found rising air surging up the valley sides. He flew along ridges, gaining altitude all the while. When he was new to gliding, he had struggled to identify the air currents that would help him to rise, and his flights had been short. Now, the countless tiny indications of where to find such currents – terrain, cloud formations, wind patterns on the ground – were noted and processed in his mind almost without conscious thought. His hands and feet moved the controls instinctively as he turned the glider to take advantage of the air currents providing the strongest lift. His eyes drank in the view and his whole body thrilled at the sense of freedom and speed.

"Who would have thought, fifty years ago, how close humans were to discovering the secrets of aviation?" It was one of Luke's father's favorite themes. "And who would have thought even thirty years ago, when the Wright brothers made their first, hesitant flights in America, that we would have come so far so quickly?" Luke could see his father holding forth at the dinner table, cigar in left hand, glass of vintage port in right, his expansive gestures slopping the ruby liquid over the white tablecloth. "And Challenger Industries is, and always will be, at the forefront of this Century of Discovery – this new Age of Science!"

Luke dragged his thoughts back to the here and now. Aside from the rushing air, his flight between the blue sky above and the white wilderness below was almost silent. He was aware of tiny creaking and pinging noises as wood and wire tensed and flexed with the glider's movement, and the more prolonged rasp of the control cables as he made adjustments to its course. The *Flying*

Wing was working perfectly. Luke thought of the falcon he had seen. Was this what it felt like to be such a creature, master of the skies, king of its airy domain? Looking down on the distant earth from a godlike height, unconcerned with the doings of the poor, struggling, earthbound wretches so far below?

Luke's reverie ended brutally and without warning. A jarring impact from somewhere above rocked his fragile glider. The whole airframe shook.

"What the...?"

He almost lost his grip on the joystick and grabbed for it convulsively. His mind raced. What had happened? A bird strike? It would have to be a very clumsy or short-sighted bird to blunder into his path. Luke craned his neck to try to see anything that might lie above the wing, just as the glider lurched under a second impact. To his astonishment, a booted foot burst through the canvas of the wing above his head, making a gaping hole and a long tear.

The boot was withdrawn and, from behind Luke's wing, a familiar swastika-bedecked glider appeared. Hagen! His glider had collided with Luke's.

Luke felt a surge of anger. "You idiot!" he yelled, with little hope of being heard. "Are you blind? Why don't you watch where you're going...?"

Then he caught sight of the German pilot's leering

face and an icy hand clutched at his heart as Hagen, with slow deliberation, drew a gloved finger across his throat.

It wasn't an accident. Luke was thunderstruck. *Hagen deliberately rammed me. Twice. He must have flown into position just above my glider and dropped like a stone, to stomp on the wing...*

And, as Hagen made a banked turn to come around behind him, Luke had no doubt that his intention was to do it again – and again, holing the canvas, breaking spars, damaging control wires, until something vital broke on Luke's glider to send him spinning to a terrible death on the jagged, snow-covered rocks two thousand feet below.

For several terrible frozen seconds, Luke was paralyzed with shock. Hagen must be insane! How could he hope to get away with this? He must have lain in wait to see which way Luke would turn, and followed him. Luke groaned aloud – and he had played into Hagen's hands by not following the other competitors, but heading for this lonely landscape. There were no farms or villages this high in the mountains. The skies were empty. If Luke fell, there would be no witnesses.

"I'm not the falcon after all," he muttered to himself, "Hagen is. And I'm the pigeon."

With this sudden understanding, and the shock of

another impact on the wing, Luke's paralysis broke. He thrust against his left-hand stirrup, and the drag rudder at the tip of the wing swung down, biting into the air. The effect was immediate: the glider pivoted on its left wingtip, turning through a hundred and eighty degrees in little more than its own length. Luke caught a momentary glance of Hagen's startled face as the German overshot, but he had no time to rejoice in his enemy's discomfiture. The violence of the maneuver had sent the glider into a spin, and Luke had to wrestle with the controls for several chilling moments before he succeeded in recovering the aircraft.

Luke skimmed across the mountain face, gazing around frantically. Where was Hagen? He was answered by yet another juddering impact and the snap of breaking timber as a wing spar gave way. The German had followed him down.

Grimly, Luke pushed the stick forward, sacrificing height for speed. His mind raced. How could he shake off his enemy? Hagen was a far more experienced pilot than Luke. His glider was larger and heavier than Luke's *Flying Wing*, and probably more robust. In any case, Hagen was sitting in his glider, his legs dangling below it in an ideal position to bring his feet into play, as the damage Luke's glider had already suffered made clear. In order to retaliate, Luke would not only have to get above Hagen's glider, he would also have to take his feet from the stirrups to do any damage, and lose control of his aircraft as a result. Every drop of Luke's Challenger blood urged him to go on the attack; every ounce of common sense told him to retreat. After a brief internal struggle, common sense won.

Luke kept the nose of his glider down until he was skimming scant feet above the valley floor. He glanced back: Hagen was some distance behind him. Luke's glider was evidently faster and more maneuverable than his enemy's. He filed the information away for later use and concentrated on not crashing.

The glider tore along the valley at breakneck speed. A small stream of meltwater tumbled over rocks, winding its way to the distant river. Luke followed its path down the twisting valley, banking from left to right, swooping over snow and jagged rocks, jinking around giant boulders and taking advantage of the momentary wind shear created by the largest to increase speed. He flew a zigzag course between isolated pine trees, then rose briefly to clear a clump of conifers. For a despairing moment he thought he wouldn't make it, then, with an agonizing slap of needles in his face, and a bomb-burst of powdered snow, which his hurtling body brushed from the topmost branches, he was clear.

He was coming to the end of the valley. The gliders

would soon be over more populated areas. Hagen would have to give up his pursuit, or he would be spotted. Luke glanced back and his eyes widened in horror as he saw Hagen take a hand off his controls, reach inside his flying jacket and bring out something metallic that glinted in the morning sun. It could only be a pistol. The German had no intention of letting Luke escape.

Grimly, Luke wrenched his eyes forward again. Dead ahead was a curving line, black against the snow, that climbed up the valley wall, supported at intervals by pylons. Dull red cars crawled toward each other from either end of the line. A cable car!

There was no time for thought. Luke pulled back on the stick to put his glider between the cable car and Hagen's line of sight. He hoped that the German, concentrating on stopping him, had not noticed the obstruction.

He dimly heard the crack of Hagen's pistol, but the bullet had already zinged past with a noise like an angry wasp. Another bullet shattered the altimeter just in front of his head and Luke felt a sharp jab of pain as a shard of broken glass seared his cheek. A third shot hit a bracing wire, which snapped; the glider yawed, creaking in protest. The joystick jerked against Luke's hand. He fought the sudden instability, wrestling the aircraft back under control. Then, the cable car was upon him.

Luke hauled on the stick and his glider shot over the cable, missing it by inches. He turned his head just in time to see the sudden look of horror on Hagen's face as he realized his peril. A split second later, the German glider slammed into the wire cable and disintegrated. A wing broke off and tumbled to earth like an autumn leaf. The tail was torn to shreds. The rest of the fuselage and the remaining wing, spinning like a boomerang, flailed across the sky and smashed into the hillside with bone-breaking force.

Luke found that his whole body was trembling. Hagen had suffered the fate he had planned for Luke. His destruction had been swift, complete and catastrophic. Strangely, only now that he was safe did Luke have time to feel fear. Adrenaline flowed through him, chilling him more thoroughly than the freezing air, as he flew past the nearer cable car. Its windows were plastered with the horrified faces of passengers who had evidently seen the accident and followed Hagen's aircraft in its final dive.

Luke spiraled to lose height and brought his glider in to a shaky landing beside the stream, kicking his feet from the stirrups to run through the springy, sharp-bladed grasses as he touched down. His foot caught in a tussock and he fell forward, the glider made a sudden nosedive into the boggy ground and stopped dead.

With shaking fingers, Luke undid the clasps on his harness and shrugged himself free. He ran across the grass and patchy snow on stiff legs that felt only partly under his control, toward the wreck of Hagen's glider. The swastika on the wing was scuffed and torn. An aileron hung drunkenly from a single wire. The fuselage was shattered.

Hagen lay a few feet further up the hillside. Luke had torn the glove off the German pilot's left hand and pulled up the sleeve of his flying jacket, automatically reaching to feel for a pulse, before fully registering the sight before him. There would be no pulse. The wire of the cable car had caught the German clean across the throat.

Luke fell to his knees as waves of nausea washed over him. Turning from the grisly spectacle of Hagen's severed neck, his eye was drawn back to the dead man's wrist, and the strange tattoo he had uncovered when pulling up Hagen's sleeve. It showed a striking snake coiled around the shaft of a spear.

As tears of shock came to his eyes and every muscle in his body began to shiver uncontrollably, Luke wondered what it meant.

3 A WARM WELCOME

Southern England
May 1933

The three-engined Junkers JU 52 dropped through sullen, rain-heavy clouds to land at Croydon Airport.

Luke stared glumly out of the rain-lashed window as the cumbersome aircraft came to rest. He was not looking forward to this homecoming. Since the events in the Austrian Tyrol, his life had become very complicated.

Hagen's death had caused a huge furore. Luke had made no mention of the German pilot's attempt on his life, largely to try and avoid an investigation that might rumble on interminably and strand him and Nick in Austria for months. In spite of his insistence that he had merely been an unfortunate witness to Hagen's spectacular demise, the Austrian authorities had asked some very difficult questions with stony-faced persistence. Worse than that, they had impounded Luke's glider. And when it became clear that Luke and Nick had lied about their age, the British consulate had become involved and telegrams had been sent to Luke's father. The replies to these had not actually set their envelopes on fire, but they must have come close.

After that, the Austrian officials had decided to believe that Hagen's death had been a tragic accident and Luke and Nick had been unceremoniously booted out of the country. One set of unsmiling consular officials had escorted them from Innsbruck to Zurich and another set from Zurich to Paris, where they had been politely but firmly ushered onto a flight to London. They knew they were being ordered home to face the music, music that was likely to make the *1812 Overture* sound like *The Dance of the Sugar Plum Fairy*.

The airliner nosed toward the terminal building and stopped. Luke and Nick followed the other passengers down the short flight of steps and into the arrivals hall. They trudged past the time zone tower without bothering to check what o'clock it was in New York, Rome or

Tokyo, and out to the parking lot. Here among a scattering of Rolls-Royces, Lagondas and Hispano Suizas they found a rakish black saloon car with wire wheels and silver trim. A stern-looking man with a bulldog face and a peaked cap was waiting beside the open rear passenger door. He nodded as the boys approached.

"Good morning, Bateman," Luke said glumly.

"Master Luke," replied Bateman austerely.

Nick was entranced. "A Daimler Double Six! She's a beauty. Twelve cylinders – actually two six-cylinder engines, set in a 'v' configuration; aluminum crankcase, steel valves…"

"It might as well be a police van," Luke told him sourly as they clambered into the luxurious, leather-upholstered interior. "It's been sent to cart us off for trial, after all." Nick's momentary good mood faded. He nodded morosely as Bateman slammed the driver's door and started the engine.

As the car headed west, Luke stared out of the window at the dripping countryside. As heir to Challenger Industries, he led a privileged life. He knew that, but sometimes the cost of that privilege weighed heavily upon him. He was being dragged home – if you could call it home – in disgrace. Kingshome Abbey might be a gilded cage, but it was still a cage for all that.

Nick knew perfectly well what Luke was thinking. "Cheer up. You know what they say. 'Stone walls do not a prison make.'"

Luke gave his friend a jaundiced look. "Yes, they most certainly do."

"I think it's supposed to mean that even if you're in prison, you can still think about the world as if you weren't. In prison, that is. Who was it who went on about 'Infinite riches in a little room'?"

"I don't know," Luke snapped. "The Governor of the Bank of England?" Nick gave up on him. He knew from experience that the best way of dealing with Luke in this mood was to leave him to find his way out of it in his own time.

The drive to Salisbury Plain took over two hours. After passing through an army checkpoint, the Daimler took a series of ever-worsening roads before eventually turning off a country lane to nose through an impressive gateway and up a long drive flanked by beech trees. Topping a rise, the car began to descend toward an extraordinary-looking house.

Kingshome Abbey was not an abbey, and no king had ever stayed there. It had been built for a Victorian industrialist by an architect with a taste for the Gothic and an overactive imagination. The stone front bristled with towers, turrets, arches and mullioned windows.

As the car swept around the side of the house, its wheels crunching gravel, the walls became covered with ivy and wisteria. Between the house and a distant, dilapidated stable block stretched a surprising number of ugly, low brick buildings.

Kingshome did not appear on any maps. Its first owner had valued his privacy: so did its present occupier, but for different reasons. Kingshome Abbey was now the headquarters of Challenger Industries and what went on here was Top Secret.

The Daimler pulled up outside the stable yard. Bateman opened the door for Luke and Nick. As they stepped from the car, the air became full of interesting noises. The roar of an airplane engine heralded the appearance of a sleek silver monoplane, which rose into view from the meadow beyond the house and swept into an aerobatic routine. From one of the low brick buildings came the rattle of automatic gunfire. Luke spotted a small group of men in white coats, carrying clipboards. They were halfway down the grassy slope to the lake that lay in the valley below the house. As he watched, a white streak raced across the lake toward a mock-up of a submarine's mid-section, complete with conning tower. This disappeared in a gout of water and a sheet of flame. A muffled BOOM! rolled around the valley. The men in white coats nodded and made notes on their clipboards.

Luke and Nick followed Bateman to the house. Between two of the brick buildings they had to dodge a miniature tank as it raced excitedly around the yard. Bateman condescended to say, "Radio controlled," before lapsing once again into silence.

He led the way through one of the buildings. This was full of odd-looking experimental gadgets on test. In a glass cabinet, a wind-up gramophone was playing "Sweet Georgia Brown" until, with a fizzing noise, the speaker-horn rotated to flood the cabinet with gas. Further along, a young woman in an apron using a cylinder vacuum cleaner, suddenly lifted the nozzle, pointing it at a fully dressed dummy of a man wearing a cardigan and smoking a pipe. Simultaneously, she kicked the machine's switch from "SUCK" to "BLOW." A sheet of flame emerged from the machine's nozzle, incinerating the dummy. Nick grinned as he supplied imaginary dialog for the scene. "Now will you take the garbage out?"

Luke gave Bateman a stern look. "Is Challenger Industries getting involved in assassination?"

"Special order for Lord Roxton," was the wooden reply.

At length, they emerged from the workshops and crossed the kitchen yard. A man in a dark blue suit walked from the house toward them.

Nick gave him a shamefaced smile. "Hello, Da."

"Nick." Edward Malone nodded. "It's good to see you, son."

"Hello, Uncle Ned," said Luke.

"At least you both seem to be safe and sound."

Luke was not surprised at the lack of warmth in the greeting. He knew that Nick's father really was pleased to see them – but it was several years since Edward Malone had shown much enthusiasm for anything.

Malone gave Luke a wintry smile. "You're expected."

"I thought we might be."

Luke and Nick followed Malone into the house and through a succession of corridors painted in unappetizing shades of green and beige before turning into a hallway that was every bit as extravagant as the house's exterior. Several dozen animal heads – various species of deer and gazelle, wild boar, rhinoceros, lion, leopard and cheetah – looked down on them with expressions that ranged from startlement to extreme annoyance. Above the huge stone fireplace hung a portrait of a forceful-looking man with a scowling red face, a bristling, black, spade-shaped beard and piercing blue-gray eyes beneath eyebrows like hairy caterpillars. Luke had inherited the eye color, along with his famous ancestor's legendary temper. A plaque at the bottom of the enormous gilt frame read *G. E. Challenger.*

Luke gave the portrait an affectionate salute. "Good day, Grandpa."

"I'll see if your father is ready for you." Edward Malone waved his son and Luke toward a couple of chairs. Nick's father was a well-built man in his mid forties, but his shoulders were habitually slumped as though from long and bitter disappointment. His hair was thinning, he had not shaved with any great attention and his suit was in need of pressing. Malone gave off an air of quiet melancholy that annoyed Luke and embarrassed his son. A noted rugby player who had played for Ireland in his youth, he had never gotten over the death of his wife, Luke's Aunt Enid. He was Challenger Industries' Head of Security, and efficient at his job; but Luke (though he would never have shared the thought with Nick) couldn't help thinking that Nick's father was more like a rather faded, apologetic ghost than a flesh-and-blood human being.

Malone crossed the hall, his feet tapping on the tiles. He paused outside a set of double oak doors and listened. Luke caught Nick's eye and mouthed the word "Library." After a moment, Malone half-opened one of the doors and slipped inside. In the instant the door was open, voices could be heard from the room beyond.

As soon as the door was closed, Luke slipped off his shoes and padded quickly across the hallway on stockinged feet to listen in. Nick was only a split second behind.

The first voice they heard was raised in anger. "I can't understand how on earth she found out where the blasted place was!"

Luke made a wry face. "That's Dad," he whispered. Nick grinned.

A second voice answered, "Not from me."

"That's Uncle Ned."

Nick pressed his ear right up against the door. "I was only there once," Malone continued, "when I was twenty-three – which, come to think of it, was twenty-three years ago. Your father handled the navigation. I couldn't find my way there again if my life depended on it and as for telling anyone else how to find it..." Nick and Luke could practically hear his shrug.

"She didn't hear about it from me either," a languid voice drawled. Luke raised his eyebrows. The voice was unmistakably that of Lord John Roxton. "She's been badgering me for years to tell her, but I wouldn't. However, she's an intelligent woman and the plateau's existence has been public knowledge ever since that Doyle feller put the whole story of our visit in print."

"Blasted interfering ink-walloper!" roared Luke's father.

"Just as you say. At all events, there was enough in

Doyle's story for her to work out a rough location."

"And so she goes haring off without a goodbye..." Andrew Challenger broke off as a discreet cough interrupted the conversation. "Oh, this is getting us nowhere. Ned, I take it the young blackguards have arrived?" The voice became grim. "Wheel 'em in!"

By the time Edward Malone reappeared to beckon them into the library, Luke and Nick were both back on the chairs by the fireplace, shoes on feet and looking innocent. They stood up and crossed the hall. Luke braced himself. It looked as if he was now in trouble on two fronts. The "she" under discussion could only be his mother, and he knew exactly how Harriet Challenger had located the plateau Roxton had mentioned.

Luke stepped into the library.

4 THE CHALLENGER EXPEDITION

Sir Andrew Challenger was sitting in his wheelchair beside his desk. Luke's father was an exact copy of the man whose portrait hung over the fireplace in the hallway. His face seemed chiseled out of granite: hard and eloquent of obstinacy, pride and implacable purpose. But the bull-strength of his upper body was not matched by that of the lower. Sir Andrew had been caught in a landmine explosion in the Great War, which had left his legs paralyzed. Wasted by years of disuse, they were wrapped in a plaid blanket.

The other man in the room lounged against the mantelpiece, warming himself beside the coal fire. Roxton's ruddy hair, crisp mustache and beard were flecked with gray; his skin was less tanned than it had been in his heyday as one of Britain's foremost explorers, but the curved nose, hollow cheeks and cold, ice-blue eyes were much as they had always been. In addition to being his godfather, Lord John Roxton was Luke's hero. The man had been everywhere and done everything. He'd penetrated the most remote corners of the Earth in pursuit of rare game, which had invariably become rarer still as a result of his attentions. Luke didn't approve of this – he felt an animal's head looked better on its shoulders than on Roxton's wall – but he couldn't help admiring the wiry old adventurer, both for his youthful explorations and for his later glittering career in British Military Intelligence.

Roxton drew on his Havana cigar and gave Luke a supportive wink as his father, twisting the wheels of his chair as if it had done him a personal injury, sailed to the attack. "Would you care to explain to me," Sir Andrew bellowed, "exactly what possessed you?"

"Hello, Father," said Luke stiffly. "I'm glad to see you, too."

Luke's father snorted dismissively. He reached into his pocket, hauled out a fistful of requisition slips and waved them in Luke's face. "You take it into your head to build a glider, to your own idiotic design, using *these*! Forged requisition slips! You've been plundering Challenger Industries supplies for the past year for your cock-eyed scheme. This is theft!"

"Not at all, sir." Luke's voice was cold and distant. "The glider I built with those materials belongs to Challenger Industries, not to me." Luke noticed that Roxton had put his hand to his mouth, as though stifling a chuckle. "I admit I acted without authorization…"

"Oh, you admit that, do you?" Sir Andrew's voice was heavy with sarcasm.

"But you left me no choice…"

"No choice?" Sir Andrew was apoplectic.

"You wouldn't let me build my design."

"Your design was nonsensical! Too complicated, too expensive…"

"How did it fly?" interrupted Roxton.

"Never mind how it flew!" Sir Andrew was red-faced with rage. "And this famous glider, which, I am enchanted to learn, belongs to my company – where, might I ask, is it now?"

Luke shrugged. "The Austrians confiscated it."

"I see."

"But Herr Messerschmitt said…"

"You showed your design to Willi Messerschmitt?"

Sir Andrew raised his arms to heaven. "Have you taken leave of your senses? The man is determined to rearm the German air force..."

"You said my design was garbage," Luke burst out. "Well, if it wasn't, you should have let me build it, and if it was, you shouldn't accuse me of revealing Challenger Industries' secrets to Herr Messerschmitt. You can't have it both ways."

Challenger chewed at his beard. He looked like an overheated boiler about to burst.

"If you ask me," drawled Roxton, "my godson has shown remarkable initiative."

"I didn't ask you," growled Sir Andrew.

"Nevertheless," Roxton continued, "he's managed to build a complex machine in complete secrecy and transport it across Europe..."

"On more forged documents!"

"Quite." Roxton dismissed this with a wave. "Then he flies it competitively against more experienced pilots and more established designs. He might even have won the competition, if not for his decision to go to the aid of a fellow pilot who had crashed..." Bile rose in Luke's throat at the memory; for a moment, the room swam before his eyes.

"He fooled me." Sir Andrew's voice was implacable. "He fooled my employees, including Ned here..." Malone lowered his eyes. "He fooled his teachers and the immigration authorities of three countries…"

"As I said," Roxton winked at Luke again. "He shows initiative."

"He should have been at home studying!" snapped Sir Andrew. "He put his life at risk…"

"Well, as to the former," said Roxton placidly, "you know what I think about packin' the young feller off to some stuffy university when he could learn far more here, and ten times as quickly."

"For pity's sake, Roxton, the boy's only fourteen!"

"So was I when I went into the Kalahari Desert for the first time. In Nelson's navy, midshipmen were given command of captured ships at that age. Mozart wrote his first opera at the age of fourteen. By the time he was fourteen, Tutankhamun had been pharaoh of Egypt for five years…"

"And look what happened to him!"

Roxton dropped his languid pose. Steel entered his voice. When he chose to exert himself, his personality was every bit as forceful as that of the irascible head of Challenger Industries. "You're being foolish, Andrew," he said bluntly. "You keep telling me you want Luke to buckle down and show he's ready to take responsibility, how can he do that when you're trying to wrap him in cotton? Why don't you tell him what we were talking about before he came in? I daresay the young rascal was listening at the door anyway."

Luke tried to look like someone who would never dream of listening at doors.

His father suddenly looked weary. "Perhaps you're right. After all, he has to know sooner or later."

"Know what?" Luke was puzzled and somewhat alarmed.

Sir Andrew sighed. "We were talking about your mother," he said heavily. "She's gone missing."

Luke stared at his father in disbelief. His heart thumped painfully. "Missing?" He exchanged a baffled glance with Nick. "How do you mean, missing?"

"I'd have thought my meaning was plain enough." Sir Andrew's voice had resumed its customary irascibility.

Luke stared at him, lost for words. Of course, he understood what his father had said, but the reality had hardly begun to sink in. His mother was missing? What did that mean? How could she be missing? She was his *mother*.

Andrew Challenger was speaking again. "I suppose you know where she was going when you last saw her?"

Luke gathered his thoughts and managed a nod. "She was going to Brazil."

"A fact both you and she carefully hid from me!"

"We might have told you," blazed Luke, "if either of us had thought you'd be interested!"

A heavy silence descended on the room.

Roxton cleared his throat. "Luke, this is important. How much do you know about what Harriet – your mother – was planning?"

Luke said, guardedly, "I know she'd decided to find the plateau that you, Uncle Ned and Grandpa discovered before the war."

"So that's what you were talking about, before..." Nick broke off at Luke's angry stare.

"Then you *were* listening at the door," snarled Luke's father.

"Just as well," said Roxton unconcernedly. "Saves time on explanations. So you know about this business, do you, young Nick?"

Nick cleared his throat. "I know that Dad went to South America – to the Amazon rainforest in Brazil – with you and the Professor – that is, Sir Andrew's father..."

"And old Summerlee, but he died years ago, poor chap. Cut the footnotes, young feller," said Roxton amicably, "or we'll be here all night."

"Well, you found a plateau cut off from the rest of the world by sheer cliffs and on it you found Indians, a lost tribe of apemen and dinosaurs..." Nick broke off as Sir Andrew snorted like a stallion.

"It seems that my wife has decided to pay the place a visit," he said bitterly, "in spite of my forbidding her ever to go near it."

"She's a paleontologist," Luke shot back. "Dinosaurs are her life's work. What would you expect her to do? Grandpa's expedition discovered creatures that died out everywhere else in the world tens of millions of years ago."

"Oh, and don't we know it!" snapped Sir Andrew. "The famous Challenger Expedition to the Lost World! As soon as that blasted scribbler Conan Doyle got hold of the story, it was all over the place. He should have stuck to writing about that fat-headed detective!"

"You're being unreasonable, Andrew," said Roxton quietly. "The old Prof didn't exactly keep the news to himself, you know. He even brought back a pterodactyl to prove our story..."

"Which promptly escaped and flapped off across London never to be seen again! And it was a five-minute wonder, and no mistake. But a week later the scientific establishment was saying it never happened, you were all frauds and charlatans, and the few people who were prepared to insist they'd seen a real live pterodactyl were dismissed as lunatics or victims of mass hallucination." Sir Andrew thumped the arm of his chair. "I was at Oxford. My father's report made me a laughing stock! You should have heard the taunts – fellows flapping around corridors using their gowns as wings, cartoons on all the noticeboards, the feeble jokes: *'Fetch me a pterodactyl sandwich and make it snappy.'* Even the Dons couldn't resist their little dig." He put on a high-pitched, querulous voice. *"'And so, the fossil evidence clearly indicates that all the major dinosaur lines died out simultaneously at the end of the Cretaceous period – whatever Mr. Challenger's father may say to the contrary...'* Hah!"

Roxton smiled ruefully. "You can't blame the prof for the fact that the scientific world didn't believe him – or us..."

"I can blame him for never letting the matter rest! Any sensible man would have bitten the bullet and kept quiet, but not my father. All through my university days he was thundering his claims in the press and offering to fight anyone who called him a liar! And after the war, when I was setting up Challenger Industries, so many financiers and industrialists failed to take me seriously because the so-called Challenger Controversy kept getting in the way. It took me years to win back people who thought my father was a madman."

"If it wasn't for Grandpa's inventions and discoveries," said Luke hotly, "there would be no Challenger Industries!"

"Don't be impudent!" roared his father.

Luke stood his ground. "Are you trying to tell me that you don't believe that Grandpa, Uncle Ned and Uncle John really discovered a lost world?"

Sir Andrew glanced briefly at Malone and Roxton. "I have no reason to disbelieve it," he said uncomfortably. "Though the details seem somewhat...but then, I was not there...and this is beside the point. What matters is what people in general believe." He lifted his chin. "At all events, somehow your mother managed to discover the location of the plateau and set out to find it. I gather she was sending news of her whereabouts to Ned." Sir Andrew gave Malone an angry glance.

"I tried to persuade her not to go, Andrew," said Malone quietly. "But you know how determined she can be. When I saw there was no stopping her, I agreed to keep quiet about her plans as long as she kept in contact with me. If I hadn't, none of us would have known where she was." He turned to Luke. "Her messages stopped arriving a week ago. I know she went up the River Amazon from Manaus with a local guide. After that..." He shrugged.

"So you've no idea what's happened to her?" Luke felt cold and sick.

"We're hoping," said Roxton gently, "that nothing has happened to her. She may have become temporarily lost in the jungle..."

"Or she may be so engrossed in digging up some decaying carcass that she's simply forgotten to keep in touch," snorted Sir Andrew. "We're not going to find out by just sitting here and speculating."

"You're right." Luke pulled himself together and squared his shoulders. "When do we leave?"

His father stared at him. "What on earth are you talking about?"

"My mother's lost in the jungle. Anything might have happened to her. So when do we set off for Brazil, to find her?"

"You," roared Sir Andrew, "are not going anywhere! Have you taken leave of your senses? This is no job for a fourteen year old!"

"If I'm old enough to be targeted for an assassination attempt," retorted Luke, "I'm old enough to be sent on a rescue mission."

His father was suddenly very still. "What assassination attempt?"

Luke cursed inwardly. He had not intended to tell his father the truth about what had happened in Austria, but it couldn't be helped. He gave a brief account of Hagen's attack. Nick put in details from time to time. Roxton's face clouded as the story unfolded and he stroked his mustache, apparently deep in thought.

When Luke had finished his story, Roxton said slowly,

"This symbol you say Hagen had tattooed on his wrist... Did it look like this?" He crossed to Sir Andrew's desk and turned over a piece of paper.

Luke joined him and stared at the paper. It was a photograph showing a man's wrist, on which was tattooed a striking snake coiled around a spear.

It was an exact replica of the snake-and-spear device Luke had found on the wrist of Heinrich Hagen.

5 SNAKES AND SPEARS

"**E**xactly like that," said Luke.

"That photograph," said Sir Andrew flatly, "was of the wrist of a courier who was arrested on the French-German border carrying Challenger Industries blueprints for a new rapid-fire, low-recoil machine gun for use in aircraft. Clearly he intended to pass them on to Germany. Unfortunately, according to the French authorities, he was carrying a cyanide capsule and committed suicide before he could be questioned.

"More recently, an Italian seaman was approached by

our own Special Branch as he was about to board a ship for Naples. He was carrying a sample of our new high-explosive grenades. He managed to pull the pin on one before they could jump him. After the explosion there wasn't much of him left, but the post-mortem report said that he also had a tattoo like this one. I've called Roxton in because of his position with the intelligence service, to see if he could shed any light on the matter."

"Very little, I'm afraid," drawled Roxton. "Security agencies are notoriously secretive – it is their stock in trade, after all. The French are very reluctant to pass information to British Military Intelligence and our own Special Branch is worse. However, some things are obvious. We're dealing with a new organization. It's clearly unprincipled and ruthless. It's also international, and events so far indicate that it may be acting for the emerging fascist governments of central Europe against the West.

"We live in dangerous times. Germany may have lost the Great War, but now she is growing stronger again and looking for revenge. Italy is in the hands of that lunatic Mussolini; Soviet Russia is run by Communist thugs who are capable of anything and Japan is going crazy with emperor worship. This snake-and-spear gang might be supporting any or all of them. And the fact that its agents were carrying Challenger secrets that had not been reported missing seems to indicate that you have a traitor in your midst."

"I'd managed to work that much out for myself," Sir Andrew said irritably. "Ned is already heading up an investigation into how the plans were taken. We'll find out who the traitor is, don't you worry. What I don't understand is, why would these people – whoever they are – want to kill Luke?"

"Perhaps in the hope of damaging Challenger Industries. The Challenger group is far and away the largest supplier of civilian and military equipment to the government. You know as well as I do that Germany and Italy are rearming, and Russia and Japan are saber-rattling like nobody's business. A wrench in the Challenger works would be disastrous for Britain – and you've made no secret of your plan that Luke should succeed you as head of the company. You're well protected here, Andrew. The snake-and-spear gang, whoever they are, may have decided that killing Luke was the best way they could get at you." Luke stirred, but said nothing. Roxton spread his hands. "Then again, Hagen may simply have been a loose cannon, operating entirely on his own initiative. We need more information."

Sir Andrew drummed his fingers on his desk for a few moments. Then he looked up. "All right," he said briskly. "Roxton, if you hear anything about these people, I'd be obliged if you'd share it with me."

"Naturally."

"Ned," Sir Andrew continued, "turn your investigation into the thefts over to your deputy – what's his name? – Cassidy. I want you to put together a team to go to Brazil. Work out routes, transportation, what equipment you'll need, you know the drill. I want everything in place for a force to winkle Harriet out of whatever she's got herself into." Malone nodded. Andrew turned to Roxton. "I don't suppose you…?"

"Nothing I'd like better, old man," said Roxton. "I have a soft spot for Harriet, as you know. But the Service is very stingy about letting senior officers traipse off around the world on private missions. Anyway, there's stuff piling up on my desk – crises springing up all over the world." He shook his head. "Afraid I can't offer you much official support, either. His Majesty's Government isn't all that popular in South America at the moment." He gave a regretful shrug. "Sorry."

"What about me?" asked Luke.

His father gave him a hard stare.

"Don't imagine for a minute that I've finished with you yet." He nodded to the others in the room. "Gentlemen."

It was a dismissal. Edward Malone took Nick's

shoulder and steered him out of the room. Nick gave Luke a sympathetic grimace as he left, and mouthed, "Good luck!"

Roxton gave Sir Andrew a cordial nod and Luke another wink before he followed them. He stopped in the doorway as though struck by an afterthought. "One more thing, Andrew. I said you were well guarded here, but I wonder... If Luke is a target for your enemies, the idea of getting him out of Europe has its attractions – especially if you have a traitor to deal with. Your head of security can hardly protect either of you from Brazil. If you keep Luke here with you, then one well-placed assassin's bomb could deprive Challenger Industries of both its present *and* its future." With this comforting reflection, he left.

When they were alone, Luke's father said nothing for a while. He fiddled with the papers on his desk until the silence became uncomfortable.

When he spoke again, his voice was more reasonable. "Cards on the table, Luke. You were as thick as thieves with your grandfather before he died last year."

This was true. Luke had been sent home from school, suffering from a mild case of diphtheria. During his illness, he had spent hours in his grandfather's room. To begin with, this had been because he needed company. His mother had been away on one of her trips – in

French Indochina, he seemed to recall – and his father had been wrapped up in his work as usual.

All through Luke's childhood, Grandpa Challenger had been a distant and alarming figure, all bristling beard and bad temper: the legendary explorer of Sir Arthur Conan Doyle's book, which Luke had read over and over again. On his first visit to the old man's room, Luke had hardly been able to believe that the hot-headed discoverer of the Lost World was now the wrinkled, wasted figure in bathrobe and slippers who spent so many hours staring out of the window, knowing that the world had moved on and that he was only waiting to leave it.

But even when Luke had recovered enough to go outside, he had stayed with his grandfather, partly because he felt sorry for him but also because, when he was well enough, Grandpa Challenger told the most amazing stories. In exchange for these, Luke would read him the latest scientific papers – the old man's eyes could no longer cope with the small print of academic journals – and they would discuss the contents. The glider had originated in one of these discussions, and Grandpa Challenger had collaborated enthusiastically on its design.

Then, following his return to school, when his housemaster had called Luke to his study to tell him that his grandfather had died, Luke had experienced a feeling of loss and deep personal grief. The old man was gone, leaving Luke nothing but memories, some scribbled sketches of the glider and a notebook. After that, whenever he was at home, Luke had made regular visits to his grandfather's grave, not with flowers – for Grandpa Challenger hadn't cared for them – but with papers about the latest scientific advances, which he left in an empty bottle at the foot of the headstone.

"At all events," his father continued, "my father knew you were forever going off with your mother on her bone-picking jaunts. He must have thought you were exactly the sort of young fool he could impress with his nonsense about lost worlds and living dinosaurs." Luke said nothing. "Roxton and Ned say they didn't tell Harriet where their wretched plateau was and how to get there. Assuming they're telling the truth, there are only two ways she could have known: if she had asked my father herself, or if he'd told you...and you'd told her."

"All right," said Luke heavily. "Yes, Grandpa did talk to me. He told me how to get to the plateau. He left me his notebook. He showed me maps and drawings. And yes, I told Mother what he told me. I wish I hadn't now."

"So she went haring off to Brazil on a wild goose

chase," said Sir Andrew bitterly. "I suppose you let her take your grandfather's notebook?"

"I wanted her to, but she wouldn't. She said Grandpa had left it to me, not to her." Luke thought it wouldn't be prudent to add that he was sure what Grandpa Challenger had really wanted was for Luke to follow in his footsteps and rediscover the Lost World. "She copied the stuff she needed and said she'd find local guides who'd know the way."

"Typical lack of planning! I'm only surprised she didn't take you with her."

"I wanted to go, but she wouldn't let me." This was a sore point. For as long as he could remember, Luke had accompanied his mother on her travels around the world, as much a part of her baggage as the scrapers and brushes she used in her work. He could still remember the arguments that had arisen when his father had decided that he was running wild and becoming an ignorant young savage. It was way past time, he insisted, that his son stopped going with his wife's expeditions and settled down to a real education: an argument that his mother had, at last, conceded. "She said I couldn't miss any more school," Luke went on, "and anyway, it was too dangerous."

"At least she showed sense for once! So you went gliding instead." Luke said nothing. For a man who never listened to what anyone said, his father could be worryingly astute at times. "What am I going to do with you?" Sir Andrew continued. "I've just received the latest report from your very expensive school – from which I understand you obtained leave of absence to go to Austria, using a letter purporting to be from me." He took a piece of folded paper from his desk drawer and read from it. "You were top of your year for science, outdoor activities and all forms of armed and unarmed combat." He looked up. "And, presumably, forgery." Luke remained silent. His father, like his grandpa, was incapable of letting anything go. "But," Sir Andrew concluded, refolding the paper, "bottom at everything else."

Luke shrugged. "I'm only interested in science and I know more about it than my teachers. Why waste my time?"

"I'll decide what's a waste of your time and what isn't! Challenger Industries will need a leader when I'm gone and, Heaven help us, you're it!"

"You know what I think about that," returned Luke. "I want to be a scientist, not a bookkeeper."

"Somebody has to run the business!"

"Then you can find somebody else. I wouldn't want to run Challenger Industries the way you run it, anyway!"

His father's eyes glittered dangerously. "Would you care to explain that comment?"

"I mean I wouldn't allow the production of anything, no matter how destructive, simply to make a profit." Luke gestured wildly in an attempt to make himself understood. "New discoveries are being made every day; discoveries that might save the world – or destroy it! But Challenger Industries just goes on cheerfully developing any invention your tame scientists come up with, no matter how dangerous, and selling it to the highest bidder."

"Nonsense! Challenger Industries only sells to Britain and Britain's allies!"

"From what I read in the papers, Italy used to be our ally. Now she's turning into an enemy, but she's still got Challenger guns and tanks, doesn't she?"

"Don't lecture me on politics!" roared Luke's father. "And don't accuse me of profiteering! What about the inventions we've developed for the good of mankind? Challenger Medicine's research into vitamin therapy? Antibiosis drugs? Developing an artificial heart?"

"What about your weapons program? Challenger Marine's self-steering torpedo? The Challenger Mark Six assault rifle? The radio-controlled tank?"

"How do you know about those?"

"Because, when you're not packing me off to some awful school or other, I live here. I have eyes in my head and I'm not a complete idiot! Anyway, the tank is running around the yard in circles right now!"

Sir Andrew shook his head in baffled fury. "You and your mother make a fine pair! You're both as headstrong as mules."

Luke's voice was weary. "Mother's obsessed with the past, you're obsessed with the future. I just wish both of you spent a little more time in the present."

His father returned Luke's stare for a while. When he spoke again, his voice was much calmer. "Sit down, Luke."

Puzzled, Luke did as he was told.

"I suppose your mother and I could have managed things differently," Sir Andrew went on with a defeated air that Luke found worse than his rage. "But with me stuck in this chair, what could I do but stay here and bury myself in work? And your mother never understood what I was about; never wanted to understand. So she'd go off on her fossil-hunting jaunts with you in tow." He gave his son a look that was almost wistful. "Did you enjoy them?"

Luke thought back to the months he had spent in tented camps, mostly in remote deserts, rooting around for fossils and bone fragments under a blazing sun while his mother, her tongue sticking out between her lips like a child's, brushed away the dust of millions of years...

"Not always," he admitted. "But I learned a lot."

Sir Andrew nodded slowly. "I couldn't have gone with

you even if I'd wanted to. Your mother and I each had our own interests." He spread his hands. "I tried to make this a home for all of us…"

"But you turned the place into a factory and sent me off to school," said Luke accusingly, "and Mother was never here. Not much of a home."

"I'm not saying I didn't make mistakes." Sir Andrew's voice was subdued. "I suppose you're right, our lives have become…" He waved his hands vaguely as he sought for a metaphor. "Semi-detached. But that doesn't mean I don't care about you, Luke, or your mother. It doesn't mean I'm not worried about her or that I'd spare any effort to get her back."

"I know," said Luke. "Don't worry, I'll find her. When do I go to Brazil?"

Sir Andrew colored. The momentary truce was over. "You are NOT going to Brazil! You've no idea what you might be getting into! Has it occurred to you that these snake-and-spear ruffians might be behind your mother's disappearance?"

"Yes," said Luke, "it has. I don't see that it makes any difference. I told her how to find the Lost World. If she's in trouble, it's up to me to get her out. As Uncle John said, you're always telling me to show you I'm ready to take responsibility – well, then, give me some!"

"Out of the question!"

Luke played his last card. "Anyway, you need me. I'm the only one who knows exactly where Mother was planning to go."

"Ned and Roxton were both on your grandfather's expedition..."

"As he said himself, Roxton can't go, and Uncle Ned couldn't find his way to the bathroom with a map!"

"Would you put your mother's life in danger by refusing to tell me where she is?"

"Of course I wouldn't. But what would be the point of telling you? You're not going to Brazil. Anyway, you've already ordered Uncle Ned to get a team there as fast as he can. All I'm asking you to do is send me and Nick with him. Uncle Ned will need guides. When he's found them, I'll tell them what they need to know. That way I can answer any questions they have and there's no possibility of confusion." Luke set his chin obstinately. "I *am* going to find my mother, so you'd better accept it."

Luke's father glared at his son for several seconds. Then he threw his hands in the air. "All right! We can at least hope that, in Brazil, you won't be surrounded by traitors and assassins. Let's see if you really are ready for responsibility. But your job is to brief the local guides. That's all! You tell them exactly where your mother was going, and what route she was planning to take. Once you've done that, you sit tight in Manaus while Ned and his team go up the Amazon. *They* go into the jungle, *you* stay in contact with me by telegraph. On no account are you to go further than Manaus. Is that understood?"

Reflecting that it was comfortably over 5,000 miles from Kingshome Abbey to Manaus, and that a lot might happen when he got there, Luke said, "All right."

Nick was waiting outside the library door when Luke emerged. "Well?" he demanded. "Are we going?" Luke nodded. Nick punched the air. "Ah, that's great. Travel, fresh air, golden beaches and Latin lovelies dancing the samba!"

Luke glared at him. "It won't be a vacation!"

"Oh, no," said Nick hurriedly, "not at all. We'll find your ma, never fear. Still – Brazil, eh? And you're never going to tell me that following in your grandpa's footsteps won't add a bit of spice to the adventure!"

6 DEPARTURE

Lisbon, Portugal
May 1933

The launch puttered busily across the shimmering blue waters of the Tagus Estuary, rising and falling as it rode the slight swell. Luke gazed back over the boat's pitching stern at the huddled white buildings of Lisbon; the soaring dome of the unfinished Santa Engrácia church on the shoreline and the looming bulk of the Castelo de São Jorge behind. As the city faded in the haze, he turned his attention to the blue and white fishing boats lying at anchor as their owners cast and hauled nets or set pots for crab and lobster, and the gulls and gannets that wheeled in the powder-blue sky.

Nick had eyes only for the gigantic flying boat to which the launch was conveying them. To his disgust, even in this age of technological marvels, there had been no available flight that would get the Challenger party to Lisbon faster than the despised train. Ever since they had left London he had moaned about the limitations of rail travel. "Chug-chug-chug," he had complained, "rattle-rattle-rattle. This is the twentieth century for pity's sake, can't we do better than a glorified stagecoach?"

The rail journey across Europe – by the boat train for Paris, then the *Sud Express* across France, Spain and Portugal – had taken three days. Luke had chaffed at the time lost. But all that was about to change. The Challenger party was about to be whisked across the Atlantic, as though on a magic carpet, in a triumph of German engineering: the mightiest aircraft that man's ingenuity had yet created.

Nick was in raptures. "Look at it! The Dornier Do X." He pointed. "Isn't it the grand machine of the world? The size of it! A hundred and thirty feet long, wingspan a hundred and sixty feet and, if you stood on that wing, you'd be thirty-three feet above the water. Then there are the engines – twelve liquid-cooled Curtiss Conquerors mounted back to back, each one producing six hundred and forty horsepower! And don't they need it – the maximum take-off weight is fifty-six tons…"

Luke sighed. "Don't you ever look at the scenery?"

"What scenery?" asked Nick without taking his eyes from the flying boat.

Luke gazed at the Dornier with a jaundiced eye. "My mother has been missing for ten days, now. Anything could be happening to her. So, sorry, just at the moment, I don't care what size that thing is or how many engines it's got. I just want to know how fast it'll get us across the Atlantic. It's nearly four thousand miles from here to the Brazilian coast."

"Well, let's see." Nick's brow furrowed in calculation. "She'll do around a hundred and twenty miles per hour, so that's about thirty-two hours' actual flying time – more if we get a headwind, less with a tailwind – plus two refueling stops. Two more days ought to do it."

"Another two days!" Luke groaned.

"If we'd had to take a steamer, it would have taken weeks! We were lucky to get these tickets."

Luke had to admit that this was true. This service, run by Lufthansa, the German state airline, from Lisbon in Portugal to Las Palmas in the Canaries, Praia in the Cape Verde Islands and Natal on the coast of Brazil, was experimental and infrequent. Consequently, demand for tickets was high. What strings Luke's father had pulled to get Edward Malone and two of his security team – let alone Luke and Nick – on the flight, he had no idea. He glanced at his escort, seated in the small cabin of the launch. Uncle Ned was pale and withdrawn as usual; and his men, Briggs and Stanwick, both crop-headed, heavily built and expressionless, looked out of place in their business suits among the fashionably dressed fellow passengers. "They look like a couple of gift-wrapped bricks," as Nick commented.

The launch bumped gently against the flying boat's hull and uniformed flight crew helped the passengers embark. The chief cabin attendant, wearing a spotless white mess jacket with Lufthansa badges on the lapels, examined their tickets. "Herr Malone and party?" he said. "Welcome aboard. Your luggage will be taken directly to your sleeping cabins. The smoking room and dining room will be open immediately once we are airborne. This way to the lounge, please."

"Smoking room? Sleeping cabins?" chortled Nick. "This isn't a plane – it's a flying hotel!"

The lounge was luxuriously furnished with plump seats and low tables. Newspapers and magazines were neatly arranged in racks. Luke glanced around and, to his amazement and delight, caught sight of a familiar, hook-nosed figure. As though feeling Luke's eyes on him, Lord John Roxton glanced up and gave his godson a wintry smile. "Ah – there you are."

Roxton and Malone were shaking hands before Luke found his voice. "I thought you weren't coming with us."

"Only as far as Las Palmas," drawled Roxton. "Something unexpected has cropped up. I need to do a little business for the Firm." Luke nodded. "The Firm" was a codename for British Military Intelligence, but there was no point asking Roxton what his business in the Canary Islands was. "Ned," continued Roxton, taking Malone's elbow, "I trust you have been able to make arrangements for the trip to your satisfaction..."

While Malone and Roxton talked in low voices and Briggs and Stanwick tried without success to look inconspicuous, Luke dropped into a seat and, for the hundredth time on the journey so far, checked his jacket pockets. He felt the comforting bulk of his grandfather's notebook and relaxed. All being well, he would shortly need the information it contained.

Reassured, he gazed around at his fellow passengers and was startled to catch one of them, a woman, watching him. At least, so he thought. It was hard to be sure as her eyes were hidden behind tinted glasses. She had the high cheekbones and shallow-set eyes particular to the Far East. The woman made no move to shift her gaze and the feeling that he was being observed made Luke uncomfortable. This angered him, and he returned her stare. She could have been Chinese or Korean, but the Tokyo and Yokohama labels on her hand luggage suggested Japanese. She was taller than Luke, almost as tall as Roxton, and wore a long leather coat with riding boots. These attracted attention and whispered comments from her fellow passengers, which she studiously ignored. At length, she turned her head away and Luke, with some relief, watched idly as the last of the passengers found their seats.

To his surprise, he realized that he was tired. Two nights on a so-called "sleeper" train had not been restful; sleeping was not easy when the train constantly whistled, clattered over points, roared through tunnels and clanked into stations. And he wasn't feeling the thrill he usually experienced when leaving Kingshome Abbey. This time, he felt as if he was exchanging one prison for another; swapping his father's plans and expectations for the responsibility of finding his mother.

Surrounded by the chatter and bustle of his fellow passengers, Luke's chin dropped onto his chest and he fell asleep.

He jerked awake as the first engine coughed into life. One by one, the twelve engines mounted above the wing spluttered, roared briefly and settled down to a steady throb, shaking the Dornier's mighty airframe. The chief cabin attendant waved goodbye to the last launch and closed the door. Moments later, the engine note changed. Passengers exclaimed with excitement – Nick was positively hugging himself with anticipation – as the flying boat began to cleave a path through the deep blue water.

The engines roared again and the plane gathered speed. The gentle smack of the waves against the hull became a rush: the aircraft juddered like a car driving over cobbles. Craning to look out of the circular windows, Luke saw a vast plume of spray fountaining out on either side of the fuselage as the ponderous aircraft surged forward. Then, abruptly, the buffeting stopped and the rippled water seemed to fall away beneath them as the huge flying boat rose into the sky with elephantine grace.

The hours passed slowly. Luke quickly found that this form of travel, while undoubtedly comfortable, was pretty monotonous. There was nothing to see outside the windows but the ruffled blue of the Atlantic and later, far over to port, the dark loom of the African coast. Luke made an attempt to talk to his godfather, but Roxton, apparently preoccupied by the papers he had taken from his briefcase, answered with such an abstracted air that Luke soon gave up the conversation. Other passengers dozed, read or played cards. The Japanese woman simply sat and did nothing. Maybe she had nothing to do. Maybe she was asleep. Luke gave up speculating whether her eyes were open or closed behind the dark glasses and followed Nick into the dining room. He was too restless to eat much, though Nick tackled everything that was brought to him with gusto.

After lunch, Luke settled back in the lounge. He took out a pocket atlas and once again ran through the route they would have to follow to reach Manaus in the heart of the Amazon rainforest. From Natal they would have to take a steamer to Belém at the mouth of the Tocantins River: a thousand miles, give or take. Then they'd have to transfer to a riverboat for the final leg to Manaus – another nine hundred miles. Luke worked the figures out in his head and groaned.

Nick gave him a sympathetic look. "Something on your mind?"

"It's going to be at least another month before we get to Grandpa's Lost World," said Luke savagely.

Malone looked up from his paper. "I know, Luke," he said quietly, "but there's nothing to be done about it. It's a roundabout route, but there isn't a faster one. In any case, we have a better chance of running across your mother if we take the route she used herself. And we're not actually sure that there's anything seriously wrong.

For all we know, Harriet may be waiting for us in Manaus, ready to scold us for making a fuss."

Luke made no reply. He knew Malone didn't believe this, but there was no use in further complaints. He tried to comfort himself with the thought that his mother, for all her apparent vagueness, was a resourceful woman who was used to harsh conditions and discomfort. But memories of her crowded in on him.

He hadn't had a conventional childhood. Other children learned to sing, "Baa Baa, Black Sheep." His mother's version had been:

"Bron-to-saur-us, munching on a tree
Shall I tell you what I see?
Your hide is thick and your legs are strong
Your head is really tiny and your neck is very long."

Admittedly, this made more sense than the original and was much more useful if he ever had to identify a brontosaurus. The Harriet Challenger nursery rhyme collection had contained many similar ditties: "Ride a T Rex to Banbury Cross," "Jack And Jill Went Up The Hill (To Fetch A Stegosaurus)": and the diplodocus bone that Old Mother Hubbard took from her cupboard was big enough to keep her poor doggie happy for months. Luke hadn't learned to read and write from storybooks or fairy tales. His ABC had been *Allosaurus, Brachiosaurus, Centrosaurus...*

However eccentric his upbringing, it had not been unhappy. Luke remembered the patience with which his mother had taught him to identify fossils and the hours she had cuddled him on her knee, telling him ridiculous made-up stories about Tommy and Trixie, the terrible triceratops twins. It dawned on Luke for the first time that while she was dragging him around some of the most inhospitable parts of the world, she had, at the same time, been trying her best to be a good mother. And now she was lost, maybe hurt or in danger... His throat became swollen and his eyes stung.

"Hello!" Nick pricked his ears at a change in the engine note. "The pilot's throttling back – looks like we're coming in to land."

Luke peered out of the window. Emerald-green islands were visible, rearing up from the silky surface of the ocean. The Canaries. A few minutes later, the flying boat's hull kissed the waters of the harbor. They had arrived at Las Palmas.

The Dornier was instantly surrounded by boats. Tankers replaced the fuel the plane had used. Launches arrived to bring new passengers, and take off the ones whose journey ended here. The Japanese woman, Luke noted, was going on. She sat with her customary immobility, like an island in a turbulent sea, while arriving and departing passengers flowed unregarded around her.

Lord Roxton had already collected his coat and hat. He shook hands with Malone and Nick, then he turned to face his godson.

"Goodbye, Luke," he said. "I wish I were coming with you. There's an attraction in the thought of pitting myself against the jungle one last time." He shrugged. "But – duty calls. I wish you luck."

Luke shook the proffered hand. "Thank you, sir."

Then Roxton was gone. Luke felt bereft. With the wily old adventurer at his side, he'd had no doubt that his search for his mother would be successful. Without him...

Luke clenched his fists. Without Roxton, he would still succeed. All the same... Luke sighed, and picked up a magazine. He sat and read it without taking in a word.

An hour later, they were in the air once more, and flying into the tropical night.

Luke and Nick retired to their cabins, where Luke, despite his anxiety, slept soundly. By the time he awoke, it was daylight. There was barely time for a hurried breakfast before the plane began descending once again to make its final fuel stop in the Cape Verde islands.

However, this time there was no repeat of the practiced efficiency that had seen them quickly on their way from Gran Canaria. The cabin door failed to open.

There seemed to be a shouted conversation from the cockpit windows between the pilots and one of the boats that had come out to meet the plane. The chief cabin attendant briefly disappeared. When he returned, it was clear from his expression that he bore unwelcome news.

He held up his hand for silence. *"Meine Damen und Herren.* Ladies and Gentlemen. On behalf of Lufthansa, I regret to inform you that the pilots report a slight technical problem with one of the engines." Ignoring the sudden buzz of conversation among the passengers, he continued, "I hope that this matter may be speedily resolved and that the delay will be minor. Nevertheless, I must ask you all to go ashore while repair work is carried out." He waited impassively for the outbreak of indignant protests to die away before continuing, "Taxis will be waiting to take you to a hotel, where you will be made comfortable until you are able to rejoin the aircraft. On behalf of the captain and the crew, I apologize for any inconvenience this delay may cause."

Nick snorted as he and Luke stepped into the launch that would carry them ashore. "So much for the triumph of German engineering."

Malone sighed. "Let's hope they can fix it quickly – and that this island is a little more interesting close up than it looks from here."

Luke said nothing. He had a sick feeling in the pit of his stomach. Yet more delay!

The short trip across the bay was made in silence. Luke's fellow passengers, whether upset, irritated or resigned, were disinclined to talk. He found himself facing the Japanese woman, whose lack of expression and hidden eyes made it impossible to guess whether she was annoyed by the delay or not. Malone sat gazing glumly over the launch's side. Briggs and Stanwick, seated to either side of him, responded to the situation with their usual stolid indifference.

They disembarked at a small jetty where a fussy little man in a nondescript uniform was helping passengers into taxis. Luke noted, to his surprise, that the Japanese woman had turned away from the line of awaiting cabs, and was walking briskly in the opposite direction. He gave a mental shrug. Maybe she was getting off here and had arranged for someone to pick her up. He forgot about the woman as his party joined the line. The official dispatched the group before theirs and Luke was about to turn to the next taxi in line when the man caught him by the arm.

"Your pardon, *senhor*," he said quickly. "You are five. This car is too small. Allow me." He put two fingers between his teeth and gave a shrill whistle. Some distance down the quayside, a battered Packard pulled out from the waiting cabs and stopped alongside the line.

Luke glanced at Malone, who shrugged and headed for the car. The little man scuttled in front of him and held the door open while Malone, his security men, Luke and Nick climbed inside. The man slammed the door shut and returned to his task of finding cabs for the remaining passengers.

Luke settled back into the scuffed leather upholstery as the car swung out of the harbor gates. With little interest, he gazed through the cracked and dusty window. Nick did the same. Edward Malone seemed sunk in melancholy, Briggs and Stanwick might have been carved in stone for all the interest they took in their surroundings.

None of them noticed the black sedan that pulled smoothly away from the curb as they passed and, at a safe distance, settled down to follow them.

7 AMBUSH

Praia, Cape Verde Islands

For a while, they traveled through the dusty streets of the town. Before long the gaps between the low buildings with their barred windows grew wider, and they were out in the country. They drove between scattered farmsteads, through low hills studded with thorn bushes and clumps of grass the color of burned paper. In the distance reared mountains with jagged peaks like dragons' teeth.

Malone frowned. "We seem to be going a very long way. Hey, driver! How long before we reach this hotel?"

Their driver, an ancient Creole with a lined face, swerved to avoid a donkey carrying a load of sugar cane three times its own height, and gave them a gap-toothed grin. "*Sim, senhor. Hotel.*"

"Yes, hotel! How long?" Malone tapped his wristwatch. "How long?"

The driver shrugged. "*Não digo inglês.*"

"Good grief, man, even if you don't understand English it's a simple enough question. How long? Fifteen minutes? An hour? *Uma hora?* Hello, what's this...?"

The Packard slithered to a halt in a cloud of dust. A truck was parked diagonally across the road in front of them. It seemed to be carrying sacks, some of which had fallen off the back, littering the road. Its rusty hood gaped open and a man wearing overalls and a straw hat stood gazing into the engine compartment with a woeful expression on his face.

Their driver got out without haste and made his way over to the truck. "*Olá!*" he called. "*O que está acontecendo?*"

The other replied in voluble Portuguese, with gestures that seemed to hold the weather, the roughness of the road, the failings of the engine and the malevolence of fate for his misfortune. As his complaints continued, a scrunching of tires behind the taxi signaled the arrival of another car. Luke glanced at the black sedan that

81

appeared in the Packard's side mirror and felt the short hairs on his neck bristle with sudden apprehension. "Uncle Ned," he began...

Then everything seemed to happen at once.

The doors of the sedan swung open and its occupants slid out on either side. The driver was the Japanese woman, their fellow passenger. Her two companions looked like islanders, but they had ammunition belts crossed over their frayed shirts and carried machine guns. Luke felt his mouth go dry as both men dropped into a crouch, aiming at the taxi. A split second later, the car juddered with the impact of high-velocity bullets.

As if this were a signal, the taxi driver and the owner of the truck took to their heels. The sacks in the back of the truck seemed to explode and two men, also armed with machine guns, surged from their hiding places with a yell, firing from the hip.

Inside the Packard it was as though time stood still. Luke and Nick exchanged appalled glances as holes appeared in the bodywork and glass shattered around them. Malone seemed shocked into immobility. One of the security men – in the heat of the moment Luke couldn't be sure whether it was Stanwick or Briggs – looked down stupidly at the fountain of blood that suddenly erupted from the shoulder of his jacket...

Then Malone yelled, "Out! Out!" and hurled himself against the car door. It burst open, and then they were running, running, with bullets whining around them like insects and striking little volcanoes of dirt from the ground at their feet. The security man who had been hit – Luke realized it was Briggs – ran with his left hand clutched to his right shoulder until another bullet found its mark and he spun around and fell. Luke half-turned to go to his aid, but a rough shove from Malone sent both him and Nick tumbling into the rocky ditch at the side of the road.

Luke sat with his back to the bank of the ditch and tried to control his breathing. A loud crack beside his ear made him look up. Malone and Stanwick, the surviving security man, had drawn automatic pistols from their shoulder holsters and were returning fire.

Nick gaped at Luke. "What in the name of...?!"

"Ambush," said Luke tersely. "We should have seen it coming. Remember how that taxi appeared especially for us?"

Nick swore. "Those are Challenger Mark III sub-machine guns they're firing at us."

"I told my father he should be more careful who he sells his blasted weapons to."

A female voice snapped an order. This may have been an instruction to the gunmen not to waste ammunition while their targets were temporarily out of harm's way. At any rate, the firing died. Luke heard their attackers calling to each other as they shifted positions, trying to get a clear shot at their quarry.

Malone dropped down beside Luke and Nick to reload. "We can't hold them off for long," he said, his voice quite calm, though his fingers worked with feverish haste to replace the ammunition clip. "Four machine guns against two pistols aren't odds I would have chosen... Now listen carefully. We'll give you covering fire. When I say 'Run', make for that gulley over there." He gestured with the barrel of the pistol toward a dried-up streambed that wound down the hillside.

"We're not leaving you," protested Nick.

Malone gave his son a lopsided smile. "You're unarmed. Difficult to see how you can help us, except by getting away. Hide up until nightfall, then contact the authorities, let them know what's happened."

"But..."

"No arguments. When I tell you, run and don't turn back for anything. Got it?"

Luke hesitated, then nodded. "Your da's right. There's nothing we can do against guns." He lowered his voice so that Malone could not hear. "In any case, if you and I escape, the gunmen might follow us and leave Uncle Ned alone."

Nick bit his lip and nodded. His father gave his shoulder a quick squeeze before swinging into a crouch and peering over the edge of the ditch.

"Now!" he snapped over his shoulder. "Run!"

Malone and Stanwick leaped to their feet and sprayed bullets in the direction of their assailants. Luke and Nick rose into a crouch and sprinted for the gulley. Once more, bullets whined around them. Luke zigzagged to make himself a more difficult target. From the corner of his eye he saw Nick stumble and go into a roll. Even as he reached back to help his friend, his momentum carried him over the edge of the gulley to land with a jarring thud on the stones of the streambed. A moment later, Nick crashed to the ground beside him.

"Are you hit?" demanded Luke.

Nick shook his head. "I tripped." Then, with a curse, he hauled himself to peer over the edge of the gulley. Luke followed suit.

They saw Malone and Stanwick, feet planted wide in a firing stance, still covering their escape. They saw their attackers, advancing at the run, firing as they came, with the woman striding behind. They saw Stanwick go down in a hail of bullets. Then, a moment later, they saw Edward Malone, Nick's father, Luke's Uncle Ned, buckle at the knees. He loosed off one more shot as he kneeled. Then, twisting as he fell, he sank out of sight.

Nick's face was frozen with horror. He opened his mouth to yell or scream, but no sound came out.

Luke was appalled. He could barely believe what he had just seen. How could it happen to Uncle Ned? Then the terrible reality of their situation caught up with him. The gunmen were still out there: he and Nick had to get away, and Nick was clearly in a state of shock, unable to think or act for himself. Luke would have to do the thinking for both of them. He grabbed Nick roughly by the sleeve. "Come on!"

Nick remained gazing at the spot where his father had fallen. The Japanese woman pushed between the gunmen and seemed to study the ground where Malone lay. Then her head swiveled until her eyes, invisible behind the dark lenses of her glasses, were staring directly at the boys' refuge.

"Nick!" Luke dragged his friend out of sight. "Your dad bought us time. We have to do what he said and get away." Nick shook his head, whether in disagreement or disbelief was unclear. Luke punched him in the chest. "We have to! D'you think your da would want you to sit here waiting to be slaughtered like some stupid sheep?" He grabbed Nick's arm and pulled. "This way!"

Nick said nothing, but made no resistance. Rocks slipped and clattered at their feet as they scrambled down the gulley.

For a while, they heard shouts behind them. Luke tensed his shoulders as he ran, expecting at any moment the impact of a bullet that would tear him from this world. But no bullet came. They seemed to have outdistanced their pursuers – or maybe the shots fired by Stanwick and Malone had done some damage to their attackers after all.

At the foot of the hill, the gulley petered out and the dry streambed settled in a meandering course between cane fields. Luke plunged into the tall, green stalks of sugar cane with relief. It would give no protection from bullets, but their pursuers were much less likely to find them and pin them down here among the cane than on the open hillside.

Luke turned and caught Nick's shoulders as he blundered into the field behind him. Nick's jaw was slack and his eyes were glassy. The moment he stopped running, he slumped down like a marionette whose strings were cut. For several minutes, he lay face down on the cracked earth, panting convulsively. Then he raised a stricken face to Luke.

"He's dead," he whispered. "My da's dead."

"We don't know that." Luke didn't believe his own words, but he couldn't allow Nick to give up hope. He tried to make his voice encouraging. "Maybe he was only injured. Or knocked out. Maybe they took him prisoner."

"Why would they do that?" Nick shook his head. Then his lips twisted into a snarl. "I'm going to kill them."

"Try it, and they'll kill you," said Luke flatly. "We don't have any friends here. We don't even know who our enemies are."

Nick drew himself into a crouch. He wrapped his arms around his chest as if to warm himself. His whole body was shaking. Tears started from his eyes and formed dark-edged lines down his dusty cheeks. "Then what can we do?"

"What your dad said. Hide out until it gets dark, then go to the authorities."

Nick let his forehead fall onto his knees. Luke kneeled beside him and dropped a hand awkwardly on his shoulder. "I'm sorry, Nick. I'm sorry about your da. Let's hope they just winged him, eh? He's a tough old bird. All rugby players are. He's probably had worse playing for London Irish."

Nick shook his head. Between choking sobs, he said, "I never told him...I never said..." His voice became harsh, accusatory. "I mean, ever since Ma died, it was like...he was only half alive – he *embarrassed* me! I didn't know...what to say to him. We never talked... about her...about anything. But he was my da! And I loved him, but I never said..." He shook his head, unable to go on. Luke knew exactly what he meant. He felt the same way about his own parents – it was one of the many bonds he had with his cousin – but he couldn't talk to his father either; and as for his mother, it might already be too late...

Furiously, he rejected the thought. Part of him just wanted to curl up, whimpering, and wait for someone else to take charge. But with Uncle Ned gone, there was no one else. If he and Nick were to survive this, it was up to Luke to make the decisions.

"Come on," he said, "we'd better keep moving. They may still be behind us." When Nick made no move, he helped him to his feet. "It's no use just sitting here. You know what we have to do. Run if we must, fight when we can. All right?"

Nick raised a tear-stained face and nodded dumbly.

For a long time, they wove their way through the cane stalks, treading carefully so that no movement of the grassy leaves would betray their location to watching eyes. They tried going to the left and the right, but either side of the cane fields there was only open country, offering no shelter, no hiding place from their pursuers.

At length, they came to farmstead beside a dirt road, with more featureless scrubland beyond. Between the field and the road stood a stone farmhouse with whitewashed plaster walls and a corrugated iron roof. A few animals scratched and rooted listlessly around it

– half a dozen chickens; a couple of small, hairy pigs; a disgruntled-looking goat.

To the side of the house, a couple of brooding oxen were yoked to a long beam that swept from their shoulders to a large pair of rollers, made of stone and supported in a wooden frame. A man wearing a faded checkered shirt was leading the oxen in a circular path around the rollers, which turned with a rumbling sound while another farmhand in overalls fed cane stalks between them. As Luke watched, the machine's purpose became clear. It was a mill, designed for grinding the sugar cane. The oxen's task was to turn one roller against the other, like a gigantic upright clothes-mangle, crushing the cane stalks between them to squeeze out the syrup. The farmhand, who was feeding the mill, had to duck beneath the low beam every time the oxen came around to complete a circuit. The cane creaked and groaned as the rollers ground it into a mess of fiber and pulp.

Nick crouched beside Luke, peering at the scene with the first signs of animation he had shown since the shooting. "Maybe we should go and ask them for help."

Luke wasn't so sure. "I don't suppose they speak English, and I don't think we could make ourselves understood in Portuguese."

"It's got to be worth a try; maybe one of them would give us a lift into Praia..."

"Ssssh!" Luke had noticed something else. In the shadows of a lean-to, precariously balanced against the side of the house, stood a farm truck – seemingly identical to the one that had stopped their taxi. Luke felt his neck bristle again. He took Nick's arm and silently began to withdraw into the cane field.

Then the farmhand at the mill turned from his task to collect more cane. For the first time, Luke saw his face. It was the driver of the truck.

Nick tugged at Luke's sleeve. A third man had emerged from the house. He called something to the first. Luke didn't recognize the newcomer, but his identity was not in doubt. Hanging from a shoulder strap and nestling against his hip, the man was carrying a Challenger Mark III sub-machine gun.

8 TRAPPED

everal minutes later, having beaten a hasty retreat from the farm, Luke and Nick crouched between the cane stalks trying to decide what to do next.

They looked up as a roar of airplane engines sounded from the bay beyond the town. The sound came nearer. Moments later, they caught a glimpse of a great boat-shaped hull and flashing wings as the flying boat that had brought them to the island passed low overhead. Drops of saltwater from the Dornier's take-off fell from the hull onto the parched earth and the cane stalks danced crazily with the wind of its passage. The great aircraft banked, already turning toward the distant coast of Brazil.

Nick was outraged. "They chucked us off here to be killed and now they've left us behind! I bet there was never anything wrong with the engines at all."

"Our snake-and-spear friends are behind this," said Luke. "I'm sure of it. They've outsmarted us all the way down the line. First the fake engine problem, then the taxi – and now here we are, rats in a trap. No wonder they didn't bother following us into the gulley – they didn't have to. They knew we couldn't leave the cane fields without being spotted and they knew we'd end up here. So one of them came back to the farm to wait for us."

"Two of them." Luke saw to his relief that Nick's instinct for survival was overcoming the grief and despair that had rendered him helpless. "Don't forget the driver. Where d'you suppose the others are?"

"Probably watching the open ground either side of the fields."

"Well, then, we could double back," said Nick, his voice harsh with anger and determination. "Go back the way we came. Maybe…" His voice caught in a sob. Then, more steadily, he went on, "Maybe we can find out for sure what happened to Da – in any case we can hide out until dark like he said, and then…"

He was interrupted by a rustle in the cane, seemingly not too far away. A flight of pigeons shot out of the surrounding stalks with a clapping of wings. With one accord, Luke and Nick turned away from the disturbance and snaked back toward the farm.

Luke's mind was racing. Their attackers had followed them down from the hills after all, and were clearly closing in. There were three other gunmen at least, and maybe the woman, too. What could the two of them do now? They could retrace their steps as Nick had suggested: but then they would be back where they started and, in any case, could they do it without being seen? The hunters had demonstrated that they were not fools: they were no doubt confident that, between them, they would spot any attempt the two boys made to escape.

In the open country to either side, or beyond the farm, Luke and Nick would have no chance: they would be spotted instantly and hunted down like rabbits. And at the farm itself, the fourth gunman was waiting. But also at the farm, there was the truck...

A plan began to form in Luke's mind. If they could get to the truck, not only could they make good their escape and get back to Praia, they could leave their pursuers helplessly stranded. But how could they get past the gunman at the farm? Luke's lips drew back from his teeth in a wolf-like grin. Maybe there was a way.

He caught at Nick's sleeve. "How's your throwing arm?" he hissed. Nick's accuracy with a stone, especially at sowing time, had made him the toast of local farmers and the terror of starlings and rooks for miles around Kingshome Abbey.

"Fine." Nick looked bewildered. But as Luke hurriedly explained his plan, a spark kindled in Nick's eyes. He liked it. The plan gave him a chance to strike back at the men who had shot his father. He began to search the dusty earth for suitably sized stones.

They were near the farm now. Luke and Nick split up and hurried to points some distance apart from which they could watch the yard.

The oxen still trod their endless path around the mill, the farmer still fed the cut stalks through the grinding rollers and the gunman still paced back and forth in front of the house, his eyes scanning the shimmering stalks of cane.

Then, with a sudden clatter, a stone thrown by an expert hand hit the wooden frame of the mill, bounced off and raised a cloud of dust at the miller's feet. He looked up, startled. The man leading the oxen came to a halt and the plodding beasts did likewise. The gunman spoke sharply to the farm workers and they shrugged expressively, protesting that they no more knew where the stone had come from than he did. Another stone followed the first; it hit the gunman in the chest. With a sharp cry, he ran to take shelter behind the stout wooden timbers of the mill. A further volley of stones set the two farm workers running for cover toward the house.

Luke tensed himself. This was the crucial moment.

A final stone flew from Nick's hiding place, and struck the nearest ox firmly on the rump. With a bellow, the startled beast surged forward, taking its companion with it, and broke into a lumbering trot.

The gunman, intent on spying out the source of the stone-throwing, realized his peril too late. The swinging beam caught him on the side of the head with a crack that Luke heard even as he set off in a sprint across the yard.

Luke's intention had been to cause a distraction while he made a beeline for the truck. If the oxen got in the gunman's way, spoiling his aim, so much the better.

What Luke had not foreseen was that the gunman, half-stunned by the blow from the beam, should stumble against the churning stones of the mill – and put out a hand to save himself.

The man screamed in agony. Luke glanced in his direction and felt a wave of nausea. The man's fingers were already being dragged between the crushing rollers. Luke glimpsed the snake-and-spear tattoo on the man's wrist just as it disappeared between the stones.

The man shrieked again and his other hand tightened convulsively on the trigger of the machine gun, which sprayed bullets wildly into the air.

This was no time to hesitate. Luke reached the truck and yanked the door open with a squeal of metal. He scrambled into the driver's seat. One of the advantages to being heir to Challenger Industries had been that, from the moment he was tall enough for his feet to reach the pedals, Luke had (with the connivance of his father's indulgent employees) driven anything on wheels, tracks or any combination of the two that had come his way. The truck's keys were in the ignition and the controls were a cinch. He pressed the starter. After a couple of reluctant wheezes, the engine burst into life. Luke put the truck in gear and floored the accelerator.

The ancient vehicle barreled out of its lean-to shelter. As Luke hauled at the wheel to send the truck into a tight turn, the tailgate caught one of the half-rotten posts holding up the roof, and sent it skittling out of the ground. The shelter swayed for a moment, then collapsed in a cloud of dust.

Mercifully, Luke could see nothing but the booted feet of the gunman kicking spasmodically in the shadow of the mill. The two farm hands ran from the house, waving their hats and shouting, until they were forced to leap for their lives as Luke drove the truck straight at them. He skidded to a halt opposite Nick's hiding place among the cane stalks. "Get in!"

As soon as Nick had hauled open the passenger door and climbed in beside him, Luke set off again. He swung the truck around in a clumsy handbrake turn to face the way he had come just as the three remaining gunmen burst from the cane field, only to scatter in panic as they each, in turn, found the bellowing, rust-streaked monster bearing down on them. By the time they had regained their feet, Luke was swinging onto the dirt road. The muzzles of their guns flashed as they fired after the speeding vehicle; the cab shuddered as a few shots found their target and the rear window shattered. But the rest of the wild shots went wide. The last Luke saw of their pursuers in the truck's cracked door mirror, they had ceased fire and stood shaking their fists and waving their guns in impotent rage.

"Watch out!" Nick's cry brought Luke's attention back to the road ahead. Bearing down on them, kicking up a plume of dust, was the black sedan that had taken part in the ambush earlier. The dirt road was narrow. There was no room for the truck and car to pass. Luke's lips pulled back in a snarl as he changed down with a grinding of gears, and gunned the engine.

"We'll crash!" howled Nick.

"Good." Luke could see the face of the Japanese

woman driving the car, set in a snarl that exactly mirrored his own. "We're heavier than she is."

Nick closed his eyes.

The woman evidently came to the same conclusion as Luke. At the last possible moment, she wrenched at the steering wheel. The car swung aside with a squeal of tires. The truck dealt it a glancing blow, crumpling the elegant black bodywork. Then they were past, and the car was lying in the rocky ditch at the roadside, engine roaring and wheels spinning helplessly. The truck raced on in triumph, burying its vanquished foe in the cloud of grit and dust that flew from its churning wheels.

Luke and Nick peered over a tumbledown wall at the main entrance of the Praia police station a little way down the street.

Earlier they had returned to the scene of the morning's ambush and found nothing. No survivors, no bodies. Even the bloodstains had disappeared beneath the shifting brown dust of the arid hills.

"It's as if they were never here!" Nick had looked around in despair. "We've got to find out what happened to Da, Luke. We've got to!"

"But we can't hang around," Luke had said unhappily. "There's always the chance those men will come back.

We're not going to find out what happened to your da and the others by rooting around here, anyway. The only sensible thing is to do what your da wanted, and go to the police."

So they had returned to Praia and abandoned the truck on a side street. They had arrived at siesta time and the streets had been almost deserted. Now, as the afternoon wore on, people were once more astir. It had taken Luke and Nick some time to find the police station. They had not wanted to draw attention to themselves by asking directions; at least, no more attention than was inevitable on an island where white faces were few and far between. The local population after all ranged in complexion from light coffee to midnight black. Finally, they had spotted a police uniform and followed its wearer, at a discreet distance, as he completed his round and headed back to the station.

"I still think we should have dumped that truck in the sea," complained Nick.

"No point," Luke replied. "It doesn't matter if they find the truck – they wouldn't need to be masterminds to figure out we'd head back here. Where else could we go?" He hesitated. "Do we go and see the police now? Your da said we should wait until after dark."

"But he didn't know we'd give them the slip, did he?" replied Nick. Hesitantly, as though by wishing he could make it true, he added, "You said yourself, he might be a prisoner or lying injured somewhere. The quicker the police know what's happened, the better our chances of finding him..." He broke off as Luke's hand closed on his shoulder like a vise, dragging him back behind the wall. "What...?"

Luke pointed wordlessly.

The black sedan was rolling down the street in a cloud of steam and dust. It looked very much the worse for wear. The whole side facing Luke and Nick had caved in and bare metal gleamed below the ravaged black paintwork. The front fender hung away from the hood, its smashed headlamp dangling against the wheel.

The Japanese woman got out of the car and strode up the steps to the police station. Luke noticed with grim satisfaction that she was limping. Just as she reached the door, it opened and a policeman came out – a senior officer, judging by his shiny boots and the amount of gold braid he wore. The woman confronted him and let rip with a stream of Portuguese. The policeman at first spread his hands, denying responsibility for whatever the woman's complaint was, but a further angry outburst had him wringing his hands. After this, the woman gave what was clearly a string of commands and the wretched man drew himself up in a crashing salute before ushering the woman into the police station with a great show of deference.

Nick and Luke slumped down behind the wall. "That's blown it! So much for the authorities," said Nick bitterly. "Who *is* that woman?"

"I don't know," said Luke. "You spotted her on the plane, didn't you?"

"Hard to miss her."

"I think she's Japanese, though I'm not sure even of that. But I'll bet you anything you like, if we could get a close look at her wrist, we'd find a snake and spear tattoo."

"No deal."

"Anyway, it looks as if the police are in cahoots with her. Maybe they're on her payroll, or maybe they believe whatever lies she just told them. Either way, going to them now would be putting our heads in a noose. I'm sorry, Nick, but we won't find any help here. We can't even try to send a telegraph – they'll be expecting that."

Nick was almost weeping with anger and frustration. "Then what can we do?"

"We can't stay here – they'll find us for sure, sooner or later. Probably sooner, seeing as we don't exactly fit in with the locals. We've got to get away."

"We're on an island," Nick snarled. "How can we get

away? And if we could, which way would we go? Back the way we came, or continue with the journey?" Luke said nothing. "We still don't know for sure what happened to Da. If we go back, we can get more help – from your dad, maybe even Lord John, the British government..."

Luke felt he was being torn in two. He knew how desperately Nick wanted to find out what had happened to his father, but he was sure in his own mind that his uncle was already dead. Meanwhile, Luke's mother was also in trouble and ever since the attack that morning, a conviction had been growing in his mind: their enemies had now made two attempts to kill him, their target was obviously Challenger Industries. Luke's instincts told him they were after his mother, too. If that was the case, she would need him and he couldn't afford to delay.

"We could go back," he said carefully. "But we don't know if Lord John is still in Las Palmas, or whether we could find him if he was. More likely, we'd have to go to London to get help and that's five days away even if we could get back as fast as we came. And we can't. We have no money, no passports, no tickets – only the clothes we stand up in. We could lose weeks by going back."

"We have to find out what's happened to Da!"

"Yes, and to do that we need help. We're closer to Brazil than England, and we do at least have a contact in Natal. Partridge is the local agent for Challenger Industries. He's the nearest person who can help us. We can send a telegraph to my father from Natal. And we'd still be on course to find my mother."

"So your ma is more important than my da, is that it?"

"You know it isn't," said Luke quietly. "If your da had been captured, and we knew where he was, I'd try to rescue him if it meant going to the North Pole or Timbuctoo."

"You do think he's dead, then?" Luke made no reply, and Nick's shoulders slumped. "Ah, there's no point in arguing. Like you said, we have to get away from here as quickly as we can. So if we get a chance to leave, we grab it, whichever way it takes us, on to Brazil or back to England. All right?"

Every instinct was telling Luke to press on, but he nodded reluctantly. "All right."

"Of course, it would help if we could grow wings..."

As if on cue, a low droning sound became audible. It grew gradually louder, reverberating from the walls of the buildings around them. The boys looked up. In a clear patch of sky above their heads, a slim high-winged aircraft with a seaplane hull appeared, heading for the harbor.

"Whale," said Nick.

Luke stared at him. "Are you sure? It looked like a plane to me."

Nick tutted. "That's what it's called – it's a Dornier Do J, if you want to be technically accurate, but it's called the *Wal* – that's German for whale. It's coming from the northeast, so it must be heading for Brazil, but it's no use to us. Wals are mail planes, they don't carry passengers."

Luke eyed the approaching aircraft, and a fierce grin spread slowly across his face. "I think you'll find this one will."

9 DELIVERY

The moon had set an hour earlier. Only the faint lights of the town and the distant glow of the stars rendered the oily surface of the sea and the outline of the seaplane visible in the otherwise perfect darkness.

Luke and Nick had "commandeered" a small boat from the beach and paddled out with lengths of driftwood. Abandoned, the boat floated slowly away. Luke had considered sinking it, for fear it might alert their pursuers to their avenue of escape. But he doubted that the islanders were wealthy and had no wish to deprive some poor fisherman of his livelihood. He hoped the drifting boat would be found and returned to its owner – once he and Nick were airborne and well away from Cape Verde.

They crept over the seaplane's starboard float. Above them loomed the struts that supported both the wing and the two back-to-back engines with four-bladed propellers fore and aft.

At length, Nick found the door into the aircraft's fuselage. It was fastened but unlocked, and moments later they were inside. The interior was pitch black, with only the faintest glimmer to show the portholes that gave light – when there was any to give – to the forward part of the hull.

Nick secured the door behind them as Luke checked the luminous dial on his watch. "Two hours before dawn," he said. "Get some sleep."

"I'm not sleepy." Nick had become increasingly morose as the evening had turned into night. For once, the prospect of adventure wasn't enough to cheer him. The full weight of the loss of his father had borne down on him during the hours they had lain hidden, waiting for the moon to disappear and the lackadaisical police watch on the harbor to peter out. Luke's awkward attempts to offer words of comfort had met with no response. At length he had run out of things to say to Nick and an awkward silence descended upon them.

Luke realized that he wasn't sleepy either. In any case, he couldn't afford to sleep. There was little point in exploring the aircraft in the dark and they could not risk a light that might be seen from the shore. He and Nick would have to be ready to make their plans at first light, when it was bright enough to see what they were doing but before the pilots arrived to take the plane on to Natal.

An hour crawled by. Luke sat on the cold deck with his back against the ribs of the fuselage, which seemed designed for maximum discomfort for anyone using them as a backrest, and tried to make plans; but all he could think of was the ambush in the hills, the broken-down truck, the sudden impact of machine-gun bullets and Uncle Ned and his men going down in a hail of fire...

Luke's head nodded, jerking him awake. Despite his resolution, he must have dozed off. He was furious with himself. The dim pre-dawn light was creeping through the aircraft's round windows, picking out vague details of the interior. Nick was already exploring. Luke scrambled to his feet and joined him, moving carefully and almost bent double in the cramped space.

In the forward part of the cabin, a raised cockpit

provided seats for the pilot and co-pilot. Otherwise most of the space was filled with mail sacks, secured to the fuselage with netting.

The prospect of action, and especially of putting one over on their enemies, seemed to have galvanized Nick. He kicked at a sack. "That's the only place to hide," he said. "Somewhere near the tail, where nobody will notice a couple of bags bulging in odd places. It won't be what you'd call luxurious – we'll be in there for a long time."

"Well, at least once we've taken off, the pilots will be busy flying the plane. Nobody will check the bags until we get to Brazil."

"Let's hope you're right." Nick shrugged. "But we have to be careful when they land to refuel..."

"Land?" Luke would not normally dream of questioning Nick's encyclopedic knowledge of air routes, but this sounded unlikely. "Where? There's nothing between here and the Brazilian coast."

"Yes, but this thing doesn't carry enough fuel to make the trip non-stop. So we'll be landing alongside a ship in the middle of the ocean. They'll pick up the plane, refuel it, and launch it again from a catapult."

"You're kidding!" Nick shook his head and Luke groaned. "This just gets better and better. Well, we'll have to make ourselves as comfortable as we can. We'll empty a couple of sacks and divide the mail between some of the others, then get inside the two empty ones and do a lifelike impression of a couple of packages. Come on, we don't have much time."

With the blade of his pocketknife, Luke pried open the lead seals securing several bags. Then they both set to work unwinding the coarse string. Luke hadn't been able to think of a way of resealing them, or retying the bags with him and Nick inside – they'd just have to hope nobody looked too closely. They selected sacks to hide in and then began to transfer handfuls of letters from them to the other bags.

When, twenty minutes later, the pilots arrived, yawning and chatting lazily to each other in German as they stowed their flight cases, the only sign that all was not as it should be were some half-dozen sacks from which the lead seals were missing and, had they been alert enough to notice, two unusually full sacks that bulged in unlikely places...

The aircraft, with its stowaways on board, took off and headed out over the ocean.

It was not a comfortable trip. The plane shook and rattled. The thin skin of its fuselage was not designed to keep out the noise of the engines. Luke was curled up in a cramped position, using the mail he had left in the sack as a prickly, makeshift cushion. He did not dare change position to ease his aches and pains – a mail sack that fidgeted was bound to attract attention. As the sun rose and the temperature inside the aircraft climbed, the stale air in the sack became stifling. Soon sweat was running down Luke's face and trickling inside his shirt. He was hungry – he had eaten nothing since breakfast the previous day – but his hunger was as nothing compared to his thirst.

He dozed fitfully as the flight went on, hour after hour. At long last, he awoke from a troubled nap to find that the engines had throttled back. A few minutes later, he suffered the discomfort of being bounced around inside his sack as the Wal set down on a lumpy sea and came to rest bobbing on the waves. Some time after that, their hiding place began to sway uncomfortably. Luke guessed that the plane was being craned onto the supply ship. Then came a series of jolts and mechanical clicks as the seaplane's hull was secured to the launching catapult. After that, silence.

Luke checked his watch. It was still only mid-afternoon. As the silence continued, he reached up for the mouth of the bag, eased it open and peered out cautiously. The cabin was deserted.

Nick's tousled head appeared from the next bag. "I bet the crew is having lunch," he growled, "lucky beggars." He looked around. "Nobody around." He began to ease his way out of the sack.

Luke was appalled. "Stay where you are! You'll be caught."

"I'd rather be caught than die of thirst." Nick had spotted a water bottle which the co-pilot had left hanging from the armrest of his seat. "I'm having that." He crept forward, eyeing the cabin windows carefully to ensure that he remained unobserved, and took the bottle. Then he paused, staring at a half-open flight case wedged beside the seat. He gave Luke a meaningful glance and dipped his hand into the case, drawing out a packet. He returned as cautiously as he had left, holding out the packet for Luke's inspection.

The manila covering was tied with a thin black ribbon and sealed with a dollop of red wax. Luke raised an eyebrow. "So?"

"Take a look at the seal."

Luke examined the wax more closely. Cast into the surface of the seal was a symbol he had first seen only a few days earlier, but one that was now instantly recognizable and charged with menace: the snake and spear.

Nick unscrewed the cap and raised the bottle to his lips. "I could drink the Atlantic dry." In spite of this, he barely moistened his mouth before passing the flask to Luke, who took a brief swig and passed it back. All his attention was on the package. He drew out his pocketknife, worked its blade under the seal and slit it from side to side.

Nick took another swig at the bottle and tutted. "Interfering with the snaky mail. You are in big trouble now, Sonny Jim."

Luke ignored him. The package contained several documents. Luke opened the topmost one and scanned it.

"What does it say?" demanded Nick, passing Luke the bottle.

"I don't know. It's just a series of symbols. Probably a code." Luke drank thirstily. "Still," he continued, "at least it shows this snake-and-spear group have a connection with Brazil. The co-pilot might be one of them, or maybe he's just moonlighting as a courier." Luke tapped the documents with an irritable finger. "We can't just take these – the crew would realize they had a stowaway on board right away. But if we can crack the code, it might tell us who our wiggly friends are and what they're up to." He glanced at the windows. "The pilots will be back any minute – there's no time to look at this right now. We'll hang on to it."

"What about the package?"

Luke reached into the bottom of his mail sack, pulled out a number of letters that were about the size and weight of the packet's contents, wrapped them in the manila covering and retied the ribbon. He eyed the seal dubiously. "We need heat to stick that back together."

"Leave it to me." While Luke stuffed the coded documents inside his shirt, Nick took the water bottle and the packet. On reaching the cockpit, he looped the bottle's strap back over the seat arm, delved into the co-pilot's case again and produced a lighter. He played the flame over the top half of the seal to soften it and pressed the two halves together. At the same moment, a sudden clang from outside announced the return of the aircrew. Hurriedly, Nick thrust the packet back inside the co-pilot's case and squirmed his way back into his hiding place.

He and Luke drew the mouths of their mailbags closed just as the hatchway into the cabin opened and the pilots returned. They seemed in a good humor, until the co-pilot gave an exclamation and asked an indignant question – presumably as to why there was no longer any water in his flask. The argument that arose was brief. Self-emptying water bottles or no, the men were on a schedule. The engines roared into life once more and, hardly a minute later, Nick and Luke were hurled, cursing (but very quietly), against the rear bulkhead of the cabin as the aircraft shot from the catapult, dipped alarmingly, then steadied itself and rose above the waves for the final leg of its journey.

The next time Luke peered out from his sack, the Wal had landed and was riding easily on a gentle sea. The last ghostly reds of sunset were fading from the sky. The puttering of a boat engine announced the arrival of a launch – apparently sent out to collect the pilots, because they, laughing and joking, left the aircraft. A member of the ground crew – wearing a postal services uniform complete with peaked cap – came aboard and, as the launch departed, busied himself checking labels on mailbags.

At least, this was what he was doing until Luke and Nick descended on him like a train wreck, stuffed an evil-smelling rag into his mouth – before he could utter more than a startled squeak – and dragged him, writhing and kicking, toward the tail of the aircraft.

A few minutes later, another boat arrived to collect the mail. The helmsman brought the boat alongside the seaplane while his companion clambered through its cargo door. There was a brief ruckus from inside the aircraft. The helmsman stood up, startled, and stepped forward as an unfamiliar figure emerged from the Wal and dropped into the boat.

The helmsman was taken aback. "*Quem é você?*" he demanded.

Luke, dressed in a postal service uniform several sizes too big for him and a cap that came down over his ears, wasn't prepared to explain who he was, especially in Portuguese. He gestured impatiently toward the open cargo door. "*Vamos!*"

The helmsman wasn't having any of it. "*O que você está fazendo?*"

Giving up the attempt to lure the man into the cabin, Luke pointed urgently at the outboard motor behind him. "Motor!" he improvised.

"*Que?*"

"Motor está..." Luke hesitated as he searched his memory for an appropriate Portuguese phrase. "Incendio!" he concluded triumphantly. The helmsman turned to see – and a quick heave from Luke sent him tumbling over the stern with an enormous splash.

Luke whistled and Nick, buttoning up the shirt that had previously belonged to the boat's other occupant, tumbled into the bow and cast off while Luke started the engine.

"I hate to be picky," said Nick, "but the Portuguese for 'fire' is '*fogo*', not 'incendio'."

Luke gave him a glare. "It worked, didn't it?"

Moments later, the launch pulled away from the

plane and set off across the bay. Some little time elapsed before a startled outcry from the shore indicated that the postal workers gathered there to unload the mail had realized there was something wrong. Luke ignored it and, keeping a wary eye out for rocks, steered the boat away from the lights of the harbor, aiming for the dark headland that would, once they had rounded it, take them out of sight.

Luke patted his pocket. Yes, he had remembered to transfer his grandfather's diary to his borrowed uniform. He yawned over the tiller. He and Nick had hardly slept for two days. Exhaustion was catching up with them, not to mention the shock of the events on Cape Verde. "We can't do anything until the morning," he told Nick. "If we go knocking on people's doors in the middle of the night, they'll set the dogs on us or have us arrested. Better try to get some sleep..."

At this point, he realized that he was wasting his breath. Nick was lying back in the bows with the cap he had appropriated from the luckless postal worker pulled down over his eyes. He was already snoring.

10 A COVERT OF PARTRIDGES

Natal, Rio Grande do Norte, Brazil

Early the next morning, George Partridge, Area Representative for Challenger Industries in Natal, was extremely surprised when two young men dressed as post office employees came knocking on his door. His surprise was upgraded to amazement by the revelation that the young men were impostors who were definitely not entitled to wear such uniforms. And when one of the young men revealed that he was the son and heir to Sir Andrew Challenger, his reaction could only be described as one of stupefaction.

"But...but...but...but..." was all he managed to say.

George Partridge was overweight and flustered. He wore an off-white linen suit, a hideous bow tie and, tucked into his breast pocket, a vast silk handkerchief with which he wiped the sweat from his face whenever he was agitated.

He wiped it now. "But you were supposed to be here two days ago! I had a telegram to say you were coming. I went to the harbor to meet you – and you weren't on the plane."

"No," said Luke patiently. "There was a bit of a hold-up."

"Well, yes, I know all about that."

Luke raised his eyebrows. "Do you?"

"Of course – I mean, I got your note."

"Which note would that be?" asked Nick.

"The note that said you'd decided to take a few days' vacation before coming on here and that I wasn't to do anything until I'd heard from you again. The man from the flight crew gave it to me personally."

"Didn't you wonder," asked Luke with the sort of restraint that made it clear that breaking things was an alternative he hadn't ruled out, "whether the note was genuine?"

George Partridge gaped at him. "Why shouldn't it be genuine? I mean, the man was an airline official – only a

German, you know, but he had a uniform and everything."

"So do we!" Luke pointed out. "What did you do?"

"Well, there wasn't much I could do. I came away and telegraphed Sir Andrew for further instructions."

Seeing that Luke's Challenger temper was wearing very thin, Nick put in, "Sir Andrew told us to meet you when we landed, and you'd help us. That's why we're here now. Did he tell you why we were coming to Brazil?"

Partridge seemed to feel on safer ground here. "No, not a word – he just said I was to give you every necessary assistance – you and Mr. Malone. Where is he, by the way?"

Carefully avoiding Nick's gaze, and in as few words as possible, Luke told him.

George Partridge's florid complexion bleached to ghostly white. He mopped the silk handkerchief over his face as though trying to rid it of some horrible stain. "God bless my soul," he said faintly. "Poor fellow. Poor fellow." He turned an appalled gaze on Luke. "But what am I to do?"

While George Partridge dithered, Luke drew Nick aside. "That's the question, isn't it?" he said. "The man's a nitwit, but he has the backing of Challenger Industries. So what *do* we want him to do?" Nick said nothing. Luke steeled himself. "I know you want to find out for sure about your da. We can't go back to Cape Verde ourselves without being shot or thrown in jail, but we could send to England for help and wait here for news."

"You'd stay with me, would you?" Nick looked him steadily in the eye.

Luke knew that their whole friendship depended on his answer. The more he thought about their enemies, the more convinced he was that his mother had fallen victim to them; that she was in danger and time was precious. But he owed Nick his loyalty, too. While he was convinced that Nick's father was dead, Luke couldn't bring himself to destroy his friend's last hope. He bit his lip and nodded. "If you want me to."

Nick gazed at Luke without speaking for what seemed an age. Then he sighed. "No. As you say, going back to Cape Verde would be suicide. And there's no point in waiting. I know my da's dead, I saw him shot with my own eyes, I just don't want to believe it. But I don't want to sit around here doing nothing. I want to get back at the people who killed my da, and the best way to do that is to find out what they're up to and put a wrench in their works. They want to stop us, so I say we go on."

"Sure?" said Luke. Nick nodded. Understanding what the decision had cost his friend, Luke took a deep breath, and squeezed Nick's arm. "Thanks."

Then he turned to George Partridge, who was still

muttering and moaning to himself. "What are you to do, sir? Follow your instructions. Send us on to Manaus."

"Manaus?!" Partridge's voice was practically a shriek. "No, no! Impossible! You've manhandled post office employees, stolen government property, entered the country illegally...you're fugitives from justice, for heaven's sake. And the Brazilian police have no sense of humor, you know. Very unforgiving body of men – very unforgiving. It will take weeks to sort this mess out. Months!"

Luke was dismayed. "We haven't got weeks, sir, much less months! Surely you can see..."

"What's going on here?" The voice was female, of the sort trained to gather members of a scattered hunt from three fields away. Any fox, hearing that voice, would know at once it might as well give up hope and die of a heart attack to save time.

The owner of the voice swept into the room. She had a hard, bony look about her – "A face to split kindling," as Nick later put it – and was dressed in corduroy slacks and a baggy sweater that seemed to have been used to smother a fire. Behind her came a woman with a pleasant, vacant expression. She wore a vast amount of costume jewelry and a dress so pale and floaty it gave her the appearance of a rather chintzy cloud.

"Lottie, m'dear." George Partridge looked more

befuddled than ever. "Dottie. Just conducting a little business…"

"We heard voices," barked the hatchet-faced woman, ignoring him completely. "Why's the house crawling with postmen?"

"They're not postmen, Lottie…"

"They look like postmen. If they're not postmen, who are they?"

Nick stood up and made a courtly bow. "Nick Malone, ladies, at your service."

"Well, this one certainly has better manners than the usual postman," said the woman Partridge had addressed as Lottie. "Postmen don't bow. All they do is steam your letters open. I hope you don't steam open letters, young man?"

Nick kept a straight face. "Certainly not, ma'am."

"Hmmm. What about the other one – does he have a name?"

"Luke Challenger."

The two women gave each other a startled glance. "Harriet Challenger's boy?"

Luke was taken aback. "Um…yes."

Lottie's attitude softened. "Well, that's different. Fine woman, your mother. Rode point-to-point before she took to digging up bones. Good seat. Very sound on horses. How is she?"

"We don't know," said Luke carefully. "That's why we're here."

"In that case," said the other woman in a much less strident voice, "you'd better sit down and tell us all about it."

Luke hesitated.

"Oh, sit down!" said Lottie forcefully. When Luke and Nick had done so, she continued, "Since my idiot of a brother seems to have forgotten his manners completely, I'd better do the introductions. This is Dorothea Partridge, I'm Charlotte Partridge – Dottie and Lottie to friends. Now, supposing you tell us why you're here at this ungodly hour, dressed in this extraordinary fashion."

Luke ran through the events of their journey again.

"Awful shame about Malone," said Lottie when he had finished. "Rugby type, wasn't he? Saw him play once – London Irish against 'Quins." She patted Nick's arm with rough sympathy. "Awful shame." Nick looked away and Lottie immediately became businesslike. "So, here you are with nothing but the clothes you stand up in – which aren't yours anyway."

"That's right," agreed Luke. "Everything else is in our trunks."

Lottie turned a gimlet eye on her brother. "And where are their trunks?"

"At the harbor, of course." George Partridge squirmed.

"I could hardly bring them away, could I? I had no instructions..."

"You're a fool, George!"

Dottie got to her feet and gave her brother's shoulder a comforting pat. "Never mind," she said, "I'll send Carlos." She gave Luke a winning smile. "Our driver, you know. He always knows exactly which officials to bribe – and he's very discreet." She went out.

Lottie gave a self-satisfied nod – though Luke noted that it was her seemingly woolly minded sister who had actually taken decisive action. "Well, at least you'll soon have a change of clothes," she said, "and passports – always assuming your baggage hasn't been ransacked. So, the question that remains is, what are we to do with you?"

"When you came in," said Luke, "I was asking your brother to send us on to Manaus..."

"Quite impossible." George Partridge made a desperate attempt to reassert his authority. "Out of the question. I have no instructions. In any case, the steamer for Belém left yesterday and there isn't another for a week."

Luke's heart sank. Belém was their next stop on the way to Manaus. If they couldn't reach it, they really were stuck.

Dottie came back. "That's all right. Carlos will be back by lunchtime." She gave them all a vague smile.

"We were debating what to do next," snapped Lottie, "but your fool of a brother won't lift a finger without instructions."

"He's your brother too, dear," said Dottie mildly. She turned to George Partridge. "Has it occurred to you, Georgie, that if you sent these young men on to Manaus, they wouldn't be your responsibility?"

"My sainted aunt!" George Partridge sat bolt upright. "That's true. Jackson's our man in Manaus. And once they leave here, they won't be my problem – they'll be Jackson's!"

"You've never liked him, have you, dear?" said Dottie inconsequentially.

A shadow crossed George Partridge's ample face. "But what's the good of talking? I couldn't get them to Manaus even if I wanted to."

"Not by steamer," said Dottie, "no. But I was thinking perhaps...Eduardo?"

Lottie snapped her fingers. "The very thing!"

"No!" Her brother failed to share her enthusiasm. "Eduardo? Man's a complete outsider, an absolute menace – not to mention a lunatic! And that machine of his – a deathtrap! Absolutely not! I will not entrust the son of my employer to Eduardo, and nothing you can do or say will make me!"

* * *

"Look!" Lottie pointed triumphantly. "There's Eduardo now!"

Carlos, as Dottie had predicted, had succeeded in recovering the trunks from the harbor. Later that afternoon, rested, fed and dressed in fresh clothes from their luggage, Luke and Nick stepped from the Partridge's car onto the strip of brown earth and spiky grass that was the nearest thing Natal possessed to an airport. They were accompanied by Dottie and Lottie, whose brother had remained at home in a fine sulk at the turn events had taken and his own powerlessness in the face of his sisters' determination.

"Dear Eduardo," said Dottie. "Such a dashing young man. He danced with me at the ball last year."

Her sister humphed. "You're a fool, Dottie."

"Just as you say, dear," said Dottie placidly. She went across to speak to the gangling aviator. Their conversation seemed to consist of a great deal of courtly attentiveness on Eduardo's part and a similar amount of playful coyness on Dottie's. Lottie watched them with a smoldering air.

"You mean, we'll be flying in *that*?" Luke stared, aghast, at Eduardo's flying machine. "It's a balloon!"

Nick shook his head. "It's a dirigible."

"It's the same thing!"

"Not at all. A balloon just goes where the wind

takes it. This has got an engine, a rudder, elevators, the whole works – you can steer it. It's like a Zeppelin, only smaller."

"I'll say it's smaller!"

Nick indicated the packs they'd made up from the contents of their trunks. "No problem – we're traveling light."

"But I was expecting an airplane." Luke's frustration was mounting.

Dottie patted him comfortably on the arm. "Not many airplanes in Natal, dear. Not to worry. Eduardo knows what he's doing – and this dirribbibble, or whatever it's called, will take you in a straight line to Manaus. If you had to go by water, you'd have to travel nearly twice as far. This will save you days and days!"

Luke considered. The dirigible's unkempt appearance and the patches all over its fabric hardly inspired confidence, but if it would save time… "Well, all right."

"Good. Now…" Dottie rummaged in her purse and pulled out a piece of folded paper. "This is for Eduardo. It's an instruction to Challenger Industries in Manaus to let him have as much hydrogen as he likes. That's why he agreed to take you, you see – he needs hydrogen to make his balloon go up. George's office has already filled his tanks to get you there."

Luke's suspicions that Dottie was not nearly as vague

as she seemed were confirmed. "And your brother George signed these instructions, did he?"

"Of course not, dear," said Dottie matter-of-factly. "I did."

"See, Luke?" Nick seized Dottie's wrinkled hand and kissed it with an air of gallantry. "Forged signatures. She's a girl after our own hearts."

"Oh, what nonsense," fluttered Dottie. "Now, we mustn't keep dear Eduardo waiting." Lottie snorted.

The look the airman gave them as they approached the gondola hanging beneath the billowing gasbag said very clearly that Luke and Nick could keep him waiting until Doomsday for all he cared. But the promise of unlimited hydrogen prevented him from saying so. He took their bags without a word and jerked his head, indicating that they should follow him aboard.

Dottie took Luke's arm and drew him aside. "By the way, dear, I thought you ought to know... A telegram for my brother arrived this morning. A postman – a real postman – brought it. I said I'd deliver it to Georgie and so I shall...tomorrow." She sighed. "Poor Georgie. He lacks a certain...decisiveness. Anyway, the telegram was from your father. In it, he instructed my brother not to let you go anywhere – as I recall it, his exact words were 'Sit on the young rascals if necessary' – until he'd made other arrangements."

"Why didn't you show Mr. Partridge the telegram?" asked Luke warily.

"I know my brother," replied Dottie, with a smile from which vagueness was entirely absent. "Poor Georgie – he doesn't stand up well to pressure. The minute the authorities started asking awkward questions, he'd have handed you over to them in the blink of an eye. You might have spent weeks rotting away in some flea-ridden jail. We couldn't have that. And in any case, we have to think of Harriet."

"Such a fine woman," contributed Lottie. "Very sound on horses."

"Yes. Well, goodbye, dears." Dottie gave Luke a lavender-water peck on the cheek, which Lottie supplemented with a bone-crushing handshake. "And good luck."

The sisters continued to wave as Luke and Nick climbed into the dirigible's minuscule cabin and, with an irritable buzz from its engine, the patchwork airship lifted away from the ground and disappeared into the clouds.

In the shadow of the airfield's one tumbledown hangar, a slim woman wearing a long leather coat and tinted glasses watched the departure. Her high-boned Japanese face betrayed no expression at all.

11 EDUARDO

Above the Amazon rainforest, Brazil

The dirigible was hardly more luxurious than the mail sacks.

Its tiny gondola hung below the great sausage-shaped balloon, swaying alarmingly with every gust of wind. It must have been cramped for Eduardo alone; with Nick and Luke aboard, the cabin was like an overfilled sardine can. It was made of lacquered canvas on a wooden frame and smelled of gasoline. There was one seat – Eduardo quickly made it clear that it was his and any unauthorized backsides that occupied it were due a kicking. Luke and Nick had to sit, eat and sleep on the floor. At the rear end of the cabin, the tiny engine buzzed, rattled and threw out clouds of evil-smelling smoke.

There were celluloid windows in front and to either side of the pilot's position. These were usually open, as the fumes from the engine quickly became overpowering if they were closed. The airship's controls consisted of a wheel for steering the rudder in the tail of the gasbag, and the stubby elevators that flanked it on either side. Its full complement of instruments was a battered alarm clock and an altimeter, that looked like a giant thermometer with a column of mercury in a glass tube.

If all this was alarming, Eduardo himself was scarcely less so. His long arms and legs looked as if they'd been grafted onto his body from another species, probably some form of insect. He wore a leather flying helmet with the goggles pushed up onto his forehead, a silk scarf, gray with age, and a villainous mustache. He seemed to steer the dirigible mainly with his feet. He lay back in his basket at an almost impossible angle and smoked a thin, black cigar, despite the obvious danger of fire. He glared over his shoulder at Luke and Nick.

"Gringos," he spat. "I, Eduardo, greatest aviator in Brazil, am reduce to carrying gringos."

Luke bristled. Nick, quick to spot the warning signs,

looked around with an air of appreciation. "Fine ship you have."

"Sure is fine ship. Brazilian. All best ships Brazilian. All best pilots Brazilian. First man to fly? Alberto Santos Dumont – Brazilian!"

"What about the Wright Brothers?" demanded Luke.

Eduardo flew into a fury. "Wright brothers? Frauds! Yankee doodle phony-baloneys! Santos Dumont first to fly airship! Round Eiffel Tower, 1901. Santos Dumont first to fly airplane – 1906. Brazilian!"

"The Wright Brothers flew their first airplane in 1903," said Luke hotly.

"Assisted take-off! Cheat! Like throwing paper airplane."

"Well, what about their flights at Kitty Hawk in 1904 and 1905?"

"Who saw this? Cows? Kitty-cats? Birdie-hawks? No reporters. Only photographs, who took them? Wrong Brothers, that's who. Look!" Eduardo reached into the pocket of his leather flying jacket and pulled out an old and faded newspaper cutting. It was from the *Herald Tribune*, dated 1907. The article that Eduardo stabbed at with an oil-stained finger carried the headline, "WRIGHT BROTHERS – FLYERS OR LIARS?"

"I say liars!" raved Eduardo. "Alberto Santos Dumont takes off, flies and lands in front of official witnesses.

First to fly! Brazilian! Santos Dumont Number One – Wright Brothers Number Ten!" Eduardo made a triumphant gesture with his cheroot, which he then proceeded to smoke with fierce concentration, muttering darkly to himself as night wrapped itself around the airship like a blanket.

But there were compensations for flying with Eduardo. When Luke and Nick awoke next morning, the rattling engine was silent. Their eccentric aircraft was being carried by the wind – an easterly one which, fortunately, was taking them roughly in the direction they wanted to go – while Eduardo crouched in the back of the gondola with oily engine parts around his knees, tinkering and cursing furiously.

Luke and Nick gazed out of the window. They were sailing over an emerald world of shimmering forest. Streams like silver slug-trails and brown rivers, their waters thick with silt, meandered between giant trees half-choked with vines. Clusters of bright orchids and bromeliads grew in the crooks of the highest branches. Above the canopy flew kingbirds, parrots and raucous flocks of macaws, their feathers flashing red and blue, blue and yellow. Perched in the treetops, toucans lifted their improbable beaks and trumpeters sounded a challenge. A harpy eagle soared past, inspecting them curiously with its cold, mad eyes.

A sudden chorus of unearthly yelps and moans drew a startled oath from Nick. "What on earth was that?"

"Howlers," said Luke, trying to sound like a knowledgeable forest hand. He had heard the monkeys' otherworldly dawn chorus on previous visits to South America with his mother, but it still startled him. "Loudest animal in the world."

"I'll say." Nick shivered. "It reminds me of school."

Luke raised an eyebrow. "How?"

"Feeding time for the younger grades."

Luke remembered the chaos in the cafeteria when the youngest kids were let loose at lunchtime. "I know what you mean."

A particularly violent oath from Eduardo drew Nick to the back of the cabin. "Problem?" Eduardo gave him a killing glare. "Here, let me take a look."

With a shrug of disgust, Eduardo inched past him and threw himself into the pilot's seat. He busied himself with a small kettle and a spirit stove, and a few minutes later handed Luke a tin mug half full of gritty black liquid. "Coffee," he grunted, taking another mug for himself. At that moment, the clatter of the engine refilled the cabin, drowning out even the lost-soul shrieks of the howlers.

Eduardo turned a startled glance on Nick, who sat

beside the reanimated engine wiping his hands on an oily rag and grinning. "How you do that?"

Nick shrugged. "I'm good with engines."

Eduardo said nothing, but from that moment on, the atmosphere in the tiny cabin began to thaw. Whenever the engine displayed alarming symptoms, which it did often, Nick would descend on it with wrenches and pliers and restore it to health. He and Eduardo would then embark on a long technical discussion about this latest fault. Luke was grateful to the temperamental engine: tinkering with it ensured that Nick was kept busy, and had little time to brood on his father.

In the few intervals when the engine behaved itself, Luke would chat with Eduardo about the wildlife of the forest, of which he had an impressive knowledge. Gradually, Luke began to appreciate the abilities of the cross-grained aviator. As a glider pilot himself, he recognized the skill with which Eduardo coaxed his clumsy craft through gusts that sought to blow them off course and avoided vertical currents of air that could take the airship too high or too low, wasting its scant resources of gas and ballast on height corrections.

Luke also spent a lot of time staring out of the window at the unending forest below, and making plans. His first task upon reaching Manaus would be to contact Jackson, the Challenger Industries representative so disliked by George Partridge. Then he and Nick would have to make inquiries. Which guides had his mother hired to take her upriver? Were they reliable? Had any of her party returned, or had any news filtered back of what had happened to it? And if they could find no answers in Manaus, Luke was determined to press on with the search along the Amazon; even, if the trail led him that far, to the Lost World itself.

In the meantime, he had a job to do. He needed to know what was in the messages that he and Nick had stolen from the package with the snake and spear seal. So, with grubby paper and a stub of pencil begged from Eduardo, he set himself to the task. The airman, despite his contempt for the activities of gringos, became intrigued by Luke's efforts.

As evening drew on once more, Nick asked, "How is it coming?"

"Slowly," Luke replied. He ran his fingers across his eyes; they felt heavy and sore.

Eduardo snatched up the message Luke was working on. He stared at it. He tried reading it upside down with no better result. With an exclamation of disgust, he passed it to Nick, who read:

ᛈᚹᚹᛈᛏᛏ ᛁᚾᛏᚲᚹᛇ ᛏᛉᚱᚺᛇᚦ ᚾᛄᛇᛇᚠᚱᚠ
ᚠᛗᛏᛈᚲᛏ ᛏᚱᛗᛈᛇᛁ ᛁᚦᛁᛗᚾᛇ ᛇᛇᛗᚹᚱᛈ
ᛇᛁᚠᛏᛏᛈ ᚦᚱᛈᛈᛁ ᛁᛗᛁᛇᛈᛏ ᚠᛄᚾᛇᚠ
ᛏᛈᚠᚠᚲᚾ ᛏᛁᚹᚱᛄᚦ ᚦᛋᛋᚾᛁᛗ ᚹᛁᛇᛗᚲᛇ
ᛗᛏᛁᛏᛗᛗ ᛁᚱᛄᛄᛗ ᚷᚠ ᚦᚠᚠᚲᚹ ᚾᛗᛗᛗᚾ
ᛈᛇᛏᛏᚲᛁ ᛇᛁᛇᛗᚾᛏ ᚷᚠᚦᚦᛁ ᛗᛁᛇᚾᛋᛈ
ᚱᛁᛇᛁᛇᛏ ᚾᛋᛏᛇᛗ ᛋᛈᚠᛗᛁᛇ ᛗᛁᛁᚾᛈᚠ
ᚦᛇᚦᚦᛗᛁᚠ ᛗᚹᛁᚱᛇᛒ ᛗᚱᛗᛁᛁᛋ ᚠᛈᚱᚦᚦᚲᛗ

"Where do you start with something like that?" Nick shook his head. "Looks double Dutch to me."

Eduardo seemed to have taken his failure to decode the message as a personal insult. "*Sim*. Portuguese Number One – Dutch Number Ten. Double Dutch not even in top hundred!"

Luke ignored this and answered Nick. "Lord John said this snake-and-spear gang is international, and I'm sure he was right. Hagen was German, the seaman who blew himself up with stolen Challenger grenades was Italian. We can assume that the traitor in Challenger Industries is English. We know that the gunmen who attacked us in Cape Verde were either Brazilian or Portuguese and the woman who led them is probably Japanese."

"So where does that get us?"

"My guess is, they'll use a single language to communicate with each other and that language is likely to be English, because it's the most widely used all over the world."

"Sounds reasonable," said Nick. Eduardo nodded wisely.

"It's still a guess. My next guess is that the code they're using is fairly simple, because it needs to be understood by people who aren't native English speakers. But at the same time, if it isn't complicated enough it'd be too easy to break."

"Oh-kay..."

"Now, the most basic kind of code is a substitution cipher. That's where every letter in the message is represented by a different letter or symbol in the code. It's the sort of cipher Holmes solved in *The Adventure of the Dancing Men* – that was Conan Doyle too, you know, the same man who wrote about Grandpa's adventures in the Lost World. The trouble is, it's a piece of cake. I always thought Doyle made Holmes out to be a bit of a dummy over that code. But of course, he only had a few short messages. The longer the message, the more chance you have of solving a substitution code."

Eduardo and Nick looked at each other. Eduardo said, "How come?"

"Because there are patterns in English. For a start, there's the frequency of the letters. 'e' is the most used letter in English, followed by 't', 'o', 'a', 'n' and so on. Then there's a frequency pattern of double letters, too. 'Th' is the most common combination, followed by 'er', 'on', 'an' and 're'." Short words are a giveaway. There's a pattern of frequency for two-letter words..."

"I guessed there might be," said Nick, feeling as if his head had started to revolve.

"...'Of', 'to', 'in', 'it', 'is', and all the rest. Then there are the three letter words, 'the', 'and', 'for', 'are', 'but'..."

"Right." Eduardo looked as if he'd been sandbagged.

"That's why the main weakness of a substitution code is that you can still see how many letters there are in the words of the original message."

"But the message we found is all in six-letter words." Nick pointed at the captured message. "That's impossible, isn't it? How can you write a message using only six-letter words?"

"You can't," said Luke. "That means whoever wrote this message has used another level of encryption." Eduardo groaned.

"That's why," Luke continued, "it's taking me so long to work it out. But I think I've cracked the substitution code they've used." Luke scribbled in the notebook for a minute, and showed Nick and Eduardo the result:

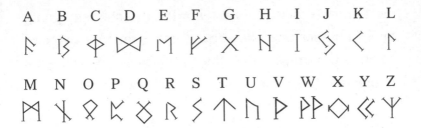

A	B	C	D	E	F	G	H	I	J	K	L

M	N	O	P	Q	R	S	T	U	V	W	X	Y	Z

"Assuming that's correct," continued Luke, "if we replace the symbols with the letters they represent, this is the message we get."

> SNNMTL IUTYFO TNRHOC UDOARA
> AELSYT TRELOI ICNEUO OOEFRN
> OIALEL CRMLNI NENOML ADUOAI
> TNAWYH TIFRDC CSSUNM FNOEKO
> ETILEE NRDMGA CAAPKF AIMEEU
> LOTTPN ONOEHT PACACI ENOUSL
> RNOIJT HSTQLU SLAEIO EIIULA
> VOWEIA EFNROB EREINS AMRWYE

"That still doesn't make sense," protested Nick.

"No. To decode it, we need number boxes."

Eduardo looked disgusted. "And what are these number boxes?"

"You write down a series of numbers – the simplest would be 1 2 3 4 5 6 7 8. Then you write the letters of each word of the message vertically downwards under each number, with the first word of the message going under number one, the second under number two and so on. So, taking the first line of this message, you get a number box like this."

1	2	3	4	5	6	7	8
S	I	T	U	A	T	I	O
N	U	N	D	E	R	C	O
N	T	R	O	L	E	N	E
M	Y	H	A	S	L	E	F
T	F	O	R	Y	O	U	R
L	O	C	A	T	I	O	N

"Then you just read across left to right and top to bottom in the normal way."

Nick read, very slowly, "*Sit-u-ation u-n-der con-t-rol* – hey, this is making sense! – *E-ne-my has le-ft for your lo-ca-tion.* Brilliant!" Eduardo applauded, not altogether ironically.

"Thanks," said Luke sourly. "The problem is, if I write out the next part of the message in exactly the same way, this is what I get."

1	2	3	4	5	6	7	8
O	C	N	A	T	T	C	F
I	R	E	D	N	I	S	N
A	M	N	U	A	F	S	O
L	L	O	O	W	R	U	E
E	N	M	A	Y	D	N	K
L	I	L	I	H	C	M	O

After scratching his head over this for some time, Nick said, "Gibberish."

"Exactly – because the number pattern keeps changing. 1 2 3 4 5 6 7 8 is too easy to break, so they've varied the number order maybe to 3 6 4 8 7 1 5 2 or 4 6 2 7 5 3 1 8, or whatever. So even though I think I've solved the substitution code, or most of it, I can't get through the number problem."

Eduardo's brow was furrowed with concentration. "But there should be a pattern to the numbers that's easy to remember, no?"

"Probably. That would make it simpler for the person decoding the message."

"Then what's the pattern?" demanded Nick. "And why eight numbers? Why not seven? Or nine?"

"That's what I can't work out. Does the number eight mean anything to you?"

Nick shook his head. Eduardo said, "It does not,

as you say, ring any bells."

"Ring any bells…" Luke's eyes widened. "I wonder."

He took more paper and began to scribble. After a while he gave a disgusted exclamation and crumpled the sheet into a ball, immediately beginning on another.

At length he sat back with a look of abstraction. "Well, I'll be a gargoyle's granny," he breathed. "Eduardo, you're a genius." Eduardo preened. "It's bell-ringing."

Eduardo looked nonplussed. Nick said, "It's *what*?"

"Church bells. I used to ring them down in the village. Mother got me involved in it – she used to say it was good exercise. Uncle Ned and Uncle John sometimes came along. There are different methods of ringing for different numbers of bells. The one they've used is Grandsire Triples for eight bells. When you write it down, it's basically a number pattern. Look… "

$$1\,2\,3\,4\,5\,6\,7\,8$$
$$2\,1\,3\,5\,4\,7\,6\,8$$
$$2\,3\,1\,4\,5\,6\,7\,8$$
$$3\,2\,4\,1\,6\,5\,7\,8$$

"…and so on. In Grandsire Triples, the tenor bell – number eight – is always at the back of the peal. It doesn't change its position in the pattern, but every other bell does. So I've put the letters in the number boxes, and we have the full message." Luke passed the decoded message to Nick and Eduardo, who read it with their heads together.

SITUATIONUNDERCONTROLENEMYHASLEFT
FORYOURLOCATIONCONTACTFRIENDSINMANAUS
FOLLOWOURENEMYANDKILLHIMCONCEALOPERA
TIONANDAIMTOCOMPLETEAUGKEEPHCSAFE
UNTILSHEREVEALSINFORMATIONWEREQUIRE
IWILLJOINYOUATBASE

"*Situation under control,*" Nick read. "*Enemy* – that's you, Luke, without a doubt! – *has left for your location. Contact friends in Manaus. Follow our enemy and kill him.* Uh-oh. *Conceal operation and aim to complete August. Keep HC safe* – HC!"

Luke was staring at nothing, but he nodded. "Harriet Challenger." He felt as if he'd stepped into a cold shower. His worst fears had just been realized.

Nick completed reading the message. "*Keep HC safe until she reveals information we require. I will join you at base.*" He whistled. "Well, that tells us a few things. We can expect trouble when we get to Manaus. Our snaky friends have some kind of operation going on that they expect to be finishing in August. They're holding a hostage and, barring an unlikely coincidence over initials, it's a pretty safe bet it's your ma – who has information they need." He whistled. "It's a good thing we found this – why d'you suppose they sent a written message? Why not send it by telegraph?"

"The telegraph office is public. Anyone sending a code would be noticed. They didn't know we'd intercept their messages." Luke closed his eyes for a moment. Then he pulled himself together and reached for the pencil. "Let's see what else we can find out from the rest…"

He was interrupted by a long peal of thunder. As he realized how dark it had grown inside the airship's cabin, a sudden blinding light picked out every detail of the gondola for a fraction of a second. Luke saw Nick's expression of frozen astonishment, and realized that it mirrored his own. Swinging around, he stared out of the cabin window at the blackest clouds he had ever seen.

"*Meu deus!*" Eduardo reached for the controls just as the storm hit them.

12 STORM

The first impact of the wind spun the dirigible around in its own length, then sent it tumbling like a falling leaf. Loose objects flew around the gondola and shot out of the open windows to fall, whirling, into the storm-tossed canopy of the trees. Struts and retaining wires twanged and creaked. Luke braced himself against the cabin sides, remembering just in time to plant his feet against the wooden ribs rather than the canvas wall, which they would have torn straight through.

The violence of the wind was appalling. It shrieked

and raved around them. Its fingers clutched at their frail craft, seeking to pluck it from the sky. The gondola lurched and shuddered. The engine's whine of protest was overwhelmed by the howl of the tempest. Thunderclaps tore the air apart. All around them, lightning flickered. Luke thought about the great gasbags full of highly inflammable hydrogen, a few feet above their heads. If lightning hit one of those, they'd make the biggest fireball ever.

Then the rain began.

It was a deluge. Raindrops the size of oranges hurled themselves at the gasbag and shattered. Water cascaded around the gondola like a curtain, dashing in at the open windows and drenching the cabin and its occupants.

Nick turned his shocked gaze on Luke. "I thought Brazil was supposed to be warm and sunny!"

"We're in the rainforest," said Luke. "The clue's in the name."

Their surroundings were now invisible thanks to sheets of rain, mist and the gathering dark. Luke peered out of the streaming window, but there was no way of telling whether they were two hundred feet above the treetops, or two thousand.

Abruptly, the rain stopped. Nick shook water from his eyes. "That's better. Maybe we're through the worst of it."

Everything Luke had ever learned about thunderstorms came back to him in a rush. "I don't think so."

The words had hardly left his mouth when the dirigible reared as though grasped by a giant hand and flung into the sky. Luke felt himself being pressed into the floor with a force sufficient to drive the air from his body.

Nick grabbed at a strut to save himself. "Now what?" he yelled.

"We're in the updraft," Luke told him. "The storm sucks air up into the troposphere. Look at the altimeter."

The column of mercury was dropping like a stone with the fall in pressure as the airship climbed.

Eduardo pushed the elevator controls forward, cursing the elements, and gave the tiny engine maximum revs, keeping the airship's nose down in a desperate attempt to slow their ascent. It seemed to have little effect. "I have to vent gas," he yelled. "We go too high, pressure in gas cells rise: too much pressure, cells split, gas escapes, we go down – finish." He reached up and tugged at a lanyard that led through the roof of the gondola. Nothing happened. He tugged again on the rope with the same result. When he turned to Luke, his face was haggard.

"Valve jammed," he said. "Not good. Okay. I steer.

You — " he pointed at Nick. "You keep engine running. No engine, no control, big smash up, *Goodnight Venezuela.*"

"Shouldn't that be *Goodnight Vienna*?" asked Nick.

"Venezuela Number One! Vienna Number Ten! Engine! Go!"

"I'm onto it." Nick inched his way to the back of the gondola.

Eduardo turned to Luke. "You. You go up there." He pointed to a hatch in the cabin roof. "Up ladder. Climb between gas cells. Don't tear! Find where line to gas valve jammed, release it, open valve for count of thirty. Got it? What you waiting for?"

Luke gazed at him stupidly. "Out there?"

"Sure out there, gasbag out there, valve at top of gasbag. Maybe you wait while I draw you picture?"

Luke steeled himself. "Do I get a flashlight?"

Eduardo, fighting the controls, rummaged in a locker and drew out a scuffed flashlight. Luke switched it on and the bulb glowed feebly.

"Don't waste battery," growled Eduardo.

Luke bit back an angry reply. He uncurled beneath the hatch and thrust it open. Immediately, the howl of the wind redoubled in volume. Luke reached for the first rung of the steel ladder, slippery with rain, and began his ascent.

The wind whipped at his wet clothing. His fingers and shoes slipped on the greasy rungs and the whole ladder pitched and swayed as the dirigible was thrown across the sky. Tendrils of cloud flowed down past the rapidly ascending airship in gray streamers and closed in behind.

The dirigible gave a particularly wild lurch and Luke's feet slipped from the ladder. He found himself holding on with one hand, his heart hammering wildly as he clung to life with his fingertips. He was about to lose his grip when the ship swung back the other way, flinging him against the ladder to which he clung now, like an octopus, breathing hard. Then he began to climb again.

The ladder went through an opening into the balloon envelope. Wiggling through this, Luke found himself among the gas cells, which heaved and billowed on either side of him. Taking a deep breath, he began to climb between them.

This was not easy. The bags rubbed and chafed against each other, with a hollow "whump"ing sound, putting pressure first on one side of his body, then the other; rising beneath him or forcing him down. The rubberized material of the cell walls smelled horrible and, when the pressure of the gas inside forced it against him, it rubbed painfully. He soon became disorientated.

It was completely dark and the balloon had not stopped its wild rolling and pitching. Half crushed and half smothered, he pressed on.

At length he found himself in the roof of the envelope. With the gasbags creaking and groaning beneath him, he fumbled one-handed in his pocket, drew out the flashlight and turned it on. The bulb glowed fitfully for a moment and then died. He shook it furiously, to no avail. Luke cursed weakly, then he nearly jumped out of his skin as a prolonged flash of lightning etched the interior structure of the balloon on his retina. He just had time to spot the failed line that had led him to make the perilous climb. A loop of the lanyard had caught around a bracing wire. Luke noted its position – naturally, just out of reach – and when the lightning glow faded, leaving him in darkness, he stretched his hand toward it.

Time after time, he strained to reach the line from his madly swaying perch. Time after time, he was jerked away from it as the dirigible executed yet another wild leap, almost tearing his arms from his sockets. At long last, his face screwed up in agony from the effort of extending his arm an inch further than nature had intended, he seized the lanyard and tugged it. He began to count off the seconds: "One anteater…two anteaters… three anteaters…" Was it his imagination, or did their rate of climb seem to have slowed? "Ten anteaters... eleven anteaters..." It was maddening. He couldn't even see the rushing clouds to gauge their ascent. But Eduardo had said thirty seconds, so he held on: "Twenty-nine anteaters...*thirty* anteaters!" Luke released the cable, clung to the ladder, breathing hard for a few seconds, then started the long climb down.

"You took your time," was Nick's greeting as Luke dropped through the hatchway and slumped on the cabin floor. The rain was back and in the last few feet of his descent Luke had been half-drowned. He bit back an angry response. Nick's haggard face revealed the tension he had been under since Luke had started his climb, and Luke understood that the blunt observation was designed to mask his relief at Luke's safe return.

He kept his reply light. "I started wondering what people went back to before they invented drawing boards and I completely lost track of time." Luke massaged his aching joints. "Have we stopped going up?"

"*Sim.* We are in level flight." But Eduardo didn't seem too happy about this.

"That's good, isn't it?" The rain had turned to ice. Nick had to yell over the drumming of golfball-sized hailstones on the canvas.

"Oh, it's terrific," said Luke. "And it'll go on being terrific right up until the moment we hit..." He broke off as his stomach collided with his diaphragm and the cabin dropped away beneath him like the floor of an express elevator. "...the downdraft!" he concluded.

Now Eduardo was hauling back on the elevator controls as the airship fell like a stooping eagle, desperately trying to keep the nose up and slow their headlong plunge with the engine. "Ballast!" he shrieked. "We must jettison ballast. Those levers – there, there, there!" While he battled with the controls, Nick and Luke tugged the levers he had indicated. It seemed unfair to Luke that some poor denizens of the forest below should find themselves pelted, not just by this monstrous rain, but by the balloon's unwanted water ballast.

The last of the ballast was gone and still the balloon fell. "Not enough!" yelled Eduardo. "Need to lose more weight. Anything we don't need!"

Luke and Nick went through the cabin stores like berserk burglars. Canned food, bottles ("Not the *cachaça!*" howled Eduardo as his supplies of cane spirit were seized) and the useless flashlight were hurled through the windows to fall to the forest floor far below. Eduardo's small collection of books and the spirit stove followed. Luke hesitated over their packs – who knew where they'd get another change of clothes? Reflecting that, if they went down at this speed, the only clothing he'd ever wear again would be a shroud, he sent them spinning down with the rest.

"We're slowing," yelled Eduardo, over the hammering of the hail and the scream of the engine. He indicated the altimeter, where the column of mercury was steadying. "We're…"

"Look out!" Nick pointed out of the pilot's window. Suddenly, horribly close and rushing up to meet them with terrifying speed, was the forest canopy.

They hit with a jarring shock. The cabin windows imploded, filling the air with flapping strips of celluloid and stinging leaves and branches. The gondola bounced high with the impact and came down again. A flock of startled birds burst from the treetops half a second before the cabin struck for a second time, dragging its passengers through the foliage. For a split second, Luke found himself staring into the black-bead eyes of a startled tree snake.

Then they were through! The dirigible clawed away from the trees and, miraculously, continued with a gentle climb. The hammering of the hail was changing to a steady drumming of rain; the thunder was already fading, the lightning flickered in the distance. Far to the west, the clouds were breaking and a half-moon was rising through them like an anxious homeowner inspecting the damage.

Eduardo throttled back the overheated engine and sat for a while slumped with his head resting on the steering wheel. Then he gave Luke and Nick a weak grin.

"You boys did good," he said. "For gringos."

Luke nodded wearily. Then a terrible thought struck him. Frantically, he patted his pockets – and sank back with a sigh of relief as he felt the reassuring shape of his grandfather's notebook, safe inside its waxed-cloth pouch. But on glancing around the cabin, he gave a low moan. The documents that he had yet to decode had disappeared, whisked away on the wind during their wild flight through the storm.

The airship that limped into Manaus seemed to be kept aloft mostly through willpower. The balloon envelope was covered with great rents, through which gas cells bulged as if straining for freedom. Struts and wires dangled uselessly and the gondola hung at a crazy angle.

Eduardo stepped from the cabin and gave a supporting strut an affectionate pat. "Brazilian! See? Very strong!" The strut gave way and the gondola sagged another five degrees. Eduardo shrugged. "I soon fix. You get me gas, some workmen: two, three days, we go upriver, yes?"

This was the agreement they'd reached during the final hours of the flight. Eduardo, completely disarmed by their adventure together, had made the offer and Luke had gratefully accepted. The dirigible would take them upriver far faster than any boat. He'd already given Eduardo Dottie Partridge's forged docket for hydrogen and promised to stir up Jackson, Challenger Industries' man in Manaus, to help with repairs.

All that remained was to find him. Waving farewell to Eduardo, who was already clearing debris from the cabin, they set off for the address they had been given.

But the Jackson residence, when they reached it, was shuttered. There was no sign of life inside the iron railings and Luke tugged at the bell pull beside the main gate to no effect.

"Nobody home," said Nick.

"There's got to be somebody – servants or something." Luke rang again. He was beginning to feel that their journey was fated. Maybe Jackson was out of town – would that mean another delay? Luke gritted his teeth and rang harder. When this summons went unanswered, he looked around and spotted a gardener sweeping a gravel path on the other side of the street. He led the way across the road and hailed the man. *"Olá! Senhor Jackson?"* He waved at the house across the way. *"Senhor Jackson?"* he said again.

The man looked up briefly, then went back to sweeping. "*Senhor Jackson é morto.*"

Luke shot Nick a startled glance. "What's that? Did he just say Jackson was dead?"

At that moment, a female voice very close to his ear said, conversationally, "You feel a sharp pain in your back? That is my knife. Do you know how a kidney can be removed from your body with just three cuts?"

"No," said Luke.

"Would you like to find out?"

Without moving his head, Luke said, "Nick?"

"Yep, they got me, too." Nick gave a weary sigh. "We're going to have to face up to it, Luke. We just don't make friends easily."

13 MERCEDES

Manaus, Brazil

"**M**aybe I'll go with you," said Luke quietly, "if you show me your wrists."

There was a startled silence. Then his captor hissed, "You are in no position to make demands."

"Show me your wrists," said Luke stolidly, "or I'm going nowhere."

There was a muttered oath from behind him. Then his captor waved her wrists in front of his face, first one, then the other. Neither had a tattoo.

The pressure of the knife was unwavering. Luke

briefly considered fighting to escape, and decided against it. The man he had asked about the whereabouts of Senhor Jackson was once again busily engaged in sweeping, pretending not to notice what was happening virtually under his nose. Luke knew that he and Nick couldn't expect any help from him. The knife at his back was another factor. Luke was in no position to take aggressive action without suffering painful consequences and, by the sound of it, nor was Nick. The third consideration was that if Jackson really was dead, he and Nick needed information. Maybe this girl, whoever she was, could supply it. At any rate, if her way of introducing herself lacked politeness, at least she wasn't one of their snake-and-spear enemies. So Luke simply shrugged and allowed the girl and her companion to guide him and Nick away from the empty house.

Another girl and a boy joined them, suggesting to a casual observer that their meeting was accidental and friendly. "We are amigos," their captor said, "just taking a walk together, relaxing, chatting. Isn't that nice?" From time to time, more young men and girls joined them, until they had an escort of around a dozen young people leading them through the darkening streets.

Before long they left the manicured homes of the wealthy, skirted the business district and entered the dark alleys of a poor neighborhood where the buildings were crammed together, poorly built and ill lit. The smells of poverty – unwashed bodies, bad cooking and raw sewage – filled the air.

Their "amigos" led them to a large building. Groups of young people were gathered around its precincts. From inside came a thunder of drums, playing a samba rhythm.

The pressure of the knife in Luke's back eased and the girl who had taken them prisoner stepped forward, allowing her captives their first look at her. She was slimly built and a head shorter than Luke. Her ancestry was difficult to guess: there was something of the Amazonian Indian in her, something of the Portuguese settler and a hint of the Caribbean. This made it difficult to determine her age, though Luke learned later that it was the same as his and Nick's. Her deep brown eyes, bold and defiant, were set in a finely molded face surrounded by long jet-black hair that was parted in the middle and gathered into a ponytail. She wore a white blouse, a scarf, gaucho pants and a scowl.

She led the way into the building. In the foyer, the noise of the drumming was ear-battering. The girl approached a gray-haired man with a dark complexion and shouted something in his ear. The man nodded. She gave him a peck on the cheek and beckoned her followers, who led Luke and Nick forward.

The main hall of the building was immense. At one end, a battery of drummers hammered out the samba. Over the rest of the floor area, people danced to the rhythm, some singly, some in couples, others in formation groups. The air was full of laughter and loud chatter as the dancers strove to make themselves heard over the drums.

Nick gazed around with an air of appreciation. "What is this place?"

"Samba school," Luke roared back. "I've heard of them. They're pretty new. It's a sort of club, I think."

Nick gazed appreciatively at two pretty girls dancing with abandon. "Where do I join?"

The girl led the way around the outside of the dance floor and through a back door leading to a set of musty rooms. The muffled beat of the samba penetrated here even when the door was closed, but it was at least possible to hold a normal conversation.

The girl drew up a chair – pointedly failing to offer seats to Luke and Nick – and sat on it backward. She stared at her visitors with flint-eyed intensity. "Which of you is Challenger?" she demanded.

Luke and Nick exchanged a glance. Then Luke said, "I'm Luke Challenger."

The girl gave a nod of satisfaction. "Then perhaps you can tell me what has happened to my father."

"Perhaps," Luke said. "And perhaps you can tell me what has happened to my mother."

The girl's scowl deepened. "I will ask the questions!"

"I might even answer them," said Luke evenly, "once I know who you are, and what you want. And if I know the answers."

The girl thought about this for a moment. Then she tilted her head proudly. "I am Mercedes da Silva. My father is Raul da Silva. He is a guide. He has his own boat.

"Three months ago, a woman comes to my father with Senhor Jackson who works for Challenger Industries. Big man here: he buys a lot of rubber from the plantations. The woman says her name is Harriet Challenger." Nick gave a stifled exclamation and Luke's heart skipped a beat. This was the first news he'd had of his mother since her messages had ceased to arrive. He forced himself to listen calmly.

"She hires my father and two of his friends to take her upriver," Mercedes continued, "to a place further than my father has ever been, on the border with Venezuela." Luke nodded: that tied in with Grandpa Challenger's instructions. "A week later, they set off in three boats – and they have not returned. I do not know what has happened to my father."

"Think of yourself as lucky," said Nick bleakly, "I know exactly what happened to mine."

Luke pressed Nick's shoulder. "Go on," he said to Mercedes.

After a pause, Mercedes continued, "Now there are new people in town – Brazilians from far away and gringos, many kinds of gringos – German, Italian, Russian – and they are trouble. The police chief says we must mount a search for Senhora Challenger. Some of the new people go to see him. Now we have a new police chief, and he is not so interested. Senhor Jackson tries to hire men to make a search. Now Senhor Jackson is dead. A car accident, they say. People who carry dynamite in their cars are liable to have accidents."

Luke stared at her. "Dynamite?"

"So we wait for you. I sent a message to Eduardo in Natal to collect and bring you here..."

"*You* sent Eduardo to us?"

"Are you a parrot? *Sim*, I sent Eduardo. He is a family friend. I know he has made himself a favorite of the foolish woman who is sister to your friend Partridge."

"Poor Dottie," said Nick, very quietly. "Not quite as clever as she thinks she is. All the time she thought she was charming Eduardo, he was really charming her."

"When Eduardo lands here, he sends word to say where you are going – so I meet you at Senhor Jackson's house."

"'Meet' is one word for it. Did Eduardo say he'd

offered to fly us upriver to search for my mother – and your father?"

"Eduardo has a soft spot for gringos."

Remembering the pilot's behavior when they'd first met, Luke gaped at her. "*Eduardo* does?"

"Compared to me, yes. Eduardo may say what he likes – I will decide."

"Fair enough." Luke gave the angry girl a considering look. "Listen, Mercedes. You must have worked out that my mother is not responsible for your father's disappearance – if he's in trouble, so is she. You want to find your father; I want to find my mother. If they're together, it comes to the same thing. There's no reason for us to be enemies. Suppose we pool our information."

Mercedes thought for a moment. Then she said, "I'm listening."

"Are you, now?" said Nick. "Well, maybe we're not ready to talk. You haven't been very friendly to us so far – whose side are you really on?"

Mercedes gave him a withering glance. "You! I don't want to talk to you. Tomasinho! Luiz!" She jerked her head at two of her companions, a giant with fists like hams and a tough-looking youth, who hustled Nick roughly out through the door. Luke took a step forward, fists raised. Mercedes's remaining friends stirred angrily until she raised a hand. "They won't hurt him," she told

Luke with contempt. "Not unless I tell them to."

Luke decided to accept this. "All right," he said. "Cards on the table. I'll tell you what we know." He told Mercedes why his mother had come to Brazil, seeking to follow in his grandfather's footsteps.

Mercedes stared at him. "Your mother came here looking for dinosaurs?" She laughed. "What – is she crazy?"

"My grandfather said they found dinosaurs," said Luke angrily. "So did Nick's father and Lord John Roxton. I believe them."

Mercedes sneered, "Then you are crazy too." She shrugged. "It figures. All gringos are crazy. Go on."

Luke kept his temper in check. "Well, then she disappeared..." He went on to tell Mercedes about their journey so far.

When he described the ambush at Cape Verde, Mercedes nodded. "So that is what your friend meant when he said he knew what had happened to his father." Luke waited, but when it became clear that Mercedes had nothing else to say on this subject, he told her what little he and Nick knew of their enemies and of the message they had intercepted.

When he had finished, Mercedes sat silently for a moment. Then she said, "This place, now it is a samba school. The president of the school, he lets us use it. He is a friend of my father. Once, it was a rubber warehouse. Then comes the war and suddenly no one wants to buy rubber. This city has trams, even an opera house, but now it is poor.

"My father is a guide – a man of resource. But my mother dies, and my father has to work all the time to put food on the table. I am mostly alone. So I make new friends." Luke glanced around. "Yes, these and others. Street kids. Their families are poor also. The police do not like us. Sometimes they shoot us, so we do not like them. We stay out of their way – we watch and we listen."

"And what do you see?" asked Luke. "What do you hear?"

"We see these new people come – the ones marked with the snake and spear. Do you know who they are?"

"No," said Luke. "But I'd very much like to know."

"I, also. We hear them tell the mayor they will bring back the rubber trade."

"And do you think they're telling the truth?"

Mercedes gave a derisive snort. "I doubt it. But the mayor believes these people and does not wish to offend them. So when my father and your mother go missing, he does nothing." She leaned forward. "And when these people say two young criminals are coming from England, the mayor gets his friend the judge to sign warrants for your arrest. You are lucky we reached you before the police."

"We're not criminals," said Luke.

"No? *We* are. In this town, if the police are out to get you, you are a criminal." She said something in Portuguese and her friends nodded in confirmation.

Luke regarded her steadily. "Mercedes, we need your help. And you need ours. I have a notebook containing every detail of the journey that my mother and your father were following."

"And where is this notebook?"

"Somewhere safe." Luke had to make an effort to prevent his hand from inching toward the pocket where the notebook lay, snug in its waterproof wrapping.

Mercedes gave him a knowing look. "I think not. You did not leave it with Eduardo, and you know no one in Manaus. I think you have it on you and I could take it right now if I chose."

Luke clenched his fists. Mercedes gave him a cool, appraising stare. Then she stood up with sudden decision. "All right. Keep the book. You can relax. I believe you."

"Even about the dinosaurs?"

Mercedes barked with laughter. "No. But that is the most convincing part of all: if you were lying, you would have made up a better story. So I think you are not lying.

You say you know where my father and your mother were going. I know the forest. We will follow them. My friends will help. Tomasinho and Luiz have already agreed to come. And Rosa and Heitor." She indicated the girl and boy who had been first to join her after her capture of Luke and Nick. "We go together. Deal?" She held out her hand.

"Deal." Solemnly, Luke shook it.

Mercedes suddenly pricked up her ears. "The drums. They do not play samba."

Luke had tuned out the drums. Now he listened – and grinned. "I think that may be something to do with my friend."

With a startled glance at Luke, Mercedes led the way back to the dance floor.

The floor was clear. The crowd stood around its edge while a single figure cavorted in the middle.

It was Nick. He was performing a dashing Irish stepdance, his upper body as rigid as a board, his legs crossing, stamping and kicking in complicated patterns as the drum battery hammered out a slightly Latinized version of a wild Gallic reel. Every high kick was greeted with cheers and whoops from the crowd, clapping along to the insistent rhythm. His guards seemed very relaxed about this: Tomasinho was beating his giant hands along to the rhythm and Luiz was whistling in approval.

Mercedes stared. "What is he...? How did he...?"

Luke laughed. "That's Nick. He has a knack for getting along with people."

Nick cut a few more capers and finished his routine by striking a pose. His audience roared its appreciation.

But the applause was cut short by the shrilling of police whistles and the sound of gunshots. Instantly, pandemonium reigned. Yelling and screaming, dancers rushed everywhere, falling over tables, chairs and each other. Abandoned drums rolled underfoot, adding to the confusion.

Luke and Mercedes fought their way through the throng to Nick, who was staring around in amazement. Luke snapped, "Trust you to start a riot!" and grabbed Nick's left arm, while Mercedes seized his right and guided them through the melee to a side door where her followers, more organized or prepared for trouble than the rest of the crowd, had already formed a wedge to keep their exit clear.

Behind the door, several men were playing a card game by the light of an oil lamp, using a large packing case as a table. This was hurriedly dragged aside to reveal a trapdoor. Mercedes leaped forward, hauled it open and beckoned urgently. "Here! Quick!"

Luke and Nick needed no further invitation. They

dropped through the hole in the floor, followed by Tomasinho, Luiz, Heitor and Rosa. Mercedes came last, hauling the door shut behind her.

When the police finally managed to force their way through the strangely obstructive crowd, they kicked open the door through which their quarry had disappeared, and found a surprised group of men drinking beer and playing cards on an upturned packing case.

"We must warn Eduardo." Mercedes led the way through a maze of narrow streets and alleyways. "They will come for him, too."

Above the huddled dwellings a sudden, blinding flash of orange and yellow flame seared across the sky, followed by the "Whumph!" of a muffled explosion. Luke stared at the expanding fireball and felt the breath catch in his throat. "I'm afraid," he said, "they already have."

Mercedes let rip a terrible oath and sprinted toward the fire-glow. Familiar with the dark, twisting streets, her friends followed. Stumbling over potholes and trash piles, Luke and Nick brought up the rear.

They reached the airfield. One end of it was lit by flames, roaring fiercely as they consumed the hydrogen from Eduardo's airship. The dirigible's twisted frame was like a blackened skeleton against the inferno, the flesh of the gas envelope that had once covered it stripped away by the blaze. Luke and Nick caught up with Mercedes as she dropped to her knees, her hair crisping in the heat, beside a huddled figure in a flying jacket.

Eduardo had been shot. Luke saw at once that there was nothing anybody could do for him. Tears of helpless rage came to his eyes.

Mercedes hugged the dying airman to her. "Eduardo!"

"Woman from Japan came." Eduardo's voice could barely be heard above the crackling of the fire. "She try to buy my ship, I tell her it is not for sale." His eyes widened with outrage. "So she shoot me! Brazilian would not do that, Brazilian would fight fair! Brazil Number One, Japan Number Te..." His head drooped. Mercedes bowed her head and rocked back and forth, her hair falling across the lifeless face like a winding sheet.

A sudden prickling in the back of his neck brought Luke to his feet. He was being watched. At the edge of the flames stood an asiatic woman in a long leather coat. Behind the tinted glasses, her face was utterly devoid of expression. His fury almost choked him and, determined to make the woman pay for what she had done, Luke took a step toward her. It was at that moment that the flames behind him reached the airship's fuel tanks.

The explosion threw Luke off his feet. By the time he had picked himself up and beaten out the patches of burning fuel that had landed on his clothes, the last glowing remnants of the airship were collapsing in on themselves with showers of sparks: and of their mysterious adversary, there was no sign.

14 UPRIVER

Amazon rainforest
June 1933

By dawn, they were twenty miles upriver.

They were traveling, not on the Amazon itself, but the River Negro, which joined the longer stream at Manaus. The river here was over a mile wide. Water the color of strong, black tea flowed sluggishly around the hulls of the two boats, long canoe-like craft with flat bottoms and narrow beams that they had taken from a small landing stage well away from the town. Along the distant banks there were still occasional cultivated lands growing rubber trees, palms and sugar cane, but these became fewer as their journey progressed, giving way to low-lying swampland, secret lagoons and tributary streams. Then the river started to divide into channels, separated by islands as long, twisting and unpredictable as smoke trails. And, little by little, as Mercedes steered her companions through the bewildering maze with practiced ease, the forest began to close in around them.

"Who do these boats belong to?" Luke had asked as they paddled quietly away from the sleeping village.

Mercedes had shrugged. "Friends of my father."

"And won't they mind us taking them?"

"I'm sure they would let us have them if we asked – unless they were mad at us – but it's the middle of the night, and if we wake them up to ask, they'll get mad; so we won't ask, and they won't get mad, and then they won't mind if we take their boats." Mercedes had given Luke a smile of ineffable sweetness and pulled the start-cord on the engine.

The battered motor failed to start. Mercedes tried again...and again. "Lazy pigs!" she muttered as the engine coughed and died for the umpteenth time. "Why can they not look after their boats?"

"You'd think they'd have more consideration for people who steal them," Luke agreed, poker-faced. Mercedes glared at him, and would probably have given her tongue free rein if the engine had not chosen that moment to splutter into reluctant life. Unhappily, the engine in the second boat, despite Nick's best efforts, could not be persuaded to start at all.

As day broke, Luke and Mercedes were traveling in the lead boat with Tomasinho and Luiz. This was towing the second boat whose passengers were Rosa, Heitor, and Nick, who sat in the stern surrounded by bits of the disembowelled outboard and whistling "The Wild Rover" as he worked. To Luke, who had spent the hours of darkness worrying about what the ruthlessness of their enemies implied for his mother, their progress seemed painfully slow. "Can't you make this thing go any faster?" he demanded.

Mercedes gave him a pitying look. "This engine is supposed to drive one boat, not two. If we try to go too fast it will stop, then we will have no engine. Anyway, this way we save gas." She chuckled at Luke's mulish expression. "Don't worry. If your friend gets the other engine going, we will move faster."

At noon, they halted at a waterside village. Mercedes was evidently well known there and was greeted with enthusiasm. She chatted with boatmen and bartered for stores and spare clothes. By the time she had finished, the expedition had modest supplies of food and a few basic medical supplies; a change of clothing, and blanket rolls for sleeping; cooking pots, tin plates and mugs as well as knives and machetes to hack through the jungle. Luke had insisted they buy candles and rope, too.

"Candles?" Mercedes stared at him. "Rope? In the forest? Are you planning a birthday party in a tree?"

Luke shook his head. "We'll need them when we get to the plateau."

He had been worried about supplies and his lack of money to buy them, but Mercedes had produced a handful of brightly colored million-réis notes to pay for their purchases. While the supplies were being loaded, he asked her, "Did you steal the money, too?"

Mercedes gave him a hard stare. "My father's life savings. If I find him, it will be worth it. If I don't, he won't need it. Anyway, if we find your mother, Challenger Industries will pay me back, no?"

"Yes." Luke was angry with himself. He knew nothing about Mercedes's life or that of her companions. He had no right to make assumptions. "I'm sorry."

Mercedes laid a hand on his arm. "Understand me, Luke Challenger, and my friends. Yes, we take when we need to. But we take nothing we do not need. And that is our rule always, in the town, in the forest. While you travel with us, it is your rule, too."

Luke regarded her gravely. "All right. Thank you."

Mercedes turned her gaze on Nick, who was

reassembling the starting mechanism of the reluctant outboard. "I am sorry for your friend."

Luke nodded. "Me, too."

"To see your father die..." There was a catch in Mercedes's voice. "I cannot imagine what I would feel if my own father..."

She was interrupted by a clatter followed by a throaty roar as the outboard, throwing out choking clouds of blue smoke, coughed into life. Mercedes's friends cheered as Nick, with a suitably modest air, throttled back the motor.

Mercedes gave Luke a quick grin. "Now we go faster."

All afternoon they traveled, with Nick's boat now alongside Mercedes's. Luke sat in the bows staring at the forest. He had half-expected it to be teeming with wildlife, but he saw little: the occasional agouti or capybara at the water's edge; a glimpse of a monkey high in the trees and birds – flashes of needle-beaked jacamars and hummingbirds, hook-billed aracaris, strutting ibises and squabbling macaws.

As they passed a sandbank, Nick gave an exclamation and pointed. Luke was startled to see a group of apparently lifeless logs suddenly slither into the water and disappear. "What were those?" he asked. "Crocodiles?"

Mercedes laughed at his expression. "Black caiman.

They grow up to thirty feet long. Some weigh three thousand pounds. But don't worry – they hardly ever attack boats."

Luke eyed the frail sides of their craft. "Hardly ever?" Mercedes's grin was far from reassuring.

At twilight, they landed on a gravel beach and pulled the boats out of the water. As Mercedes's friends cleared a campsite and collected driftwood for a fire and Luke filled a lamp with paraffin, Nick stripped off his shirt and pants and plunged into the river.

Mercedes, who was washing yams at the water's edge, said, "I wouldn't do that if I were you."

Nick splashed water over his neck. "Ah, don't be such a prude. I'm covered in oil and sweating like a hog."

Mercedes shrugged and went on scrubbing.

A sudden thought struck Nick and he scanned the river nervously. "Hey – there aren't any caimans around here, are there?"

"Oh, no."

"Good."

Mercedes took out a knife and began to slice the yams. "Piranhas ate them all."

Nick shot straight out of the water with a yell and made for the bank in a wild, splay-legged run, encouraged by cheers and catcalls. Mercedes watched him with a smirk.

But later that evening, as Luke lay in his sleeping roll, listening to the hoots and howls of night creatures and gazing at the stars, he saw Mercedes, lithe and silent as a cat, uncurl from her place by the fire. Nick had become increasingly moody and withdrawn as the evening wore on, eating little and saying less. Now he sat against a dead tree stump near the water's edge, staring out across the moonlit water. Mercedes crouched down beside him. Long into the night, they talked quietly as the fire flickered, sending sparks and shadows dancing into the trees, and the many voices of the forest rose around them.

In the morning, they found the paw prints of a jaguar in the mud at the water's edge. Though they had taken turns to keep watch through the night, everyone swore they had seen and heard nothing. They packed their meager belongings into the boats and, leaving a band of bear-like coatimundis scavenging around the abandoned campsite in search of discarded food, once more took to the river.

This time, somehow, Nick ended up in Mercedes's boat and Luke was thrown into the company of Mercedes's friends. The giant Tomasinho (meaning "little Tomas") proved to be an amiable soul, whose strength was equalled only by his shyness. Rosa was habitually silent and watchful, relaxing her guard only with the nervous and twitchy Heitor, whose hands and feet seemed too big for his body. Luiz must have watched too many American gangster movies. He spoke out of the side of his mouth and constantly played with a flick knife, but when he forgot to act tough he had an impish sense of fun and a disarming giggle. Although they spoke virtually no English, Luke got to know them all, and to appreciate their loyalty to Mercedes and each other. His Portuguese improved too.

They spent the second night of their journey on a small island. Nick had been more relaxed and talkative during the evening; by contrast, it was Luke who had become silent and morose. While Mercedes was sorting out a dispute between Luiz and Rosa, Nick joined his friend by the fire. "Are you all right?"

Luke stared into the flames. "What are we doing here, Nick? This is a job for people like Uncle John, not you and me. I mean, I'd do anything to find my mother, but from the start I've been thinking about this as an adventure, the sort you read about where wild adventurers defeat the bad guys and go home for dinner, but it's not like that, is it? I got Eduardo involved in this business. Now he's dead." Luke turned a haunted face to Nick. "And your father, Briggs and Stanwick... How many more people have to die before we find my mother – if we find her at all? What gives me the right to drag Mercedes and her friends into this?"

"Nothing," said Nick. "You haven't dragged Mercedes into anything. She wanted to find her father: if we hadn't come along, she would have set off after him anyway. She told me. The others wanted to come because they're her friends. They're street kids, so what future do they have in Manaus? Mercedes told me that Tomasinho is wanted by the police after someone died in a fight…"

"What?" Luke was startled. It seemed barely possible that the good-natured giant was a killer.

"It wasn't deliberate. Somebody got rough with Mercedes and he went to protect her. It all got out of hand: he's very strong. And Rosa – well, from what Mercedes told me, you can't blame her if the only man she trusts is Heitor, who's been bullied all his life. And Luiz – anyway, they all have reasons for getting out of town. And you know why I want to come: to finish what my da started and get back at the scum who killed him. Don't beat yourself up, Luke. We're all here because we want to be."

Luke gave him the ghost of a smile. "Thanks, Nick."

"Anyway, we can't go back now. We definitely outstayed our welcome in Manaus." Nick cursed and slapped at his neck. "Though, if I get bitten by many more of these blasted insects, I might change my mind."

On the afternoon of the third day, they turned north at the point where the bright blue waters of the River Branco flowed into the duller stream of the River Negro. The Branco, being a narrower river, had a correspondingly stronger current. Progress became slower, and the forest grew deeper, darker and taller, folding itself over the boats until they were traveling through a green tunnel with only a ribbon of sky visible directly overhead.

They passed riverside settlements with no more than a wave, eventually reaching a larger township where they took on more fuel. After that, there were few villages along the river. By the ninth day there were none at all. The boats moved on, the wake of their passage washing the riverbanks, their engines indecently loud in a landscape where human activity was an alien intrusion.

The river became increasingly shallow and difficult to follow. Three times they ran aground, and only Tomasinho's giant strength enabled them to drag the unloaded boats through the shallow water. At length, faced by a maze of sandbanks, Mercedes turned her boat's bow to the shore, cut the engine, and glided in to a natural harbor in the shelter of a fallen tree. The others followed. The boats stopped with a bump and Nick, who had been asleep in the bows, woke with a start.

"End of the line," said Mercedes. "We can go no further in the boats."

"So what do we do now?" asked Nick, still fuddled with sleep.

Mercedes picked up the improvised pack she had made from her sleeping roll. "We walk."

She stepped out of the boat. A split second later, an arrow, feathered with bright plumes, sped from nowhere to bury itself, quivering, in the bark of a tree barely a handsbreadth in front of her face.

With no change of expression and without raising her voice, Mercedes said, "Nobody move."

15 TRIBE

The travelers froze at Mercedes's command.

Nick had stepped out of the boat and was reaching to pull her out of danger, Luke's arm was flung across his chest to stop him. Heitor had moved protectively in front of Rosa. Tomasinho was caught in the act of transferring their belongings from the boats to the riverbank. Luiz had drawn out his knife. He pressed the release catch and the blade sprang out with a metallic click.

Mercedes threw him a furious glance. "Put that thing

away," she hissed in Portuguese. Luiz did so, with very poor grace. No one else moved.

Mercedes raised her head and called out in a strange, fluid, bird-like language that was utterly unfamiliar to Luke. There was no response. She repeated the call. Still nothing.

"Keep still," said Mercedes. "We don't want to frighten them."

"I don't see why not," Nick hissed in Luke's ear. "They're frightening me!"

Mercedes repeated her call a third time. For a while, nothing happened. Then, shadows shifted among the trees. At first, Luke couldn't be sure he had really seen movement, or whether light, falling through the canopy, was creating the illusion of a presence. But then leaves parted to reveal, first one, then two, then half a dozen figures surrounding the travelers. Three carried slender, lethal-looking spears; two held bows, half-drawn with arrows knocked to the string, and the last carried a six-foot long blow pipe, which he pointed directly at Luke.

"The darts in that pipe," Mercedes observed, "are poisonous."

"Thanks," said Luke. "I'll keep that in mind."

The men were slim, dark-haired and brown-skinned. Their bodies were painted with patterns of red and blue dye, and naked except for belts, loincloths and bead necklaces. They wore arm or wrist bands of bright cloth. Several had circular decorations set into their ears, others had pierced lobes that hung down as low as their jawline. They looked purposeful and far from welcoming.

"These are Arara people," said Mercedes. "My father and I have met them before, many times. Don't worry, they're friendly."

"Is that a fact?" said Nick in disbelief.

"Friendly isn't the same as stupid. They are wary and they have a right to be. Consider yourself lucky; we could have met people from more warlike tribes. Cinta Larga, Rikbaktsa, Zoró – that one means 'dried head,' and it doesn't mean they towel-dry their hair after swimming."

Nick gulped. "I get the picture."

"Well, they've stopped shooting," said Luke, "and nobody's died yet, which is a good thing. But they don't seem happy to see us."

"No." Mercedes said something in the Indians' language, holding out her hands in a clear gesture of peaceful intent. This had no effect. For the first time Mercedes's voice sounded concerned. "I tell them we mean them no harm and ask them to lay down their weapons, but they're not doing it. Something's wrong."

"We're in the middle of a trackless jungle," said Nick to the world at large, "surrounded by hostile Indians armed with spears and bows and blowpipes and it's taken her until now to work out that something's wrong!"

"Don't be a fool! I mean they're really worried about something – they were a lot more friendly last time I met them. Listen, I want you all to sit down – no sudden moves and especially no weapons. Try to look relaxed. I'll talk to them and see if I can find out what they're scared of." Mercedes folded her legs under her and sat down gracefully in the leaf-litter of the forest floor. She adopted a pose of casual unconcern, beaming at the watchful Indians. Luke, Nick and her friends did their best to follow suit.

This seemed to lighten the atmosphere, but only by a fraction. Mercedes spoke again. This time, she talked for a long time, and seemed to be asking questions. The replies to these were grudging and monosyllabic to begin with, but at length, one of the tribesmen laid down his spear and squatted opposite Mercedes. He began to talk, slowly at first, then volubly. His tone became angry. He made chopping hand gestures and pointed to the north. After a final exclamation, he became silent, seemingly waiting for a reply.

"This is the headman of a nearby village. He and his

men are out hunting. He says..." Mercedes gave Luke a glance of appeal. "Understand that I do not speak this language very well."

"You speak it a lot better than I do," said Luke.

"Well, then, I will do my best. He says that his people are always hard-pressed – by other tribes seeking land and rubber planters who clear the forest and make his people wear white men's clothes and work for them. But new people have come down from the north who are worse than any of these – white men who do not speak Portuguese and a devil woman, tall, tall – not Indian, not European – whose eyes are always hidden..."

"Our Japanese friend," said Nick savagely. "We might have known she'd be involved."

"At first, these newcomers seem friendly: they bring gifts, and promises of friendship. But then, they turn on his people. They use guns. Some are killed. They drive the men off, up the river, toward the..." She hesitated. "The high, flat land, is as near as I can come to what he said."

"The plateau," said Luke quietly. "Grandpa's Lost World."

Mercedes nodded. "It could be. The Arara have only seen it in the distance, they have never been so far."

"Ask him about these new people. What were they like? Did they have any markings – or tattoos?"

189

Mercedes asked the question. The tribesman scowled. Then he cleared leaves with the flat of his hand to leave a patch of bare sandy soil, took up a stick and drew a picture of a striking snake coiled around a spear.

Nick took in a sharp breath. Luke felt a lead weight settle in his gut: his worst fears for his mother's safety had been realized. Keeping his voice steady with an effort, he said, "Tell him that these people are our enemies. And ask him whether he has seen your father and my mother."

The question took some time to ask, but once it was understood, the change in the atmosphere was marked. Spears, bows and blowpipes were lowered. The Indians grinned and chuckled to each other, their spokesman becoming positively genial.

"Yes," Mercedes translated, "they came through here...I think he's saying, two months ago." The tribesman said something else and she gave Luke a mischievous grin. "She went to their village. All she asks them about is...bones, yes, that's it, bones. Bones of dead animals, old bones..." She gave Luke a mocking glance. "Dinosaurs?" Luke nodded and she snorted. "Then she..." Mercedes broke off and said something to the Indian, apparently checking whether her translation was correct. In reply, he gave an unmistakable mime of measuring something with calipers, and Mercedes laughed. "Yes, I am right. He says she measured their heads, everyone – young, old, man, woman, boy, girl. She measured them all and made marks on white leaves – I suppose he means in a book. He says it tickled. They all thought it was a huge joke." She gave Luke a wry smile. "They like your mother, but they think she is a little *luoco* – crazy, you know?"

Luke sighed. "I wouldn't argue with that. If she couldn't find any fossil bones, she'd resort to anthropology – study of humans. She has a thing about skulls – and quite a collection back home."

Mercedes gave him a rueful look. "I'd better not translate that. They might think she was a Zoró in disguise."

"And did she and your father go on, upriver?"

Mercedes asked the question and translated the reply: "Yes – they left their boats here and went on in canoes." Luke gave her an inquiring glance. "Beyond here, the river is too shallow for boats, but with canoes they could go on for maybe three days, carrying the canoes where there was not enough water for them to float."

Luke nodded. "So they left their boats – may we see them?"

The question was put but the tribesman's reply was evasive. Eventually, by gentle but persistent questioning,

Mercedes established that the boats had been left in the care of the Arara, but that the snake people had destroyed them. "He is afraid we will blame him," said Mercedes heavily. "He says he can show us where the boats were sunk."

All the animation had left her face suddenly. She had become withdrawn, shrunken, grieving for the boat in which she and her father had made so many trips along the river.

"Do you want to see?" Luke asked.

She shook her head. "Do you?"

"No. If our enemies were as efficient in destroying the boats as they've been with everything else, we won't find anything. Your father and my mother were fine when they left here – at least that's something. Was that before or after the snake-and-spear men arrived?"

Mercedes put the question. Her face was troubled as she gave Luke the answer. "Before."

Luke's heart thudded painfully. "Then they may have met somewhere between here and the plateau."

Mercedes's voice was savage. "If they have harmed my father..."

"Ah, now, let's not count our chickens before they've – uh – come home to roost." Nick's intervention was clumsy, but kindly meant, and Mercedes rewarded him with a smile.

"Well, we're not going to find anything further by sitting around here." Luke shook off his apprehension. "Will they lend us canoes to go on?"

The request caused much discussion among the tribesmen. Mercedes translated as much as she was able. "They won't exchange the canoes for the boats – they have no use for boats as they never go downriver from here. Their canoes are important to them for fishing. They are afraid that, if we take them, they will never see them again."

Luke pondered for a moment. "Well then – tell them we are going to find your father and my mother. Tell them that we'll try to find out what has happened to their friends who were driven away by the snake people. Say that, if we can, we will bring their friends back to them."

Mercedes translated this. The Indians were a polite and dignified people. If they thought it unlikely that Luke and his ill-assorted band would be able to rescue their friends from a well-armed and ruthless foe, they gave no sign of it.

After further discussion, Mercedes announced, "He will let us have four canoes and two men to guide us. When we leave the canoes, the men will wait for one month: that will give us time to get to the plateau and return. If we do not return, the men will bring the canoes back."

Luke nodded. "That's more than fair."

"Fair? I call it handsome." Nick stepped forward impulsively, holding out his hand. At first the spokesman recoiled in alarm: then, understanding the meaning of the gesture from Nick's manner, he took the proffered hand and shook it.

They spent that night in the Indian village. The hunting party that had met them was greeted with consternation upon its return, but as soon as they learned that the strangers they had brought were connected with the crazy woman with a taste for bones and skulls, and not the snake people, Luke and his companions were surrounded by curious Indians – men, women and chattering children.

Luke's blond hair was a novelty to the dark-haired Arara, and a huge hit, much to his embarrassment. At Mercedes's insistence (which Luke suspected was partly due to a determination not to offend their hosts, and partly to delight at his discomfiture), he allowed the villagers to run their fingers through it. They exclaimed with delight at its color and softness. Surprisingly, Luiz's flick knife was also popular, especially with the young men, until Mercedes angrily told him to put it away.

That evening, around the fire, the travelers and villagers cemented their friendship with a feast of yams, cassava and plantains, accompanied by fish and meat.

"What's this?" asked Nick, taking a generous helping of fish.

"Piranha," said Mercedes with her mouth full.

"Man eats piranha!" observed Nick.

"Better than the other way around," said Luke. Mercedes laughed, nearly choking on her food.

Another dish was presented to Nick. He turned to his other neighbor, a member of the hunting party, with an inquiring gesture. "And what's this?"

The man gave a spirited impersonation of a monkey.

Nick turned a delicate shade of green and waved the dish away. "Thanks, I'll stick with the piranha."

The food was followed by singing and dancing. The festivities went on well into the night. Drinks were brought around, adding to the jollity of the occasion. Luke was careful to avoid a lethal-looking concoction that Mercedes told him was made from fermented cassava, and was relieved to see that she and Nick did the same. Heitor and Luiz succumbed however, and were suffering from sore heads and grumbling stomachs when the time came to depart next morning.

* * *

They traveled by canoe for the next three days.

Their new craft were dugouts, twelve to fourteen feet long. They were made, according to Mercedes, from trunks of the marupa tree, carefully hollowed out to have thin hulls for lightness. They were a little tricky to manage, but with the help of the Indians, the travelers soon learned to paddle, suffering only the occasional capsize. Their dwindling supplies had been replenished by the Arara and they now carried spears, bows, arrows and blowpipes, in the hope that they would be able to hunt more food on their journey. Luke was doubtful of their hunting skills, but glad of the weapons nonetheless.

By now, the forest – with its clinging vegetation, stifling heat and biting insects – had folded itself around them completely. It seemed to encompass their whole world, so that they could hardly imagine anywhere else existed. They were constantly surrounded by strange noises and furtive rustlings. From time to time, they disturbed forest creatures: troops of inquisitive monkeys, indignant snakes and pop-eyed frogs (which their guides caught as a source of poison for their darts).

The Indians were adept at fishing and shooting birds for the pot. Luke was used to an English longbow and found it difficult to master the hunting bow of the Amazon, but eventually he succeeded in bringing down a curassow – a bird about the size of a turkey. Nick managed to shoot a jacana with his blowpipe, much to his surprise and delight. Though neither he nor Luke enjoyed killing, they felt less like useless passengers once they had made a contribution to the company's food supply.

The occasional hunt aside, their days consisted of paddling and, where the water was too shallow, carrying the canoes on their backs, three to a canoe, so that with only their legs visible beneath the upturned hull, they looked like an overgrown insect.

At length they came to a spot where their guides indicated that further progress by water was impossible. Leaving the canoes, the travelers shouldered their packs.

Luke shook hands with the Arara. "Please say goodbye to them," he said to Mercedes, "and tell them we will see them in a month's time." Mercedes translated. Leaving the Arara squatting amid their canoes and talking in low voices, Luke checked the map in his grandfather's notebook. Then he and his companions lifted their machetes and began to hack their way into the jungle.

They made better progress than Luke had expected. He soon realized why: they were following the stream, where the vegetation was less dense, along a trail that someone had made before them – the growth they were clearing was new, with cut and broken branches on either side.

By Luke's reckoning they had barely gone a mile when they found five more canoes drawn up on the riverbank. The hulls had been smashed, the paddles snapped. Mercedes stared at them. She began to shiver uncontrollably.

Panic threatened to engulf Luke. He took refuge in action. "Spread out," he said harshly. "See what you can find."

It was Nick who discovered the bodies. He called Luke over.

There were five, each little more than a skeleton to which scraps of skin and wisps of hair still clung. The scurrying insects of the forest had disposed of the rest of the remains. They wore western clothes: shirts, pants and sturdy boots. Frayed holes in the material surrounded by brown stains revealed where they had been shot.

None was female. Luke let out a shuddering breath. Whatever had happened to his mother, she had not met her death here.

"What do we do?" asked Nick in a choked voice. Luke kneeled by the nearest body. More deaths! He felt a surge of pity for these men he had never known, callously murdered by people with whom they had no quarrel. His eyes stung. Without looking up, he said, "Get Mercedes."

Nick gave him an appalled look. "We can't let her see this!"

"It's not up to us to decide what she can and can't see. She has the right."

Nick stumbled off, returning with Mercedes and her friends. They stood around the killing field, silent, as Mercedes, her face a mask, moved from body to body.

At the fourth she stopped. She reached beneath the ragged shirt and withdrew a small silver medallion in the shape of a leaping dolphin.

She said, "This is my father."

Her howl of despair sent monkeys scurrying for the treetops.

16 CLIMB

Guiana Highlands, Brazil
and Venezuela

It was late in the day by the time they had finished burying the bodies, scratching out shallow graves with sticks and their bare hands.

Mercedes would allow no one else to dig her father's grave. She took his dolphin medallion and hung it around her own neck. She scraped at the soil with fierce intensity, hacking at tree roots with knife and machete. When the body was placed in the grave, she covered it with earth and made a cross out of wood lashed together with vines, which she planted at the head.

She remained kneeling by the grave while the others cleared a campsite. Tomasinho began to gather wood for a fire, but Luke stopped him from lighting it. The wood was wet: it would smolder, and they had no idea how close the killers of Raul da Silva were. Their enemies might be all around them and a column of smoke would be the surest means of giving away their presence.

Mercedes spent the hours before darkness fell alone, refusing her friends' offers of condolence. She had made it clear to Luke that she didn't want his company. She even spurned Nick, who was desperate to return some of the sympathy she had shown him during the journey. Her rejection made Nick miserable too. So it was a silent and cheerless company that Mercedes rejoined at sunset.

Luke had also been thinking hard, and had reached a decision. "Tomorrow," he told Mercedes, "you go back."

"Tomorrow," Mercedes replied, "we go on."

Luke shifted uncomfortably. "I *have* to go on. They have my mother. But you don't. We've seen what these people are capable of. And now your father... I can't ask you to go on after this."

Mercedes's eyes were burning rubies in a mask of stone. "We've always known what they were capable of. Remember Eduardo? Do not try to make my choices for me, Luke Challenger. Do you think that I would let my father's killers go scot-free? You may do what you like: but even if everyone else goes back, I shall go on."

Her friends had remained silent while Mercedes was speaking English. Now she translated what she had said into Portuguese. Luiz listened intently, flicking his knife open and closed.

"But it won't be safe…" protested Luke.

"Would I be any safer in Manaus? Do you think I want to be safe now? We go on. You to find your mother, I to avenge my father."

"I was afraid you'd say that." Luke glanced around Mercedes's companions. "What about the rest of you?"

Tomasinho rumbled something. "He says, he will go where I go," said Mercedes. Heitor and Rosa nodded in agreement.

Luiz burst into a torrent of Portuguese. Mercedes translated: "'I, Luiz Tavares, say this. Whatever I do, I decide. No one makes my choices for me – not my parents or my family; not the church or the police; not bosses or big-shot politicians, not my friends or my enemies. How I live – and yes, if it comes to that, how I die – while my heart beats and blood runs in my veins… I decide!'"

A heavy silence followed Luiz's outburst while darkness gathered around them. At length, Luke said,

"We might as well risk a fire, now. The smoke won't be seen."

The fire was lit, filling the campsite with unearthly smoke. Nobody suggested cooking a meal.

Mercedes sat with her back to the others. After a while, her shoulders began to shake as she wept. Nick kneeled beside her and put an arm around them. This time, she let it stay there.

Ten days later, they stood at the foot of the plateau. It rose into the sky, its distant summit an island in the clouds. Basalt ramparts reared up before the travelers like the walls of some huge, impregnable castle. Greenery spilled over the clifftop high above and clung precariously to ledges. Streams of white water tumbled down immeasurable distances, dashing themselves to spray where they fell. Luke gazed upwards with a mixture of elation and foreboding. There it was, the goal of their expedition. The land about which Luke's grandfather had told him so many stories, where now he thought, with fierce determination, he would find his mother. The Lost World.

The trek to this point had been long and hard. Mercedes had begun by hacking her way wildly through the undergrowth as though the ferns and vines had done her a personal injury, lips set in a snarl. Within a few hours her hands were blistered and her breath came in ragged gasps.

Luke was concerned for her, but he knew that in her current mood, sympathy would not be well received. "Take it easy," he advised.

"Don't tell me to take it easy!" she stormed. "I want to find the men who killed my father."

"By the time you do, you'll wear yourself out. What are you planning to do when you find them? Collapse with exhaustion and hope they trip over you?"

Mercedes swore at Luke: but she calmed down after that. During their midday halt, she had offered him a drink from her water flask as a peace token.

Their way had led them through dense forest where, even though the band that had captured the Arara and (Luke supposed) kidnapped his mother had blazed the trail before them, the going was hard. To add to their misery, the fine weather broke and it rained for at least an hour or two every day. This mattered less when they reached swamplands. They were forced to wade through evil-smelling, stagnant water and ooze, sometimes up to their necks, getting so thoroughly soaked in the process that the heavy showers that pelted them from above made little difference. The swamp held other dangers and discomforts: vicious biting insects and supple, aggressive and highly poisonous snakes that seemed to lie in ambush behind every half-sunken log.

And now that they had finally reached the plateau, filthy, footsore and exhausted, there seemed to be no way forward. Vast cliffs rose above them, red and chocolate brown, a thousand feet high and sheer. Nick stared at them in dismay. "We'll never climb that!"

Mercedes glared at the cliffs. "The raiding party that killed my father – how did they get up there?"

"I don't know." Luke was poring over his grandfather's notebook. "Maybe they had a balloon – Grandpa was going to build one to escape from the plateau – or some sort of crane. Whatever they used, I don't suppose they'll have left it for us to find." He closed the book and pointed to a pinnacle of rock. It stood upright, like a needle, its narrow top just forty feet from the edge of the cliff. "The first expedition went up that way and crossed to the plateau on a fallen tree."

Nick stared at him. "You're kidding."

"Don't worry, the tree isn't there any more. One of Grandpa's guides pushed it over the cliff to strand them on the plateau. So we can't use that route."

"I can live with that," said Nick fervently.

"So if we can't go up the way they went up," said Mercedes, "what are we going to do?"

Luke gave her an encouraging grin. "We're going to go up the way they came down – if I can find it. Come on..."

The words died in his throat as a strange cry, like that of a hawk but many times deeper and stronger, echoed from the cliffs. Moments later, a creature out of nightmares soared over the cliff edge and wheeled above them.

Despite the distance from which they saw it, the creature's size was stupendous. Tomasinho let out a hoarse yelp of alarm. Rosa put her hand to her mouth, stifling a moan of terror. Luiz and Heitor raised their bows – and lowered them again, stunned at the size and outlandish appearance of their would-be quarry.

"*Meu deus!*" Instinctively, Mercedes shrank back toward the shelter of the trees. Shielding her eyes with her hand, she squinted into the sun. "What is that thing? A condor?" She shook her head in wonder. "But condors live in the Andes – that's a thousand miles west of here."

"It would have to be very, very lost," said Luke, his voice shaking with suppressed excitement. Perhaps, of them all, he alone had been expecting something like this. "Anyway, you'll never see one *that* size."

The creature repeated its cry, veered sharply, and disappeared from view.

There was a moment of complete silence.

Luke stepped to Mercedes's side. "If my grandfather was such a crazy old gringo," he said softly, "how do you explain that?"

"I don't know how to explain it," said Mercedes, her voice troubled. "I have traveled through the forest many times and that is like no bird I have ever seen."

Any lingering doubts Luke might have had about the truth of his grandfather's story had been dispelled by the appearance of the creature from the plateau. He felt a surge of renewed energy. "We have got to get up there." He set off along the foot of the cliffs with a determined stride.

Nick gazed after his departing friend. "He sees a monster like that, and he's in a hurry to get to where they live?"

Mercedes shook her head. "Like his mother: *luoco*."

"Here we are," said Luke. He was gazing at a page of his grandfather's notebook with an air of triumph. His companions looked around and, one by one, sank to the ground, tired and dejected.

Nick was incensed. "What do you mean 'Here we are'? *Where* are we, exactly?" He indicated the cliff wall towering above them. "We've no better chance of climbing here than anywhere else! These cliffs just go on forever."

Luke ignored him. He put the book away and set to work clearing moss from a gigantic trunk that grew from the base of the cliff – the monstrous specimen was well over a hundred feet tall.

Nick glared at him. "And would you stop messing around with that blasted tree!"

"It isn't a tree," Mercedes told him, "it's a strangler fig."

"What's the difference?"

"It's a tree-killer." Mercedes pointed into the canopy. "And it doesn't grow up, it grows down. The fig starts its life as a tiny seed, way up in the treetops. Then it starts to grow down the trunk of the tree, until it reaches the soil. Then it really gets going, and wraps itself around the tree like an anaconda wraps itself around its prey, and strangles it. This is an old fig and it's completely destroyed the tree that it grew around. If you look carefully you can see it is hollow in the middle."

Nick looked. "Yes, very interesting. But why are we wasting time on it?"

"Because it's the way up." Luke stepped back. Carved deep into the trunk, invisible until he had cleared away the moss, were the initials *GEC*. "George Edward Challenger," he said in a voice that shook with excitement. "Grandpa. When he came down from the plateau, he carved his initials in this trunk." He punched the air and let out a whoop of elation that sent birds rocketing nervously from nearby trees. Mercedes and her companions stared at him in alarm.

Nick was unimpressed. "Your grandpa's initials: very nice – but what do they tell us that we don't already know?"

Luke pointed. "You see up there, that projection of rock that looks like a spear head?" Nick looked up and nodded. "According to Grandpa's notebook, there's a cave just below it. You can't see it from here because the cliff overhangs, but it's there all right. And a tunnel leads from that cave right into the caves the Indians used up on the plateau."

Nick nodded reluctantly. "All right, but how do we get to it? You may be able to climb that cliff but I'm sure I can't – anyone else want to try?" Mercedes pursed her lips and shook her head, her friends followed suit.

Luke thought for a moment. "I reckon I could climb to the cave."

"And throw a rope down for the rest of us to climb up?"

"No," said Luke. "I don't think I could do the climb with a coil of rope weighing me down. In any case, the rope wouldn't be long enough. But the rest of you could climb up the inside of the fig. It'd be like climbing inside a chimney, but with lots of handholds and footholds. Shouldn't be too difficult."

"Yes, but how do we get across from the trunk to the cliff?"

"You're pretty good at climbing trees." Luke pointed upwards. "The crown of the fig is about level with the ledge above that overhang, but there's a branch that stands out above it. You shin up there with a rope and tie it off. You throw the other end to me. Then you tie another rope in the middle of the first. I loop the first rope around the projecting rock, then you all use the second rope to swing across the gap."

"You mean like Tarzan?" Nick's eyes gleamed. He had seen the movie *Tarzan, the Ape Man* the previous year and been very impressed by Johnny Weissmuller in the title role.

Mercedes folded her arms. "*Luoco.*"

"If anyone has a better suggestion," said Luke sharply, "I'd be happy to hear it."

Nick, recognizing the danger signals, picked up two coils of rope. "No point in arguing about it. We may as well try. Let's get going." He headed for the tree.

Immediately he began his ascent, Luke knew that the cliff was the most difficult climb he had ever attempted – and he had to do it without equipment, knowing that any slip would be fatal. Handholds and footholds were few and little more than tiny crevices in the rock into which he could only insert his fingers or the toe of his boot with difficulty. There was no opportunity to rest. It was not long before he was dripping with sweat and every muscle in his body was aching with the strain of hauling himself up and maintaining his position while he searched anxiously for the next precarious hold.

The overhang nearly finished him. The cliff wall here leaned outwards, so that Luke felt like a fly on a sloping ceiling. At one point, his feet lost their grip when a tiny ledge crumbled beneath them, and he found himself hanging by his arms alone. He could never remember afterwards the extraordinary feat of gymnastics with which he had regained his hold. But at long last, exhausted and trembling, he hauled himself onto the ledge and discovered that Nick, whose climb had been simple by comparison, had already secured the crossing rope to the branch, and the swinging rope to it. He was now waiting impatiently to throw the free end of the crossing rope to Luke.

"You told me you were the climbing expert," called Nick. "I thought you'd never get there at all."

Luke was too exhausted to rise to the bait. "Just throw the rope."

Nick's first throw fell short, but on the second Luke

succeeded in making the catch. The climb to the projecting rock was far easier than the ascent he had already made and he had no difficulty in securing the rope around it. By this time, Mercedes and Luiz had joined Nick in the crown of the fig: it was time to make the crossing.

They tested it out with the packs. The first flew across the gap above Luke's head. He had to climb back and slacken off the rope. Nick swung the pack again: this time, Luke was able to catch it. The rest of their stores and weapons went across in the same way.

Then it was Mercedes's turn. Nick had made a loop in the bottom of the swinging rope and tied a knot at shoulder height to make it easier to hold on to. Mercedes was clearly terrified of the crossing, but she would not ask her friends to do anything she was not prepared to do herself.

"Ah, it's just like a swing," Nick said to encourage her.

"I hate swings."

"Well, look on the bright side. You only have to do this once."

"What about coming back?"

"We'll cross that bridge when we come to it."

Mercedes glared at Nick, then took a deep breath and launched herself into space. She swung across as easily as the packs had done, and Luke caught her. He couldn't help noticing that her whole body was shaking, but he made no comment.

The others followed. Luiz did his tough-guy act on taking the rope, then screamed all the way across, much to Tomasinho's amusement. Heitor and Rosa seemed to view the crossing as one more trial in a life full of trouble, and made it stoically. Tomasinho had more difficulty – his weight made the whole assembly creak and the first time he reached the ledge where the others were gathered, his impetus failed to carry him quite far enough for them to reach him. He swung back across the gulf. Nick caught him as he reached the other side, and gave him an almighty shove. This time he came just within reach of his anxious friends, who managed, after a perilous struggle, to draw him over the ledge to safety.

Luke glanced up as Mercedes prepared to swing the rope back, and felt cold horror flood through him. "Nick!" he yelled. "Watch out!"

He had been so preoccupied by the difficulties of the crossing that he had failed to keep a good watch. Luke cursed himself – he should have been prepared for trouble. His grandfather had told him of the gigantic flying reptiles that lived on the plateau. They had even seen one – Mercedes's so-called "Condor" – and now, perhaps alerted to their presence by Luiz's scream, one had found them.

The creature was a pterosaur, but bigger than any Luke had seen in his mother's books. Its head, which terminated in a vast yellow bill, stretched out far in front of its body; its wings, leathery and bat-like, must have spanned nearly thirty feet. It had no tail, but its legs, pink and naked, trailed behind it.

"*Meu deus!*" Mercedes and her friends exclaimed in horror and disbelief as the creature swooped out of the clouds like a destroying angel. It was already diving toward the crown of the fig as Luke yelled his warning. Nick had just time to duck back before its wicked talons clutched at the branches. The hideous beast gave a screech of frustration and rose clumsily into the air, circling for another attack.

Luke snatched up the bow the Arara had given him and notched an arrow to the string. The others followed suit: Luiz and Rosa fitting arrows to their bows and Mercedes loading a poison dart into her blowpipe.

A chorus of harsh cries from above made Luke crane his neck to stare upwards. "Nick!" he yelled. "There are more of those things on the way. You'll have to come across now!"

Nick waved to show that he had heard and understood. Mercedes flung the rope across the gap. Nick reached up and caught it. Without hesitation, he launched himself into space.

The first pterosaur completed its turn. With the others close behind, screaming with the cold rage of the hunter, it dived to attack.

17 THE LOST WORLD

Luke raised his bow and loosed the arrow: it went through the pterosaur's leathery wing. The creature screeched, but continued its attack as arrows from Luiz and Rosa flew wide. By the time Luke had readied himself for another shot, the pterosaur had reached Nick. It barreled into him and Nick nearly lost his grip on the rope. The pterosaur clawed at him with its talons, flapping its wings for balance and snapping at Nick's head with its long, pointed beak. Time seemed to slow down. The swinging rope was bringing Nick and his attacker inexorably closer to the cliff ledge, but Luke did not dare loose an arrow for fear of hitting his friend.

Then, Nick tore his foot free of the loop at the end of the rope, and kicked out at the pterosaur. The beast shrieked as it lost its grip and fell back. Seizing his chance, Luke let his arrow fly. It thumped into the creature's scaly breast, followed a split-second later by arrows from Luiz and Rosa. The pterosaur gave a screech of mortal agony and tumbled from the sky, its wings fluttering uselessly. The other reptiles, seeing the plight of their stricken companion, dived after it, clutching and biting at its still-living body, tearing it to pieces in mid-air.

Luke dropped his bow and, with Mercedes, grabbed at Nick as he completed his swing. His clothes and skin were torn in at least a dozen places and he was bleeding profusely from several jagged scalp-wounds. They dragged him, half-fainting, onto the ledge. Then Luiz and Rosa gave covering fire as they retreated with the rest of the group into the cave behind them. Outside, the rest of the pterosaurs wheeled to attack. Arrows accounted for two of them; a third tried to follow them into the cave, only to fall back, screaming, with a dart from Mercedes's blowpipe embedded in its throat. The remaining creatures broke off the attack. When Luke checked, a few seconds later, the sky outside their refuge was clear. Their assailants had evidently returned to the plateau.

Luke returned to the companions to find Mercedes bathing Nick's wounds with drinking water from her own flask. "Are you all right?" he asked.

Nick glared at him. "All right?" he repeated incredulously. "I've just been pecked half to death by a flying dinosaur with a six-foot beak and he asks if I'm all right!"

"It could have been worse," Luke told him.

"Oh, really? How?"

"It could have been a seven-foot beak."

Nick stared at Luke for a moment. Then he burst out laughing. Luke joined in. The relief at their escape made even the feeblest of jokes incredibly funny.

Mercedes eyed them both with exasperation. "Boys!" She dabbed at a deep cut with a ragged edge.

"Ow!"

"Hold still!"

As Mercedes continued to dab away, Nick said, "That was a pterodactyl, wasn't it?"

"Strictly speaking," said Luke, "a pterodactyl is a lot smaller than the beast that attacked you. That was a pterosaur – a big one. Bigger even than a pteranodon, I think."

"A pterosaur – so that's what it was. Thank you," said

Nick gravely. "I couldn't help feeling it was very rude, trying to rip my throat out before we'd been properly introduced."

While Mercedes completed her running repairs on Nick, Luke rummaged in the pack to find the candles they had brought. As soon as Nick (his head swathed in bandages torn from spare shirts and his skin liberally daubed with purple iodine) was on his feet, Luke handed around the candles he had bought, and lit them. Then he led the way into the cave.

A little over two hours later, they emerged blinking into daylight. The climb through the caves had been steep, but uneventful. As they neared their goal, Luke had called for silence and scouted ahead, expecting to meet the Indians of the plateau who, his grandfather had told him, used the caves as barns and storehouses. But all he had found were bat-roosts and a few wrinkled vegetables and withered ears of corn, with no sign of humans anywhere.

Now, here they were, standing with low cliffs and caves behind them and the plateau laid out before them. "The Lost World," said Luke. He closed his eyes and very quietly, so that only Nick heard him, he added, "Well, Grandpa, I'm here."

"If we're right," said Nick, "so's your ma."

"I know," said Luke. His Challenger chin jutted pugnaciously. "Let's go and find her."

The plateau was shrouded in mist and low cloud. What they could see of the landscape consisted of flat granite blocks like great irregular flagstones. The thin soil between these supported a range of unearthly looking, ancient plants: scrub and thorn brush, fern and sisal, monkey puzzle and conifer. From far away, invisible in the murk, came the harsh, unfamiliar cries of animals that had died out elsewhere on earth over sixty million years ago. Luke gazed into the shifting mist, enraptured. "Incredible," he breathed.

Nick sniffed. "If you ask me, it looks like parts of Galway."

Luke gave him a disgusted look and dragged his gaze away from the landscape, angry with himself for daydreaming when there was so much to explore. He took out his grandfather's notebook, opened it at a sketch map of the plateau and studied it. After a few moments, he pointed. "The Indian village should be nearby, and the central lake is over there."

Nick squinted into the mist. "I can't see anything. But I can smell smoke."

Luke sniffed. "You're right. Woodsmoke. And – listen!"

As they fell silent, all the companions heard the sound that had caught Luke's attention – a rhythmic tapping or hammering noise, muffled by distance.

"Hammers?" suggested Nick. "Or picks?"

Luke was equally puzzled. "A quarry?" he said. "Or a mine?"

Nick shrugged. "There's only one way to find out."

"All right," agreed Luke. "But – carefully."

Their way led them through the Indian village. It was deserted and looked as if it had not been lived in for some time. Some of the huts had been burned. Others were missing part of the roof or walls.

Mercedes gazed around and gave a shudder. "What happened here?"

"I don't know," said Luke, "but I'm beginning to get an idea. Why do you think the snake-and-spear gang went out raiding and carried off the men of the Arara tribe? Didn't kill them – carried them off?"

"How should I know…?" Mercedes broke off as light dawned. "To work for them?"

"That's my guess. As labor – slave labor, from what we know of them. And it's a good bet that they'd already have forced the local tribe into working for them before they went to all the trouble of sending out a raiding party." Luke led the way forward and they moved off into the mist.

For a long time, nothing seemed to alter. Then they climbed up a slope and crested a ridge. From this point, with every step they took the noises became louder and more distinct. As well as the hammering noise there were others – shouts in an unknown language that sounded like orders, wails and cries. They inched toward the sounds – and came upon an unexpected barrier.

"Barbed wire," said Nick. "Now, that's something you don't expect to find on a remote plateau, inhabited by Indians who've been cut off from the rest of the world for thousands of years."

Tomasinho reached out to touch the wire. Before Luke could hiss a warning, there was a crackle and a blue flash. Cursing, Tomasinho sucked at his burned fingers.

"Electric fence." Luke beckoned urgently. "Everyone back!" Moving as silently as he could, he led the way to a thick clump of ferns growing on a slight rise that overlooked the fence. The companions squirmed through the stiff green fronds, finding vantage points from which they could see what was happening below without being seen.

After a short pause, indistinct shapes appeared on the other side of the fence – huge, cumbrous shapes that snorted and snuffled like shire horses with bronchitis.

Mercedes gripped Luke's arm so tightly that he almost cried out. Rosa buried her face in Heitor's shoulder. Tomasinho clenched his great fists. Luiz swore softly and continuously in Portuguese. Nick stared at Luke. "Are those *dinosaurs*?" he hissed.

"Oh, yes," said Luke with relish. He wanted to dance in triumph. "Iguanodons. Grandpa said when he was here, the Indians kept them like we keep cattle. They branded them and everything…"

He broke off. Now that the iguanodons were close enough, he was amazed to see that both had riders. His enemies had clearly gone one better than the Indians – they were using dinosaurs not merely as cattle, but as horses!

The riders were dressed in kepi-style caps and gray uniforms with knee-length boots. They wore riding goggles around their necks. Luke watched avidly from his refuge among the ferns as they detatched themselves from their mounts and moved toward the fence. "*Was war das?*" demanded one.

"*E' stato un animale?*" replied the other.

A third iguanodon approached: a tall, booted figure wearing a long leather coat threw itself from the creature's back and approached the earlier arrivals. "What is happening here?" The voice was female and heavily accented. Nick stiffened and Mercedes gave an angry hiss. The Japanese woman! Luke gestured them both to silence. They glared at him, but made no further sound.

The men who had arrived first immediately sprang to attention. "There is nothing here, Colonel," said the German speaker. "It was probably an animal blundering into the fence. Some of them are very stupid."

"But not as stupid as guards who make idiotic guesses where security is concerned!" The Japanese woman turned her tinted glasses toward the fence and stared into the mist. Luke and his friends flattened themselves onto the ground. Luke could have sworn he felt her gaze sweep over them like the beam of a searchlight. Finally she said, "It seems the fence remains unbroken. Security has not been compromised. Continue your patrol."

She stalked back to her mount and vaulted into the saddle. The German waited until she was out of sight and earshot before spitting out a Teutonic oath and making a rude gesture. His companion added an Italian curse. Talking in low voices, the men returned to their steeds. The beasts lumbered off into the mist.

Luke straightened up and brushed earth from his clothes. "No wonder my mother couldn't stay away from this place," he said, awestruck. "It's where all her dreams come true – at least as far as dinosaurs are concerned. But she didn't know about the snake-and-spear gang."

His tone hardened. "That Japanese woman has been dogging our steps ever since we left Portugal."

"She killed my da," said Nick bleakly.

"My father, too," said Mercedes. "And Eduardo." She spat on the ground. "She will pay."

"She and her friends are up to something here," said Luke, "something they don't want the rest of the world to know about: something big."

Nick nodded. "Big enough to throw a huge great fence around it."

"They can make a fence as strong as a mountain and as high as the sky," said Mercedes grimly. "It will not keep them safe from me."

"In the end, no," said Luke, "but it'll keep them safe for now. We're not going to get through here tonight. We can't cut a hole in the fence without electrocuting ourselves and setting off an alarm, and we've nothing to cut metal with anyway. What's more, it's getting late. We don't want to be out in the open after dark."

As if on cue, a strange, savage roar bellowed out of the mist. The companions instinctively drew closer to each other.

"So where do we go?" asked Mercedes.

"We need to be among trees. Grandpa was pretty sure there's an allosaurus up here somewhere."

Nick groaned. "That's not a good thing, right?"

"No. It's a meat-eater, a big one."

"Perfect." Nick gazed at his friend in wonder. "How can you be so – matter of fact about all this? Lost worlds? Dinosaurs? I mean…" Nick waved his arms to encompass the whole of the plateau as words failed him. "It's just all so…strange," he concluded lamely.

"Not to me," said Luke firmly. "I mean, the reality, yes…I suppose I'm more prepared for it. My mother has been bringing fossil bones to life for me since I was knee-high to a velociraptor. Dinosaurs have always been as real to me as – well, zebras, say, or giraffes."

Nick shook his head in bafflement.

"Anyway," said Luke, "the allosaurus is a plains hunter, a runner. It likes to chase its prey over open ground. If we can get among trees, its size will be a disadvantage and we should be safe." Luke considered. "Saf*er*."

"Then let's go and find some trees. I *like* trees."

For a while, the companions skirted the wire fence. When a tall structure loomed up – "A watchtower," Luke hissed – they shrank back and turned away from the fence. Gradually, the noises of human activity died away and were replaced by silence, punctuated from time to time by the shrill and eerie cries of unseen beasts. They walked for some distance across the flat landscape of a fern prairie, then they skirted a marsh and pushed through a stand of giant horsetail ferns. Here they suddenly came upon a beast the size of a delivery van, covered in armored scales. The creature gazed at them with bleary eyes, gave a shrill grunt of alarm unexpected in such a giant, and lumbered off as fast as it could waddle.

"*Nossa!*" Mercedes whistled softly. "Look at that shell! You could use it as a boathouse."

Nick turned to Luke. "I suppose there's no chance you don't know what it is?"

"Glyptodon," said Luke. "It's a sort of primitive armadillo." His quirky upbringing was certainly paying off in ways he could never have dreamed of. "It's harmless."

"Thank you," said Nick. "When one of those runs me over, it'll be a real comfort to know that I'm being trampled to death by something I know the name of – and that it's harmless."

As the light was beginning to fail, they came to the edge of the plateau. Beyond it, cliffs fell away for a thousand feet to the forest that lapped its great stone ramparts like waves breaking against a ship's hull.

Near the cliff-edge was a stand of deciduous trees, broad-leaved and much like those found in the forest below. Luke peered into the shadows between the trunks. "It looks all right so far," he said warily, "and certainly safer than open ground. At least this close to the edge nothing can creep up on us from behind. Come on, and keep your eyes peeled..."

"Wait!" hissed Mercedes. She pointed. "What's that?"

A bird had emerged from the trees to their left. It was huge, taller than an ostrich and far more powerfully built, with an enormous hawk-like beak, a high crest and silly little wings, obviously of no use for flying.

"That," said Luke, "is a phorusrhachos – a terror bird."

"Why," said Nick, "and I realize I may not like the answer to this, is it called that?"

"It's a hunter." Luke bent down, very slowly. His hand curled around a stout fallen branch. "It can kill a horse. Everyone pick up a branch. We can't outrun it: our best chance is to drive it off."

The phorusrhachos raised its head and screeched a challenge. Then it charged.

The beast hit Heitor with the force of a pile driver, knocking him to the ground. It turned with a speed remarkable in such a gigantic creature, and raised a foot tipped with razor-edged claws to disembowel its helpless opponent – only to find Rosa, her face set in a wolf-like snarl, standing over her friend, thrusting and slashing with a long, sturdy branch. The bird gave a shrill cry and flapped its ridiculous wings. Luiz and Mercedes, hastily stringing their bows, let fly a number of arrows that bounced uselessly away as the creature's leathery skin with its mail coat of feathers turned them aside. Now the phorusrhachos's attention was drawn to them instead. Tomasinho stepped between the terror bird and his friends. His club was smashed from his hands and a blow from the great bird's beak sent him reeling from the fray.

But that was the last blow the phorusrhachos landed. Roaring and yelling, Luke and his companions drove it back, jabbing at its chest and belly, clubbing at its flanks, which sent up clouds of dust like a beaten carpet. At length, the great bird, overwhelmed by numbers, turned tail, and with a final scream of frustrated rage, fled.

Bruised and aching, Luke's party entered the shelter of the trees. They had gone only a little way into the woods when they came across a small clearing, at the center of which lay a vast nest, thrown together higgledy-piggledy with debris from the forest floor. Sitting in the middle of the nest was one huge speckled egg.

"That's why it was so aggressive," said Mercedes, almost ruefully. "It was defending its nest."

Nick regarded the egg and licked his lips.

"Oh, no!" said Luke. "Don't even think about it. That bird may be the last of its kind. It's an endangered species."

"You call it endangered?" Nick reached for the egg. "I call it supper."

18 HELL-MOUTH

The following morning, the mist had cleared. Two hours after sunrise, Luke, Nick and Mercedes, who had begun their journey before first light, were back at the fence. Luke had refused to allow the others to join them, on the grounds that a small group was less likely to be spotted than a large one, but he left them all the weapons, along with strict instructions to remain in the safety of the woodland. His scouting party had found a small hill from which they could survey their enemies' entire encampment.

It was, as they had suspected, a mine. It lay some distance from a wide lake that occupied the center of the plateau. The fence they had encountered yesterday was in the shape of an irregular pentangle that completely surrounded the camp. It had watchtowers at each corner and a gate facing the lake. At the center of the enclosure stood a strange, stunted tower – a sort of Eiffel tower in miniature – the purpose of which Luke could not guess. Some distance from this lay a pit. A crane alongside it was operated by two iguanodons turning a windlass. Every now and then, a bucket would emerge from the pit and the crane jib would be swung over to allow clay from the mine to be emptied.

"You were right." Mercedes nudged Luke's shoulder and pointed. "Over there – slaves."

A line of Indians carrying empty baskets wound its way toward the pit. They were hobbled, with fetters on their ankles connected with a chain, to prevent them from running away. They filled their baskets with clay from the mine, lifted them to their shoulders and headed for a large wooden building with a chimney, from which belched clouds of steam and smoke. Their loads were heavy and the Indians staggered beneath them, many clearly near the end of their strength. Uniformed guards carrying machine guns stood around watching beadily, occasionally stepping forward to beat one of the workers for slacking on the job.

Another line of Indians, with fully laden baskets, emerged from the building, heading toward a wagon way. Here they tipped their burdens into trucks that ran on wooden rails. These were in trains of six, pulled by dinosaurs with three horns and huge shield-like frills emerging from the back of their heads.

"I know that one," said Nick. "Those are triceratops." Luke nodded.

When each train was full, the giant reptile at its head was led through the gate with its line of trucks rumbling along behind. The wagon way led to the shores of the lake, where another gang of sweating laborers shoveled the spoil from the trucks into the water, staining it a filthy yellow-brown.

The air was filled with noise. Pterosaurs wheeled above the camp like vultures over a corpse, shrieking protests. The guards in the watchtowers fired warning shots if they came too close. Dinosaurs roared and trumpeted. These cries, added to the sounds of hammers and picks, the yelled orders of the guards and the rattle of machinery from the smoking building, created such a din that Luke and his friends could talk normally with no fear of being heard.

"I know what this place is," said Luke. "Grandpa called it the 'pterodactyl rookery'."

Nick gave him a grin. "Shouldn't that be the 'pterosaur' rookery?"

"Classification wasn't an exact science back then."

Mercedes looked skywards. "That's why those things are making such a fuss. They've been turned out of their nests."

"Da told me about this place," said Nick. "He said there was a volcanic tube full of blue clay here. Lord John spotted it. When they all got back to London, he shared out some diamonds he'd found there."

"Diamonds?" Mercedes's eyes glinted.

Nick chuckled. "Girls!" Mercedes made a face at him. "Lord Roxton and my da were going to come back here to see if they could dig up a few more, but the war got in the way, so they never did."

"Well, it looks as if someone else has found it." Luke was studying the encampment carefully. "They're digging clay out of the mine..." He pointed at the crane as it lifted another bucket load. "The building with the chimney must be where they wash the diamonds out of it – yes, look, you can see there's a hose from the lake and they've dug a channel to run the dirty water back. The other Indians are taking the spoil away. That pit may be hundreds of feet deep. The snake-and-spear gang wants diamonds." His voice became hard and angry. "And they're forcing the plateau Indians and the Arara they captured to do their dirty work for them."

Nick pointed at a double row of badly made huts surrounded by another fence with more watchtowers. "I'm guessing they keep their slaves in there."

"Yes. The outer fence must be to keep dinosaurs out, the inner fence to keep the prisoners in."

"What about the tower in the middle? Another watchtower?"

"Shouldn't think so – it's in the wrong place. You wouldn't be able to see half the prison perimeter from there. I have no idea what it's for." Dismissing the problem, Luke went on, "Those must be the guards' huts over there, where the iguanodons are picketed. But where's my mother?" he added, half to himself.

Their examination of the camp was interrupted by a sudden commotion. The crane had hauled up, not a bucket, but a cage seemingly made of bamboo.

"What are they doing?" asked Mercedes.

"Looks like they're changing shift," replied Nick.

But though the cage was swung away from the pit, the Indians were kept inside. Moments later, there was a dull boom beneath their feet. The earth shook. A cloud of smoke and debris shot from the pit.

"They're blasting," said Luke excitedly. "They must have an explosives store somewhere..." He cast his eyes across the compound. "Yes, that little shed there – it's as far as it can be from everything else."

The cloud from the mine dispersed and the crane operators prepared to swing the cage back over the pit. But the Indians inside suddenly raised their voices in protest. Fingers were pointed. The Indians expostulated fiercely, with angry gestures.

Nick was puzzled. "What are they doing?"

Luke focused on the cage. "I think they're telling the guards that the cage isn't safe."

Whether or not the guards understood the Indians' complaints, they reacted with ruthless violence. Protesters were clubbed and kicked through the bars, their howls of pain and fear completely ignored.

The crane jib was swung back over the pit. As soon as it was in position, the cage began to disintegrate. The bottom gave way suddenly, precipitating the screaming occupants into the gaping maw of the pit. A few lucky ones clung to the bars, their legs kicking frantically over the drop. The guards cursed and bellowed orders. The jib was swung back over the brink, and the survivors were beaten and set to work repairing the cage.

Luke struggled to get to his feet. The brutality of the scene, the senseless waste of life, was more than he could stand. The temper he had inherited from his father and grandfather had turned his blood to molten lava. It took all Nick and Mercedes's strength to hold him back.

"Leave it!" panted Nick. "There's nothing you can do."

"They're dying!" snarled Luke.

"Yes, and if you go off at half-cock and try and attack dozens of armed guards single-handed, so will you! Remember what you told me in Cape Verde?"

Luke took a deep breath and waited for the red mist to fade from his vision. Nick was right: the odds were too great. There was a time to act – and a time to watch and wait. Once he had himself under control again, he said, "Sorry. It's just..." He shook his head. "That's no mine. It's the gate of hell."

Mercedes pointed at the circling, screeching pteradons. "With its very own demons."

"Hell-mouth mine," said Nick. "Very apt." He glanced back at the mine and grabbed at Luke's arm. "Over there!"

The door of a small hut in the prison compound had swung open. A guard walked down the steps, followed by a woman.

Luke's heart gave a jolt. Breathing was suddenly painful. Even at that distance there was no mistaking the slight but erect figure with fiery red hair: Harriet Challenger. His mother.

Luke immediately felt some of the tension of the past

weeks flow out of him. She was alive! He had been so afraid...

His relief turned to anger as the guard prodded his prisoner in the back with the muzzle of his machine gun. Luke instinctively clenched his fists, but then he groaned as his mother instantly turned on the guard to tell him in no uncertain terms what she thought of his behavior. "No," he muttered, willing his mother to be sensible. "Pipe down, for goodness' sake." Harriet Challenger was usually mild-mannered and vague, but she could be a holy terror when roused, as Luke had often found at his expense. He might almost have felt sorry for the guard, except that the man had a deadly weapon pointing straight at his mother and had only to pull the trigger...

But he didn't. With a final toss of her head, Harriet Challenger turned on her heel and headed across the compound with the guard slouching along behind her in a rather hangdog manner. They disappeared into another hut.

Luke breathed a sigh of relief. Then he began to think furiously. He had found his mother. So far so good. Now – how was he going to get her out of this?

Before he could reach any sensible conclusion, an outburst of roars and terror-stricken trumpeting echoed across the encampment.

Nick stared wildly around. "What's happening now?"

Luke tore his eyes away from his mother – and gaped in wonder at the sight that met his eyes.

A huge dinosaur was charging over the plain toward the mine encampment. It must have been nearly forty feet long. It ran on long, heavily muscled legs, which ate up the ground with gargantuan strides. Its front limbs were short and held close to its chest. It ran with its back as flat as a tabletop, its head thrust forward and balanced by a long, swinging tail with a whip-like end. Its mouth, filled with jagged teeth, was wide open, and it roared as it came.

"Tyrannosaurus rex," breathed Nick.

"No," said Luke. "It's the allosaurus. Just as big; just as deadly."

A triceratops had just hauled a train of spoil out of the gates. As soon as it saw the giant predator bearing down on it, the poor creature had panicked and tried to run, only to find its efforts hampered by the line of wagons it was pulling. The train had instantly jumped the tracks. Half the trucks now lay on their side and the ones that were still upright had become hopelessly bogged down in the loose sand of the lakeside. The triceratops's handler drew a knife and began to saw at its harness.

The Indians, who were shoveling waste into the lake,

dropped their tools and fled. One threw himself into the lake, swimming strongly – until the water boiled around him, and a huge head broke the surface and caught the screaming man in its vast jaws, which clamped shut around his struggling body. The creature's neck, chest and gigantic forelimbs reared out of the water. After what seemed an age, the vast predator fell back into the waters with a titanic splash and disappeared.

"A liopleurodon," breathed Luke, his horror at the man's grisly fate warring with his awe at the power and majesty of the gigantic reptile. "Amazing!"

"Remind me not to go for a swim," said Nick grimly. "Give me piranhas any day."

Its handler's action saved the triceratops: the last rope of its harness snapped moments before the allosaurus arrived. It lumbered to its feet and sped away with shrill squeals of alarm. The handler was not so lucky. He had barely managed to turn and run for the gates before the huge reptile was upon him. Its first bite nearly tore him in half: it dropped his twitching corpse to the ground and raked the flesh with razor-sharp claws.

Inside the mine encampment, someone had managed to drag the gates shut. More guards arrived, firing as they ran: the dinosaur was so big they hardly had to aim. But the bullets bounced off the allosaurus's hide, merely seeming to irritate it, as an attack of gnats or mosquitoes might irritate a man. The great beast gave a bellow of defiance and advanced on the fence. There was loud *snap*, a flash of blue light and the dinosaur, bellowing in rage and frustration, backed away. It turned tail and, pausing occasionally to crane its head back and bellow defiance, loped off across the plain toward the distant conifer forest from which it had emerged.

Luke, Mercedes and Nick gaped at each other. The speed and scale of the events they had just witnessed had left them speechless with horror.

Eventually, Nick cleared his throat and said, "Well, at least you know your ma's still alive."

"She won't be for long if she keeps on throwing tantrums around people with guns." Luke stared down at the camp. "We may as well go. We've seen everything we can from here, and the whole camp's stirred up like a hornet's nest now – we haven't a hope of slipping in without being spotted."

"Could we not wait until another load of waste is dumped and get through the gates in the empty trucks?"

Luke considered Mercedes's suggestion. "It's tempting – but how do we get to the trucks in the first place? There's no cover along the lakeshore. The guards will spot us for certain."

"We could swim across the lake..." Nick remembered the liopleurodon and shuddered. "On second thoughts, no. Bad idea. Forget I mentioned it."

Luke led the way down from the hill. "Our best chance is a night attack. But if it's to work, we'll need a diversion."

"What sort of a diversion?" asked Mercedes.

"I'm not sure yet, but I think I may have the germ of an idea...if the allosaurus has its lair in that forest, maybe we can..."

"What happened to the pterosaurs?" interrupted Nick.

Luke and Mercedes followed his gaze skywards. At some point in all the excitement of the allosaurus's attack, the flying reptiles, which had been circling above the encampment all morning, had disappeared.

"I don't know," said Luke slowly.

"Maybe the allosaurus frightened them off," suggested Nick.

"Why would they be scared of an allosaurus? It can't fly." Luke stared across the plateau. Could he just see, at the edge of his vision, a cluster of V-shapes, circling, hovering and diving to earth? "But if they had spotted some different prey..." A wave of horror washed over him. "The others!" He began to run. With a startled glance at each other, Nick and Mercedes followed.

* * *

As they approached the woodland where they had left their friends, their worst fears were realized. Luke ran, his heart pounding with more than fatigue, toward the clifftop where Tomasinho, Luiz, Heitor and Rosa crouched at bay. Above them, like a flock of gigantic bloodthirsty gulls, pterosaurs circled. Even as Luke and his companions sped to their friends' aid, the terrible beasts dived to attack.

19 ON THE EDGE

Luiz and Rosa overcame two of the attackers with their bows. Tomasinho and Heitor laid around them with clubs made from tree branches, taking down several more. But the odds were overwhelming. Luke, Mercedes and Nick snatched makeshift weapons as they ran, but by the time they arrived to join the fray, the pterosaurs were swarming all over their companions.

Luke raced to a group of pterosaurs that were stabbing and tearing at Rosa. She had lost her footing and lay face down, unable to beat them off. Heitor, roaring at the top of his lungs, was swiping at the creatures that surrounded her, but it was a hopeless effort: the pterosaurs seemed blinded by bloodlust and their attack was unceasing. For every one Heitor struck down, two more took their place.

Luke's arrival had little effect. The branch he had snatched up, dry and brittle, shattered immediately. He was reduced to waving his arms and shouting – until he spotted Rosa's bow, which she had dropped as she fell. He snatched it up and kicked furiously at a pterosaur that was clawing at her back. As the beast fell away, Luke tore Rosa's quiver from her, pulled out an arrow, fit it to the string and let fly.

Firing as fast as he could, Luke brought down several of the winged terrors. From the corner of his eye, he saw that Luiz was still firing: that Tomasinho had plucked a pterosaur from the sky and, his face set in a snarl of animal rage, was twisting its head back to snap its spine. Nick and Mercedes, using spears improvised from bamboo, were laying around them with a will, but Luke spotted movement in the air above them, and yelled a warning...

"Nick! Behind you!"

Nick looked up, but too late. A diving pterosaur dashed the spear from his hands and both he and Mercedes went down beneath a flurry of leathery wings.

"Nick!" Luke cried again. The moment of distraction cost him dearly. His bow was knocked from his hands and a pterosaur, its great beak agape in a scream of fury, was clawing at his chest. He could see nothing but its flapping wings, hear nothing but its battle cry, smell nothing but its foul breath, feel nothing but the tearing of its claws... He staggered back, and the ground crumbled beneath his feet. Luke teetered on the brink of the precipice.

Then, suddenly, he was free. The terrible reptile had released its hold and was flying away with shrill cries of alarm. Luke threw himself forward just as the crumbling rock gave way and, with a clatter of stone and a rush of earth, disappeared into the void. He wiped blood from his eyes and glanced about him. The whole flock of pterosaurs was taking to the skies. His friends were staggering to their feet.

Luke gazed around in puzzlement. "Why are they giving up? They were all over us!"

Nick pointed across the plain. "I think that's why!"

Luke turned his head to follow Nick's pointing finger – and his heart failed him.

The allosaurus, frustrated in its attempt on the mine, had arrived in search of new prey. The pterosaurs circled its head, shrieking with rage. The giant predator paid them no heed. It was bounding toward Tomasinho and

Luiz, who stood at the very edge of the cliff. Seeing that its prey had nowhere to run, the beast slowed, and stalked forward with terrible deliberation. Luke and his companions stood transfixed with horror, powerless to help.

With a roar, Tomasinho rushed forward, swinging his club. The solid branch smacked against the beast's scaly muzzle and broke. The allosaurus blinked: then it took a step to the side, and its long tail whipped around with incredible speed, smashing into Tomasinho with a force that lifted him high into the sky and way out over the cliff edge.

Rosa gave a scream of horror. Mercedes howled, "No!"

Luke watched helplessly. As their giant companion disappeared from view without a sound, he found himself hoping that Tomasinho had been killed outright by the allosaurus's blow.

The monster turned its attention to Luiz. The boy from the streets of Manaus looked around desperately. He was standing on an outcrop of rock with a drop of thousands of feet on three sides and the dinosaur blocking the fourth, crouched and ready to pounce. There was a faint metallic click as Luiz opened his beloved flick knife. He looked down at the tiny blade then up at the deadly teeth of the allosaurus. He turned to his companions and gave them a rueful smile and a shrug.

Mercedes's eyes widened as she guessed what he had in mind. "Luiz." Her voice was no more than a whisper. "Luiz, don't do it – *não faça isso...*"

Her plea went unheard: Luiz raised his free hand to his forehead in a salute: "so long." Then he flung the knife, overarm, straight at the creature's muzzle. Without waiting to see the result, he turned, sprinted and hurled himself over the cliff edge. The allosaurus lunged forward, jaws snapping, but its prey was already out of reach, following Tomasinho in his long fall to the jungle far below. Mercedes sank to her knees, burying her face in her hands.

This was the spur that drove Luke to action. Were all his companions to suffer the fate of Luiz and Tomasinho? Not if he could help it. He gazed around and spotted a cleft in the rocks. It was little more than a water-runnel, but it looked deep; it was certainly the only cover he could see. With a cry to his companions of "Come on!" he beckoned them toward this meager shelter.

They ran, following his pointing finger. Spotting the cleft, they dropped into it without hesitation. The allosaurus turned to see its prey escaping. Bellowing with rage, it swung around to cut off their retreat. But it was too slow: despite its agility, the beast weighed several tons and needed time to maneuver. Even so, as Luke threw himself after his surviving friends, he felt its hot breath on his neck as he dropped into the cleft. The creature's jaws clashed and its muzzle slammed into the rock behind him, dislodging earth and stones, which rained down on the companions as they crouched deep inside the cleft. The infuriated dinosaur tore at the gap with its talons in an attempt to reach them, but the rock held firm. After what seemed an age, the allosaurus's great head withdrew from the aperture above them and they heard it move away, bellowing its frustration. As the tension drained out of him, Luke felt weak and light-headed.

Heitor and Rosa were in each other's arms. Both were crying. Mercedes was silent, stunned by the loss of her friends. Tears coursed down her cheeks. Nick was the first to find his voice. In a shocked whisper, he said, "Poor Tomasinho. Poor Luiz. Why did he do that?"

"Luiz chose his own death." Mercedes's voice was harsh with shock and grief. "Remember what he said after we found my father? 'I decide.' He would not let that monster choose his fate for him."

Luke felt on the verge of tears himself. "But what happened?" he demanded. "They were safe in the woodland. What on earth possessed them to leave it?"

Mercedes repeated the question in Portuguese. Gradually, the story emerged from Heitor and Rosa.

The phorusrhachos had come back. Thomasinho, Luiz, Rosa and Heitor had been no match for its rage when it discovered its nest despoiled, its precious egg gone. It had driven them out of the woodland and to the cliff edge, retreating once the pterosaurs arrived.

Luke groaned. "It's my fault for making them stay behind. If only I'd let them come with us..."

Nick shook his head. "It's my fault for taking that egg."

Mercedes was using her scarf to wipe blood and tears from Rosa's face. "And mine for bringing them from Manaus," she said savagely. "It doesn't matter whose fault it is – we have to decide what to do now. We've lost our weapons; we have to find a safe place to hide, and I don't want anyone else to die..."

"Ssssh!" Luke held up a hand in warning. He had heard heavy footfalls outside their refuge.

For a moment there was silence. Then they heard the snorting of a large animal, the faint jingling of a harness.

Nick raised his eyebrows and mouthed, "The allosaurus? Has it come back?"

"No," Luke hissed grimly. "This is something worse."

There was a short silence. Then a mocking voice called, "*Herausgekommen!* Come out, come out, wherever you are!"

"Scatter!" Luke hissed, and he clambered swiftly out of the cleft.

In the brief moment it took to haul himself over its lip, he took in the situation. Three iguanodons carrying gray-uniformed guards with rifles surrounded their refuge.

Luke scrambled up and made straight for the nearest dinosaur. The iguanodon reared, startled by the figure that had risen from the earth at its feet and now seemed to be attacking it. At the last moment, Luke swerved aside and raced past. Cursing, the iguanodon's rider brought it under control and turned in pursuit.

Having gained a head start, Luke risked a glance over his shoulder. All his companions were running for their lives: Nick and Mercedes in one direction, Heitor and Rosa in another, both pursued by iguanodons and their riders. Then Luke heard the pounding of the iguanodon's feet behind him, and had no further time to wonder what was happening to the others.

The woodland loomed ahead of him. He shot beneath its eaves and found himself tearing through ferns and leaf-litter, swerving around trees as the canopy blocked out the sun. The iguanodon was never far behind. It could run faster than Luke, but was less maneuverable and too big to squeeze through gaps that Luke could slip between with ease. But Luke was getting tired. He had already run and fought to the limit of his strength. He knew that he could not outdistance his pursuer forever.

Taking advantage of the cover of a dense thicket, he dove into the undergrowth. The iguanodon galloped past; its rider, realizing Luke was now behind them, brought the beast up short in a cloud of leaf-litter. He turned his mount and sat, scanning the scene, waiting for Luke to emerge from hiding.

Luke checked the position of the sun and the growth of moss on the trees. He had little chance of escape against a mounted man armed with a rifle, unless... He grimaced. It wasn't much of a hope, but the only alternatives were death or capture. He made up his mind, chose his direction carefully and broke cover.

A guard gave a cry of triumph and spurred his mount forward. They were right on Luke's heels when, nearing the edge of the woods, he burst into the clearing they had found the previous evening.

As Luke had hoped, the phorusrhachos was there, still grieving over its despoiled nest and lost egg. Luke dove through the startled bird's legs, but the iguanodon, following close behind and unable to pull up in time, barreled straight into it.

There was instant chaos. A single rifle shot rang out. The iguanodon bellowed and stamped its great feet. The phorusrhachos gave a screech of rage. A dense cloud of dust and feathers arose, obscuring Luke's view. When it settled, the iguanodon had disappeared. The phorusrhachos remained, however, busily tearing the luckless guard to pieces.

Leaving it to its grisly feast, Luke staggered from the trees. Every muscle seemed to scream in protest as he followed the eaves of the woods away from the plateau's edge, desperate to put distance between himself and the deadly terror bird, equally desperate to find out what had happened to his friends. His efforts were rewarded more quickly than he had dared to hope. He had gone hardly half a mile before he met Nick and Mercedes emerging from the trees, leading an iguanodon by the reins.

Luke gaped at them. "How did you get a hold of that?"

Mercedes smiled grimly. "Its rider followed us into the woods. It went under a low branch and he forgot to duck. His neck was broken." She shrugged. "Small loss." Luke stared at her, dismayed by her callous reaction.

"We followed this feller. It didn't go far without its rider." Nick patted the iguanodon's scaly nose. "We tied it to a tree and went to see what had happened to Rosa and Heitor." He shook his head unhappily. "They were captured. We saw the guard lead them off. So we came to look for you..." He broke off as an inquiring hoot sounded through the trees. Nick jumped as the beast he was leading raised its head and bellowed a reply. Shortly afterwards, the iguanodon that had chased Luke appeared and lumbered over cautiously to join its stable mate.

Luke caught its head-harness. "Two iguanodons. Better than one." He looked gravely at his remaining companions. "We've been running long enough. Not any more. It's time we took the fight to the enemy."

Luke gave Nick a critical look. "You sit your iguanodon like a sack of potatoes."

"Don't you mean 'sit on'?"

"No. It's a horse-riding term. Remember Lottie? She'd say you have a very poor seat." Mercedes snorted. Nick was sitting behind her and she hauled him upright just as he began to slip from the saddle.

"I've heard enough personal remarks about my seat," said Nick bitterly. "I shouldn't think *yours* is exactly an oil painting. We weren't all born in the saddle, you know." Luke had been riding on his mother's expeditions practically since he could walk: horses, mules, camels – even, on one occasion, a yak.

"I've never ridden anything bigger than a seaside donkey," Nick complained, "and that was when I was six. Anyway, this isn't a horse I'm *sitting*, in case you hadn't noticed. It's bigger than an elephant and it's got the brains of a turnip. When you pull the reins it takes half a minute for the stupid beast to realize you want it to do something."

There was some excuse for Nick's ill-temper. The iguanodons were as obstinate and cross-grained as camels and a lot smellier. They had saddles, which fit above their shoulders, where their backs were broad enough to be horribly uncomfortable but not quite wide enough to make their riders do the splits. "It's like riding an elephant," he moaned.

"Actually, it isn't," said Luke, "because there's a lot of neck stretching in front of you and even more tail behind. It's really different. Easier, in fact."

"Oh, I might have known you'd ridden elephants, too." Nick couldn't help feeling resentful of the effortless ease with which Luke rode his iguanodon, especially as Mercedes, who casually announced that she had learned to ride with gauchos, had no trouble keeping her seat either. Only Nick had suffered the indignity of having to be helped onto the mount he shared with the Brazilian girl. Only he had fallen off (twice). Only his iguanodon had persisted in trying to eat every tree, bush and fern they passed and, when Nick attempted to make it behave itself, had tried to bite him. At this point Luke had insisted that Mercedes should take the reins of their second mount, with Nick riding tandem behind her. Though he knew this was the most sensible arrangement, Nick's pride was dented and as the iguanodon missed its footing, he smacked it hard on the shoulder. "Stop swaying like that, you half-witted makingmybottomsaurus!"

They lumbered on through the gathering darkness with a surprising lack of noise. Night fell and now the only light came from the last crescent of the waning moon and the cold glimmer of the stars. They were almost invisible to each other before Mercedes, who had said little since her friends' deaths, broke the silence: "We're getting near the allosaurus's forest."

Luke could see the loom of trees just ahead. Black feathery spears thrust upward into the star-dusted sky. Upon leaving the forest, they had headed away from the edge of the plateau. Just before sunset, from a safe distance, they had watched the allosaurus enter its forest lair; they had not seen it come out. Luke's mount gave a nervous hoot and reared on its back legs to sniff the air. Nick cursed as the mount he shared with Mercedes followed suit and tightened his grip on her waist just in time to stop himself from slipping backwards over the animal's rump.

Mercedes patted her iguanodon's neck to comfort it. "They're nervous," she said.

"*They're* nervous," Nick echoed bitterly. "How do you think I feel?"

"Do you think they can smell the allosaurus?" asked Luke.

"No. The wind's coming from behind us, so he can smell them and they can't smell him. But they know he went into this forest. They aren't *that* stupid!"

"I think this is close enough." Luke reined in his iguanodon. Mercedes did the same, but the mount she shared with Nick blundered on for a few steps before coming to a halt and stood, shifting its weight from foot to foot, snuffling nervously.

They sat and waited, while the moon disappeared behind a wisp of cloud and the sounds of the plateau rose around them – yips, barks, grunts and stealthy rustling noises that would be sufficiently alarming even without the presence of the unseen threat in the darkness. But of the allosaurus, there was no sign.

"Maybe we missed it?" Nick suggested hopefully.

"It's in there, all right," said Mercedes softly. "It's just being cautious. It knows men with guns ride these creatures. We'll have to annoy it."

"Annoy it?" Nick was incredulous. "How are we supposed to do that? Shout rude things about its mother?"

"I think tempting it out might work better," said Luke.

He shrugged off his pack and brought out a bundle wrapped with leaves. He tore it open, and a rich, meaty smell arose causing Nick and Mercedes to exclaim in disgust. "I went back for it while Nick was learning to fall off his iguanodon. Sun-braised leg of pterosaur," said Luke. "One of those we shot this morning. Twelve hours old, getting a bit gamy. Do you think he'll go for this?"

"It'll drive him crazy!" Mercedes's voice was alarmed. "Luke, have you gone out of your mind...?"

In that moment, with the crash of breaking branches and a roar like the end of the world, the allosaurus was upon them.

20 ATTACK

The moon reappeared just in time for the companions and their terrified mounts to glimpse the allosaurus's gaping jaws and mad, reptilian eyes as it raced toward them like a sprinter. Its tremendous legs pumped rhythmically, taking enormous strides that ate up the distance between the beast and its prey.

The giant carnivore had evidently been waiting in ambush. But its roar had been a miscalculation. It alerted the nervous iguanodons and gave them just enough time to spin around with screeches of alarm and take off before the predator was within striking range. They lifted their forefeet off the ground and ran on their hind legs, making astonishing speed for such heavy beasts. They had every incentive to do so. The allosaurus was right behind them.

Mercedes was using the reins to lash her mount to greater efforts. Roaring dreadful Irish oaths, Nick hung on for grim death behind her, the allosaurus's pounding footsteps hammering in his ears, certain that he could feel its hot, meaty breath on the back of his neck. Luke was alongside them, riding neck and neck, still waving the gory haunch of pterosaur meat as if the allosaurus needed further encouragement. "Are we heading for the mine?" he yelled.

Nick gawped at him. "How would I know?"

Luke's reply was partly lost in the noise and jarring of their passage. "That's where…stables are…may think they'll be safe there…"

"It doesn't matter!" howled Mercedes. "There's no way we can steer these beasts anyway. Just hang on and hope – *Vamos!*"

Whether the iguanodons really were making for their stables, or whether they just happened to be running in the right direction, it became evident that they were indeed headed for the mine. Ahead stood the fence with its lights and watchtowers. The noise of the pursuit had already alarmed the camp. Searchlights stabbed from the darkness. Luke caught glimpses of startled guards unslinging their weapons and heard the urgent clamor of an alarm bell.

Their mounts were headed straight for the gates. These were closed, but with five tons of maddened allosaurus behind them, that wasn't going to stop the iguanodons. With spectacular blue flares of electricity as the current shorted out, the gates splintered like matchwood before their charge, and they were inside the camp.

Guards in various stages of dress were scurrying in all directions. Some, instinctively reacting as though the missing iguanodons could be rounded up and calmed down, stepped forward. Crazed with fear however, the beasts were no longer the placid creatures the guards knew. With deadly sweeps of their powerful tails, the iguanodons swept aside their startled handlers like bowling pins. One was lifted high into the air to crash through the roof of the guardhouse. Luke's iguanodon smashed into the supports beneath a watchtower, which lurched drunkenly, tipping its screaming occupants out to be trampled beneath the feet of the frantic beast. The tower's oil lantern smashed as it hit the ground. The contents of its reservoir ignited, further terrifying the iguanodons as a stream of fire added to the chaos.

The guards began to shoot at the iguanodons. The bullets had little effect, other than to madden the beasts further.

"*Halt!*" One of the guards was quicker on the uptake than his fellows. "These are not wild animals! Shoot the riders!" He raised his rifle to his shoulder and aimed at Mercedes. "*Feuer!*"

But the allosaurus had arrived. Following the iguanodons through the shattered gates, it spotted a target of opportunity. As his finger tightened on the trigger, jaws like excavator buckets closed on the guard. With a muffled crack, his rifle went off in the allosaurus's mouth, and a fountain of red burst from its muzzle. The beast screamed with pain and fury, spit out its victim's lifeless body and instantly went on the rampage, tearing down buildings and mine machinery and pouncing on howling guards. The defenders scattered.

Nick's desperate hold on the saddle of the bucking iguanodon broke, and he was tossed through the air to land on the sandy floor of the compound. Winded, he lay gasping and helpless as the great feet of his former mount trampled the earth around him, until a steely hand grasped his arm and dragged him to the shelter of a wall of a hut that had so far escaped demolition. A voice in his ear hissed, "Stay there!" and he watched in fascinated horror as Luke ran across the compound.

His breath caught as he realized that Mercedes, too, had been thrown from their mount and was lying, dazed, between the frenzied iguanodons and the enraged allosaurus.

"Good boy! Fetch!"

Luke held aloft the stinking pterosaur leg he had used as bait, and lobbed it toward the allosaurus, which darted out its neck and caught the morsel like a gigantic dog snapping up a tossed biscuit. The momentary diversion as it swallowed the meat gave Luke time to grab Mercedes around the waist and haul her to her feet. Nick staggered forward on unsteady legs to help Luke half drag, half carry the stunned girl out of harm's way, just as the blazing oil from the smashed lantern reached a stack of oil drums behind the iguanodons. The diesel fuel inside the drums went up with a thunderous explosion and a huge jet of flame. The scurrying guards were blown off their feet and burning oil rained over the whole compound. All the lights went out.

For a moment, the allosaurus backed off in alarm. But its helpless prey was too near and too tempting. The iguanodons picketed inside the camp were trapped. As they backed away, bellowing hopeless defiance, the allosaurus charged. It slammed into the nearest iguanodon, bowling it over. The terrible jaws descended on the helpless creature's neck. While the remaining iguanodons broke their tethers and stampeded into the night, the allosaurus completed its kill. In the unearthly light of burning tents and buildings, it began to feed.

Luke helped Nick and Mercedes to the shelter of a wagon train. "Everyone all right?" he hissed.

"Never better," said Nick, feeling for broken bones. Mercedes gave a dazed nod. "Well, that didn't exactly go as planned," Nick added, "but as distractions go, it seemed to be a success."

"You could say that. Keep your heads down. I'm going to find my mother."

The remaining guards, realizing that their bullets had no effect on the allosaurus, were organizing themselves into bucket chains to fight the fires that threatened to overwhelm the camp. Luke hurried away from them and the allosaurus, toward the prison compound, dodging puddles of blazing oil. But halfway to his goal, he was brought up short as a figure stepped from the shadows directly into his path.

His Japanese nemesis was wearing her familiar outfit: the long leather coat, now colored red as it reflected the flames, and the riding boots Luke had first noted on their departure from Lisbon. The tinted glasses still hid her eyes.

She gave Luke a mocking bow. "Luke Challenger."

Luke stood his ground, his whole body tense, ready for action. "Who are you?"

The woman shrugged. "Does it matter? I am your enemy – that is all you need know."

Fury welled up in Luke. "You killed Uncle Ned. And Mercedes's father, and Eduardo."

His opponent gave a thin, hard smile. "Such a catalog of crimes. To that list of casualties, you can add – yourself." She hurled herself into the attack.

From the first blow, Luke knew that he was outclassed. His fighting prowess had impressed his tutors, but he was a beginner compared to this woman, who had been taught by the finest masters in a country that had turned unarmed combat into an art form. What's more she was taller than Luke, and had a longer reach. She came at him, arms and legs a blur, coat-tails flying, with the force of an avalanche.

Luke caught the first flurry of blows on his forearms, which felt as if they had been broken. A front kick to the chest knocked him off his feet, sending him rolling through a puddle of blazing fuel. He scrambled upright, beating at the flames where oil had caught in his clothing. The woman dropped down and swept a low-level kick that cut his legs from under him. He landed on his back with an impact that knocked the air from his lungs.

The woman danced back, laughing. "Come! Surely the famous Luke Challenger can do better than that!" Her face transformed into a demonic mask by the flickering glare of burning oil, she beckoned him on.

Luke spit blood, beat out the last of the flames and clambered to his feet. He launched his counterattack with the heel of his palm and had the satisfaction of feeling it connect. But the woman jerked her head back at the same moment, dispelling the force of the blow. She caught his lunging arm and delivered a knee strike into Luke's stomach and an elbow to the kidneys. He went down gasping. With the last of his strength, he raised his head. His mistimed blow had dislodged the woman's tinted glasses. They lay at her feet. He looked into her eyes. Their centers were black, with no apparent difference between iris and pupil: two black holes, the surrounding fires reflected in their depths, as hot and merciless as the lowest pit in hell.

"I am disappointed." The woman was openly mocking now. "You are only a child. After all the times you succeeded in eluding me, I thought I had found an opponent more worthy of my skills."

"Your skills are not as great you think," said Luke. His eyes were focused, not on his gloating enemy, but on the hideous shadow that loomed behind her. "You let your mind be clouded with triumph. And you talk too much. You don't listen. Goodbye."

The woman's eyes widened and she spun around just as the allosaurus's gigantic head descended, jaws gaping, to engulf her. Whether it had been driven away from its kill by the guards, or attracted by the movement of their fight, Luke never knew: nor did he care. He was no more than half-conscious as he hauled himself to his feet and limped toward the prison compound. The sounds of rending flesh from behind him spurred him on.

Nick and Mercedes caught up with him just as he reached the wire fence surrounding the prison enclosure. Nick gave Luke a clap on the shoulder. "We saw what happened. We were about to come and help you when the allosaurus turned up."

Mercedes's face was livid in the firelight, her eyes shining with feverish intensity. In a fierce, harsh voice, she said, "My father is avenged." Luke thought her expression was the most frightening thing he'd seen all day.

"What now?" demanded Nick.

"Jailbreak," said Luke. He pointed at the prison compound. "I'm going to get my mother out of there."

"And Rosa and Heitor," Mercedes reminded him.

"I hadn't forgotten. We'll release everyone we can."

They could hear panicked sounds coming from the locked huts. The prisoners could not have seen the allosaurus's rampage through the mine compound, but from the explosions, roars and gunshots they certainly knew that something was up. As Luke and his friends watched, a panting officer ran up to the main gate of the stockade, where the guards stood fingering their rifles and exchanging nervous looks, uncertain of what to do. The officer barked a series of commands, waving his arms urgently. The gates were opened, and most of the guards rushed through, following him toward the main compound. They looked far from happy. The officer relocked the gates and followed his men – but at a speed that suggested he had no intention of overtaking them.

"That should make things a little easier," hissed Luke, "but we need to get in there while they're busy with the allosaurus. We don't have much time." He eyed the sturdy wire fence with its coils of barbed wire along the top. It didn't look too high: it didn't need to be. Anyone trying to climb it would be shot by the guards – but at the moment, most of the guards were otherwise engaged.

Luke clapped a hand on Nick's shoulder. "What do you say to breaking bounds?"

Nick grinned as he gathered Luke's plan. Mercedes looked puzzled. "What do you mean?"

"It means getting out of school without being spotted

– going 'out of bounds', you see?" Mercedes still looked bewildered. Luke winked at her. "We used to do it all the time: we're experts. And I'm betting the man who built this fence never had to deal with two boys desperate to get out of an English private school."

Luke slipped away. Nick beckoned to Mercedes. She followed him to one side of the fence, well away from the gate, and watched in perplexity as Nick half-crouched with his back to the fence, and cupped his hands just above knee level. A moment later, Luke appeared, running, his feet kicking up little spurts of sand. Without breaking stride, he stepped into Nick's cupped hands. In one fluid movement, Nick thrust with his legs and hauled upward with his arms to send Luke sailing above his head. He cleared the barbed wire by a hairsbreadth, did a somersault on the way down and landed, rolling.

Nick winked at Mercedes. "Allez-oop!"

Mercedes stared at him. "You learned how to do that just to get out of school?"

"You should see our school! Come on." Nick took Mercedes's hand and ran back the way they'd come.

Four guards remained at the gate. One felt a tap on the shoulder and turned in surprise. Unlike Luke's Japanese foe, the man had not been trained in martial arts from childhood, and a pile driver karate blow from the heel of Luke's palm lifted him off his feet. A second guard opened his mouth to shout and raised his gun. Luke's high-level roundhouse kick almost took his head off. And then there were two.

The third guard managed to get his gun to his shoulder, and fired at Luke. But Luke was no longer there. The man was still looking around for his disappearing opponent when his legs were scythed from under him. He landed on his back with stunning force, any breath he had left was driven from his lungs by an elbow in the solar plexus. Then there was one.

The remaining guard had backed against the gate. By the time Luke had rolled away from the unconscious body of his last opponent, his rifle was at his shoulder. Knowing that he was too far away from Luke to be rushed, the man favored him with an evil grin. Luke gave a slight shrug and a rueful smile. Then his eyes flicked to a spot just past the guard's left shoulder. The man's grin widened. The old look-out-there's-someone-behind-you ploy, eh? He wasn't falling for that one. He eased back the trigger. Luke was helpless. This time there was no allosaurus to save him. He shut his eyes.

21 ESCAPE

The bullet never came. Instead, the guard gave a kind of high-pitched shriek, which instantly turned into frantic gasping.

Mercedes was at the gate with her arms thrust through the wire. Her scarf was around the man's neck, choking him. His hands convulsed and the rifle went off, the bullet passing harmlessly over Luke's head. Eyes bulging, he dropped his gun and scrabbled at the tough material of the scarf with frantic fingers. Mercedes's teeth were bared in a grimace of pure animal rage as she tightened her grip. The guard made horrible gurgling sounds, his heels drumming on the soil of the enclosure.

Luke leaped off his right foot and landed a perfect snap-kick on his opponent's jaw. The man collapsed.

Mercedes glared at Luke. "You didn't have to do that! I had him!"

Quietly, Luke said, "I didn't want you to kill him." He liked Mercedes, but he feared what anger at her father's death was driving her to do. "Please. Don't let yourself become like them."

Mercedes glared at him for a moment longer. Then her head dropped. She fell to her knees and began to sob. Nick kneeled beside her and put his arm around her shoulders. Luke felt a surge of relief. Mercedes's tears were of grief, not anger; not a bottling up, but a letting go. With them, a dark beast, more fierce and deadly than the allosaurus, that had dogged their steps for many days, had suddenly departed.

"Thanks, anyway," he said awkwardly. He turned his attention to the guards' belts and found a bunch of keys on the third. Ten seconds later the gate was open.

Luke listened for a moment to see whether the guards' gunshots had attracted attention, but a burst of renewed firing from behind them reassured him. On a night like this, no one was going to notice a couple more shots.

Mercedes wiped her eyes with the backs of her wrists. "Are you all right?" Luke asked her. She nodded. "Remember the plan?" Another nod. "The explosives store is over there." Luke pointed. "It'll have a skull and crossbones on the door. Bring all the dynamite you can carry, fuses and blasting caps." Mercedes, in full control of herself once more, gave a final nod and sped away.

Nick grinned appreciatively. "That's my girl."

"Come on." Luke jangled the keys. "My mother first – then the others." With Nick at his shoulder, he slipped across the enclosure and stopped at the door of the small hut from which his mother had been led the previous day. He began trying keys in its lock. After some fumbling he found the right one, and the lock clicked. Luke threw the keys to Nick, who caught them deftly and ran across to the larger huts. Luke opened the door of his mother's prison and slipped inside.

A slim woman with a mass of red curls scraped up to the top of her head sat at a table on which a single candle burned. She was wearing a safari shirt, a fisherman's waistcoat, with an improbable number of bulging pockets, and jodhpurs. A number of irregularly shaped brown, earth-colored objects lay on the table in front of her. As Luke watched, his mouth suddenly dry, she lifted one to the light and peered at it minutely through the glasses she used for close work.

"If you've brought my supper," she said, without turning around, "leave it on the chair by the door. How many times do I have to tell you I never eat while I'm working? And I don't know what all that rumpus is – some new devilry you've devised to torment your poor workers, I don't doubt – but whatever it is, tell them to keep the noise down. I can hardly hear myself think."

Luke swallowed. "Hello, Mother," he managed.

Harriet Challenger spun around. "Luke! What on earth are you doing here?"

"I've come to rescue you."

"You mean, your father's sent in the troops to get me out?" Luke's mother gave a prim little smile. "I suppose that's what all the noise is about. He always did go around doing things like a bull in a china shop. I suppose he's sent a regiment and half the Royal Flying Corps..."

"It's the RAF now, Mother," said Luke firmly. "And no. There's just me. And Nick. And Mercedes."

"Mercedes?" Harriet's eyes narrowed.

"She's a local girl. From Manaus. You'll like her."

Harriet dismissed this with a wave. "Never mind all that! What was your father thinking of, sending you into this nest of vipers? Do you have the slightest idea who you're dealing with? They're perfectly frightful people. They killed poor old Raul, you know, my guide."

"Yes, Mother, I know. Mercedes is his daughter."

"Oh, poor girl." For a moment, Harriet looked downcast. Then she rallied and slapped Luke's arm. Her eyes were fierce behind her glasses. "Don't change the subject! I asked you what you were doing here. You should be at home, studying and staying out of trouble."

"Well, I'm not." Luke's temper, always short at the best of times, was beginning to get the better of him. "I came all the way across the Atlantic to get you, and now I've found you – so are you coming or not?"

Harriet gave a little gasp. "Impossible! This plateau is a treasure trove of prehistoric species…"

"I know," said Luke tightly. "We've met some of them."

"…quite unique," continued Harriet, ignoring him, "and some of them completely unknown to science. I couldn't possibly leave now – I've only just begun to classify these bones," she pointed to the tabletop, "and there are boxes and boxes more awaiting my attention. The forest out there is simply crawling with life that hasn't been seen on earth for over sixty million years…"

"Yes, and it's also crawling with armed lunatics who kill anyone who gets in their way!" snapped Luke. He grabbed his mother's satchel and thrust it into her arms. "We are leaving! Now! And we're going to make the brutes who run this place very sorry they ever laid hands on a Challenger!"

"Yes, that's all very well, but what about my collection?"

Luke stared at her open-mouthed. "What collection?"

A guard burst into the hut, gun raised. He looked from Harriet to Luke and back again with astonishment. "*Hände hoch*," he said without much conviction.

Harriet continued on as if he had not been there. "I've found fossils from two new species of coelophysis, an entirely new subgroup of ornithopods, and the thigh bone of a titanosaurid that makes a diplodocus look like a chihuahua…"

Luke followed his mother's eyes. "Is that it?" When Harriet nodded, he picked up the bone and looked at it closely. "Are you nuts?" he demanded. "This isn't a titanosaurid bone. Look at the muscle attachment! It's clearly from a large theropod." He held out the bone to the guard. "Does this look like a titanosaurid bone to you?"

The guard gaped. "*Was?*"

Luke brought the bone down on his head. The man's eyes rolled up and he slumped to the floor.

Harriet gazed at the shattered specimen and groaned. "Look what you did!"

"Mother!"

"Oh, all right, all right! I'm coming." Harriet made a

sudden rush at her son and gave him a fierce hug. After a startled pause, Luke returned it.

Harriet stepped back, holding him at arm's length. "You always were so headstrong." She cast her eyes around the hut. "Now, where did I put my badger-hair brush...? Oh!"

Seething, Luke snatched his mother's hand and dragged her from the hut. Outside, he met Nick with Heitor and Rosa – who seemed none the worse for their capture – and a grim-looking deputation of Indians from the mine.

"Hello, Lady Challenger."

"Good evening, Nick." Luke's mother might have been greeting an acquaintance at a charity fundraiser.

Nick turned to Luke. "I've opened all the huts. The rest are making a getaway, but these wouldn't go."

Luke shook his head. "The best way they can help is by making a getaway themselves. The snake-and-spear gang can't work the mine without them – they'll have to go out and round them up. That gives us a chance to do what we have to do here."

"And what might that be?" demanded Harriet.

"Blow the whole place to kingdom come."

"Oh dear. Do you think that's wise?"

"Mother!" Luke got a grip on his temper with difficulty. "Whoever these people are and whatever they want with these diamonds, they're up to no good. They kidnapped you, they tried to kill me, they're stealing Challenger secrets, they're slavers and murderers and it's time we put a stop to their little game."

Mercedes rushed up carrying bundles of small sticks that looked for all the world like seaside rock. She dumped them in Nick's arms in order to greet her lost friends. Nick held the sticks gingerly, like an unexploded baby.

"I take it this is Mercedes?" said Harriet. Luke nodded, and she went on, "I'm sorry about your father. He was a good man."

Mercedes caught her breath and nodded.

"Mercedes." Luke's voice was low and urgent. "Please ask these people to lead the guards into the forest. Heitor and Rosa too."

Mercedes translated. Her words were greeted with angry mutterings. She turned back to Luke. "They want to fight."

"I know they do. If the guards come after them, they can do what they like. But I want them out of the compound. Tell them why."

Mercedes launched into a rapid explanation, pointing at the dynamite. Heitor settled the argument by taking Rosa's hand and leading the way. Still muttering discontentedly, the Indians followed.

"See how much I found," Mercedes crowed, returning to her find and holding up a bundle for Luke's inspection.

Nick eyed the dynamite with alarm. "Are you sure you know how to handle that stuff?"

"I told you! We used to dynamite fish all the time." Mercedes reached into her pockets. "And blasting caps, to set off the dynamite..." She pulled two loops of what looked like rope from her shoulders. "And fuses. The yellow is the slow fuse, thirty seconds per foot. The white is the fast one, five seconds per foot." She half-closed her eyes. "Or is the white fuse the short one, and the yellow fuse the fast one?" Nick goggled at her. "No," she went on briskly. "The yellow one is the slow one, I'm certain."

"Certain?" said Nick.

"Practically certain. Well, pretty sure, anyway." Ignoring the stricken look on Nick's face, she went on, "Do you have any matches?"

"Matches?" Luke patted his pockets and groaned. "Matches!"

Harriet dipped a hand into one of the pockets of her fisherman's jacket and pulled out a small rectangular box. "I never go anywhere without them."

Luke gave her a quick hug. "Mother, you're wonderful!" He tipped the contents of the box into his hand and quickly sorted the matches into three piles, giving one each to Mercedes and Nick.

Several volleys of shots rang out from the direction of the main compound, followed by renewed roaring. Luke frowned. "Someone's getting the defenses organized. The allosaurus won't hang around for long. Those bullets may only sting him, but enough stings will drive him off." He grabbed three of the dynamite bundles and a handful of blasting caps. He used his clasp knife to cut off a length of yellow cord. "Aren't we supposed to crimp the fuses into the caps?" Mercedes nodded. "Then we'll need pliers, or pincers or something."

Mercedes made an impatient noise. "Tsk. There's no time for that. Use your teeth."

Nick regarded her with horror. "My teeth?" He held out a blasting cap as though expecting it to bite him. "What if it goes off?"

"Oh, they hardly ever do that."

Nick's eyebrows shot into his hairline. "*Hardly ever...*? If one of these goes off in my mouth it'll blow my head off!"

"Maybe, but it's more likely to blow your teeth out." Mercedes gave him a wicked grin. "I hope you like soup."

"Nick, take the crane." Luke pointed. "Mercedes, the generator. I'll take the processing plant. Set your fuses for one minute and light them on Mercedes's signal." He turned to her. "That bird call you used to contact the Arara people." Mercedes nodded. "Let's go." Nick and Mercedes faded into the darkness. Luke took his mother's hand. "Come on."

Harriet sighed. "Oh, well, if we must."

The main compound was quiet when they reached it. The allosaurus was gone, presumably driven off by the guards' rifles. The body of the iguanodon, partly eaten, lay where it had fallen. The most serious fires had died down. There were few guards around, the ones that were in view were bringing buckets of water to dump on the flames or standing around exclaiming at their losses.

The power had been restored and the watchtower searchlights that were still working were directed out of the camp, watching for further attack, or for the prisoners whose escape must by now have been discovered. The moon had set. The compound was a place of silence and shadows. Luke pointed toward the processing plant. His mother nodded. Bent double, they scuttled across to the building and slipped through the open doors. The steel girders of the machinery inside the plant looked like the stripped ribcage of the unlucky iguanodon in the light of the guttering fires around it.

Luke jammed a bundle of dynamite sticks into the

frame of a machine and hacked at the fuse with his clasp knife.

Harriet was crouching behind him. "Luke," she said quietly.

"Not now, Mother." Luke pushed a two-foot length of fuse into the base of the blasting cap and bit down on the tube to crimp it.

"Luke..."

"No," hissed Luke, "we cannot go back for whatever it is you've forgotten." He reached into his pocket for a match and held it against the rough rusted ironwork of the machine, ready to strike.

Something hard and circular ground into the back of his neck. Luke closed his eyes, understanding what his mother had been trying to tell him. With a groan, he dropped the match, raised his hands above his head, and turned around slowly.

A guard was covering him with a Gewehr 98 rifle. Luke would have taken a chance and jumped him, but his mother was being held at pistol point by another guard and he knew he couldn't take them both. Slowly and carefully, he handed the dynamite to the guard and clasped his hands behind his neck.

The guard twitched the barrel of his rifle to indicate that he wanted Luke to move out into the compound. He did so, followed by Harriet. Two more figures emerged from the shadows: Mercedes and Nick, each with their hands clasped in surrender, each being urged forward at riflepoint by stern-faced guards.

A man waited in the center of the compound. He was bareheaded and wearing a trench coat. The prisoners were brought to a halt before him. No one spoke.

Then a stray fuel drum exploded with a roar of flame. In the angry red glare, Luke caught sight of the man's face – and his stomach suddenly felt like lead.

The man who had captured them was Edward Malone.

22 CONSPIRACY

Nick stepped forward with a shout of incredulous joy. "Da!"

Luke stared at Malone as if he was seeing a ghost. "Uncle Ned?"

"Hello, son. Luke." Malone took the dynamite bundle from the guard and examined it as though he'd never seen such a thing before.

"But..." Nick struggled for words. "We thought you were dead. We saw you..." The memory of that dreadful moment on Cape Verde seemed to overcome him. "What happened?" he managed at last. "We went back, after we stole the truck, and you weren't there. Did they capture you? Are you their prisoner?"

"He's not a prisoner." Harriet Challenger's voice was low and filled with contempt. "He's with them. Aren't you, Ned?"

Nick was aghast. "Da?"

Luke stared at his mother. "What are you talking about?"

"He arrived days ago. I've seen him with the guards and that Japanese woman. They're as thick as thieves."

Luke's mind began to clear. As the first shock of revelation passed, a great deal of what had been puzzling him over the last few weeks suddenly made sense. Who but Uncle Ned had known of his mother's plans, when she set out to find the Lost World? Who could have told the raiding party led by the Japanese woman where to find her? If there was a traitor in Challenger Industries, why hadn't Edward Malone, trusted Head of Security, rooted him out – unless the traitor in question was Malone himself? And who had arranged Luke and Nick's journey across the Atlantic, which had terminated in such tragedy on Cape Verde…?

"It was all a set-up, Nick," said Luke heavily. "The car that picked us up, the broken-down truck, the gunmen: they killed Briggs and Stanwick, but they were instructed not to kill your da."

"Or to kill you." Malone held up a bandaged hand. "I'm afraid they rather exceeded their orders. Colonel Mochizuki has a habit of that."

"The Japanese woman?" Luke's voice was icy. "She won't be doing it again."

"No," said Malone. "I understand the allosaurus got her. I can't say I'm sorry. A soldier kills at need, and with regret. But for some, killing becomes a pastime – a pleasure – a joy. The late Colonel was of that mind."

"You...with them?" Nick's voice was hardly above a whisper. He stood shaking his head like a boxer who had taken one punch too many. He stared at Malone as though straining to see his real father in the stranger, the impostor standing before them. "It can't be. Da, tell me it's not true."

Malone said nothing.

Mercedes looked from father to son with burning eyes. "You told me your father was dead."

"I thought he was," said Nick. His voice hardened. "I *wish* he was." His voice cracking, he yelled, "You would have let them kill us! Me and Luke! You did your little play-acting and left us to die!"

Malone shook his head. "That wasn't the plan. You were supposed to escape and go to the authorities. You would have told your story and the police would have been shocked and appalled – why didn't you, by the way? Go to the police, I mean?"

"Because we saw your Japanese friend and the Chief of Police chumming up together like long-lost twins," Luke told him.

"Colonel Mochizuki again." Malone shook his head. "The Cape Verde authorities would have sent you back to England. Everyone would have thought I was dead: had I remained with Challenger Industries, suspicion would have fallen on me sooner or later. With my death, my role in the whole sorry business would never have been suspected."

"That mattered to you, did it?" demanded Nick bitterly.

"Yes. Not because I didn't want to be known as a traitor, but because I didn't want you to go through life known as the son of one."

Nick said nothing.

"My employers agreed to the scheme because they knew it would take time for Andrew to send out another expedition, especially without me, and time was what my employers needed.

"Instead, you escaped and managed to reach Natal. Colonel Mochizuki followed you. Acting on her own initiative, she killed your pilot…"

"And Jackson," said Luke, "the Challenger Industries

agent we were supposed to meet in Manaus. Or was he blown up in a car full of dynamite by pure accident?"

"No," said Malone heavily. "He was murdered. The High Command was very angry."

"Aren't you the High Command?" demanded Luke.

Malone gave a rueful smile. "No. Merely its creature."

"A vile creature," spat Harriet.

Malone regarded her steadily. "Perhaps. But I kept you alive, Harriet, when others would have you put out of the way." He turned to his son. "Nick, no doubt I deserve everything you're thinking about me at this moment. But I'm not a killer…"

"What are you then?" Mercedes's voice was a shriek. "On whose orders was my father killed? Filth! *Desgraçado…!*" She launched herself at Malone.

The guards raised their guns. Luke and Nick threw themselves on Mercedes and hauled her away.

As they were still struggling with the furious girl, the deep throb of an aircraft engine sounded across the compound. The captives looked up as a vast, gray cigar-shaped airship hove into view. Six mighty diesel engines roared, kicking up dust and fanning the flames of the burning compound, sending the hair of the watchers flying and their pants-legs flapping. Searchlights played over its huge envelope. Ropes snaked from the nose of the great flying machine and water ballast poured from its belly as it prepared to land.

"A Zeppelin," breathed Nick. "So that's what the tower was for. It's a mooring mast."

Luke nodded. "And I daresay that's how the raiding party got the Indians up to the plateau."

A panting orderly appeared. While he reported to Malone, Nick did his best to calm Mercedes and Luke whispered to his mother, "If Uncle Ned isn't in charge here, who is?"

"Don't call him that. He may be my brother-in-law, but he's a traitor. And I don't know who's in charge. I've only ever seen the Japanese woman and your precious uncle. The bigwigs come and go in *that* thing." Harriet Challenger dismissed the Zeppelin with a sniff. "The Sons of Destiny don't show themselves to mere prisoners."

Luke gaped at her. "The what of how much?"

"That's what they call themselves. All absurd nonsense and mumbo-jumbo. They run this place. They're some kind of secret organization, an offshoot of the Thule Society."

"Thule Society? I've never heard of it."

"Well, you should have. They were behind the German Workers' Party, which Hitler turned into..."

Light dawned on Luke. "The Nazi party! That's the German connection."

"Exactly. But they're not just a bunch of political thugs, they're lunatics as well. They believe all kinds of supernatural hogwash. They think they're members of some Aryan master race that comes from a lost land called Ultima Thule, somewhere in the frozen north…" She broke off and squeezed Luke's hand. "I keep forgetting to say this: you shouldn't be here at all, but I am glad you are."

Luke returned her smile. "I'm glad, too."

Malone gave the orderly a series of instructions and turned his attention back to his captives. "It seems the allosaurus has been driven off and the boundary secured. The Sons of Destiny have almost completed their business here." He gave his son and Luke a thin smile. "I'm afraid the damage you caused tonight makes very little difference to their plans. The workforce is no longer required, so the prisoners' escape does not matter. The mine is all but played out, most of the accessible diamonds have been extracted. The schedule has been brought forward and the Zeppelin is landing here tonight for the last time. When it leaves, the diamonds will be aboard – and so will you."

"And what will happen to us then?" demanded Nick.

Malone's expression was wooden. "That isn't my decision." Nick glared at him and Malone was the first to drop his eyes. "Follow me, please."

He led the way through the dying fires. Any ideas Luke might have had of escaping were dispelled by the alertness of the guards and the bright lights of the landing area, where the Zeppelin lay tethered to its mast. They trailed after Malone up a flight of rickety steps that wound up the tower and onto a ramp that had been lowered from the nose of the airship. An interior staircase and a long corridor led into a luxurious passenger lounge.

Guards took up positions around the walls as Malone waved his captives to their seats. "Please make yourselves comfortable. The members of the High Command are assessing the situation on the ground and issuing their final orders. They will be joining us shortly." Absently, he placed the dynamite bundle Luke had prepared on a gold-legged table near the doorway.

Mercedes and Nick sat together: Nick still shell-shocked by the revelation of his father's treachery; Mercedes overawed and subdued. Harriet Challenger sat with her arms folded and a thunderous expression on her face.

Luke gazed around. At both sides of the room were observation windows, overlooking the ruined mine compound. The night was warm and several of the windows were open. On either side of the door was mounted a display of swords: sabers and rapiers, great broadswords and delicate épées, curved scimitars and straight-edged Japanese katana. On the opposite wall, completely covering it, hung a banner: a golden snake, wrapped around a silver spear on a blood-red background. "So what's that all about?" Luke asked. "The snake and spear?"

Malone looked uncomfortable. "Legend has it," he said slowly, "that the spear used by the centurion Longinus to pierce Christ's side at the crucifixion is still in existence. It became known as the Spear of Destiny. The Sons of Destiny believe the spear passed through the hands of some of the greatest leaders in world history: the Emperor Constantine; Charles Martel, the greatest warrior prince of all time; and his grandson, the Holy Roman Emperor Charlemagne. It is said that whoever possesses the spear will rule the world…"

Harriet snorted. "And the snake is self-explanatory. Ridiculous! Rampant male fantasy and unmitigated balderdash! I knew you and Enid were into some pretty silly spiritualist eyewash, Edward, but are you seriously telling me you believe this bunk?"

Malone winced at the mention of his dead wife. "I wish you'd leave Enid out of this, Harriet, if only for Nick's sake…"

"You haven't shown much consideration for your son up to now!"

"In any case, I didn't say I believed it. But the Sons of Destiny take the legend seriously."

"The spear is on public display in the Hapsburg Treasure House in Vienna," Harriet informed him. "It's hardly a secret."

"They believe that spear to be a copy – a fake. It's rumored that Herr Hitler has his eye on the Vienna spear and will seize it when the time is ripe. The Sons of Destiny are happy to let him: they seek the real spear and the real power they think it contains."

"If you don't believe all this," said Nick harshly, "why are you working for them?"

Malone sighed. "Because I knew them – some of them – when your mother was ill, and her care was expensive. Then a man I knew well told me that one of our competitors had developed a treatment he believed could help Enid, maybe even cure her. The medicine was a secret and they were unwilling to sell it to me, but my – friend – thought they might trade some for something of equal worth: some of Challenger Industries' secrets. It was small potatoes to begin with, stuff of little real value." Nick put his head in his hands. "I knew it was wrong," Malone went on quietly, his eyes on his son, "but your mother was so sick…" After a pause, he continued, "Of course, once I'd started to pass secrets to them, I was in their power. And my friend told me they had improved the formula of the medicine, but in return for it he would want more important secrets. Military secrets."

Nick stared at his father. "And you believed that?" he demanded scornfully.

"I was desperate enough to believe anything." Malone's voice was low and hopeless. "Of course, their medicine did no good in the end. Your mother died just the same. But by then, I had gone too far to turn back. I couldn't accuse the person who had led me into betraying my country without revealing my own guilt. And in any case, after Enid's death, what did anything matter?" He looked his son straight in the eye for the first time. "But I'm sorry that my weakness has led us all to this pass."

Harriet gazed at him. For the first time, Luke saw pity in her eyes. "Oh, Edward! You utter fool."

Malone spread his hands. "Guilty as charged."

"So you tried to persuade Mother to give up her expedition here," said Luke, "and when that didn't work, you sent that Mochizuki woman to kidnap her..."

"But *not* to kill her guides," said Malone. "That was her own idea." He looked at Mercedes's set, bitter face and turned away quickly. "I'm sorry."

"And then," said Luke, his anger rising, "I was the only person in the world who knew where Mother was going. You found out about the glider competition, so you sent Hagen to kill me!"

"No!" Malone's denial was vehement. "I knew nothing of that! I would never have agreed to it."

"So who did give Hagen his orders?" demanded Luke. "Who is the leader of these maniacs?"

"Good evening, Luke."

The well-bred drawl was all Luke needed to identify the speaker. He turned, knowing exactly who was behind him.

The lean, hook-nosed figure lounging against the doorway, regarding the scene with sleepy, amused eyes was his godfather, Lord John Roxton.

23 REVELATION

Roxton picked up the bundle of dynamite from the table where Malone had left it, and tossed it casually from hand to hand. The guards in the room exchanged nervous glances.

"Demolition charges on an airship, Ned?" Roxton chuckled. "You're getting careless in your old age."

"Luke prepared it," said Malone evenly. "He was trying to blow up the mine."

"I told you he showed initiative, didn't I?" Roxton sounded delighted. "You should have let him get on with it. It would have saved us a job." He winked at Luke.

Luke groaned. "Bell-ringing."

His mother stared at him. "What are you talking about?"

"Bell-ringing. I should have known. The code we solved on Eduardo's dirigible – the number code, set out in Grandsire Triples. I knew that code could only be devised by someone who knew bell-ringing, but I forgot one thing. That sort of bell-ringing – change-ringing – is only done in Britain. The person who devised the code had to be British, and a bell-ringer – and he's both. I just didn't make the connection."

"Always been partial to a spot of Grandsire Triples," Roxton confirmed jovially.

Nick swore. "And the diamonds!" He glared at Roxton. "I told Luke and Mercedes you'd discovered them and were planning to come back and get them before the war came along. And then we saw them being mined and I thought someone else had discovered them. It never even occurred to me that the most obvious person to be digging for them, was you!" Roxton gave him an ironic bow.

Luke felt as though his mind was unraveling. These were the enemies he'd tracked across an ocean and two continents. First Uncle Ned, and now Roxton, a man he had idolized from his earliest childhood. His father's two closest friends. And as if that wasn't enough, Roxton was a senior officer with British Intelligence. What secrets had he passed on to the Sons of Destiny over the years? Then another suspicion arose, and quickly grew to a certainty. "You were the one who got Uncle Ned involved in all this, weren't you? The one who pretended to have medicines that could cure Aunt Enid."

Roxton sang,

"If I can help somebody as I pass along,
Then my living shall not be in vain..."

Nick flung himself at Roxton. Casually, the old adventurer gave him a back-handed slap that took him, spinning, halfway across the room. Mercedes sprang between Nick and Roxton, fists clenched, her face a snarling mask. Luke and Malone stepped forward.

"As you were!" There were whips and knives in Roxton's voice. The languid aristocrat had stepped aside, giving way to the steely adventurer. Roxton put the dynamite down where he had found it, and with a return to his former nonchalant manner, continued, "Displays of temperament really won't do any good, you know." Nick sat up, rubbing his jaw, and stared at Roxton with hate-filled eyes. Mercedes crouched protectively beside him. Luke choked down his rage:

attacking Roxton would do no good at this moment. He must bide his time.

A man dressed in the uniform of an airship captain entered the room and spoke quietly to Roxton, who nodded. "Very well, bring them aboard." The man saluted and went out again.

"Your diamonds, I presume," said Harriet scathingly. "Really, John. For all your airs and graces, you're nothing but a vulgar thief."

Roxton shook his head. "Oh no, my dear. If you think I or my associates are doing this simply for the money, you're in error."

"Very well, then." Harriet's voice dripped irony. "Tell us what higher purpose caused you to betray your best friends, commit murder and subject helpless people to slavery."

Roxton's eyes glinted, but his voice remained level. "Gladly. I heard Ned's potted history of our organization..." Malone shifted uncomfortably. "It was fascinating, but incomplete. The Sons of Destiny..." He leaned back in his chair and steepled his fingers. "Where to start? Well, we're an international organization – you'll meet some of my colleagues presently. As to our objectives..."

Roxton leaned forward, casting off his air of indolence. His voice was clear and hard. "Some of us can see what's happening to the world. Everywhere you look, nothing but chaos and decay. Discipline goes by the board in the name of democracy, progress, freedom: governments tremble at the word of the Common Man. Hah! The common donkey more like! The meek really shall inherit the earth, the way things are going, and verily shall they mess it up.

"And what's the consequence? Our governments are full of old women while strong men find their hands tied. Empires, that have taken centuries of blood and sacrifice to build up, crumble. Lesser races bleat about human rights and self-government – let me tell you, I've been around natives all my life, and the ones I've met are no more capable of governing themselves than of flying through the air!"

Luke thought of all those who had helped him and his mother – he assumed Roxton's definition of "lesser races" would include people like Eduardo; Raul da Silva, Mercedes's father; Mercedes herself, and her friends, Tomasinho and Luiz, Heitor and Rosa; not to mention the Arara Indians who had welcomed his party with such generosity. He stared at his godfather as though seeing him for the first time. As he did so, he remembered details of Roxton's adventures that he had dismissed as a child – of native guides and porters beaten or shot for theft or desertion, or dying of exposure and exhaustion in pursuit of Roxton's goals. In fact, hadn't he shot Gomez, his guide on the first Challenger expedition? Allegedly it had been for treachery, but who knew the truth of that now? As a child, Luke had glossed over such shady incidents in his hero's adventures. He could do so no longer.

"There are those of us," Roxton continued in more measured tones, "among the establishment, the nobility – even the royal family – who can see where that kind of independence leads. That is why we have joined the Sons of Destiny – along with like-minded spirits in Germany, Italy, Russia and Japan – anywhere a strong leader is emerging to turn back the tide. To rid the world of parasites and degenerates. To instill discipline. To restore power to those who were born to rule."

"Like you and your chums?" scoffed Harriet. "And Herr Hitler no doubt – there's a fine specimen of Aryan manhood! Not to mention Mussolini, the self-aggrandizing son of a blacksmith and Stalin, the murderous savage whose father cobbled shoes for a living. What are their aristocratic credentials, exactly? And these are the pillars of your new world order? Hah!"

Roxton gave her an angry glance. "I always said it was a mistake to give women the vote." The corner of Luke's mouth twitched: his mother really was good at getting under an opponent's skin.

She followed up her advantage. "No doubt. And it is for these half-baked notions that you have betrayed your country..."

"I have betrayed no one!" bellowed Roxton. "Our politicians – the appeasers, the disarmers, the bleeding-heart liberals – they're the ones who have betrayed their country." With a visible effort he controlled himself. "I'll not bandy words with you, Harriet. Hitler, Mussolini, Stalin – yes, even the Emperor of Japan – each may reign in their own lands, or at least be permitted to imagine they do. But they will hold such power as we allow them for precisely as long as they are useful to us. And all the time, the real power will lie elsewhere."

"With you, I imagine?" said Harriet.

Roxton gave her an ironic bow. "And others – both here and elsewhere."

"As I said before," snapped Harriet, "a real nest of vipers."

Luke's attention was diverted from the verbal battle between his mother and his godfather by the arrival of a procession. The airship captain entered the lounge, accompanied by three other men in uniform. They were carrying a large crate, which, from the efforts they were making, was very heavy. Placing it in the center of the lounge, its bearers stood back, flexing arms and fingers freed of their heavy load. "Allow me to perform the introductions." Roxton's urbanity was fully restored. "Kapitän Vogts, commander of this vessel. Gruppenführer Hartmann of the new SS division of the German Army. Admiral Khostov of the Soviet Navy. General Okada of the Imperial Japanese Army. Our High Command." While the members of the High Command stared at the captives in mild confusion, Roxton stepped forward and threw open the lid of the chest. It was filled to the brim with diamonds. Even in their uncut state, the brilliant gems gleamed and sparkled in the electric light of the room.

"Pretty little things, aren't they?" said Roxton softly. "And useful. No, my dear Harriet," he went on, "I am not a vulgar thief. These diamonds will be used to finance the rearmament of our allies: Germany, Japan, Italy, Soviet Russia. Within two years, with the wealth you see before you, the world will be at war – a war for which the West is pathetically unprepared. The Eastern powers will triumph, a new world order will arise, and the Sons of Destiny will take our rightful place as its leaders."

Kapitän Vogts saluted. "My Lord – may I remind you that the demolition charges have been set, and the fuses fired. The mine will be destroyed in…" He glanced at his watch. "Ten minutes and fifteen seconds precisely."

"Very well, Captain." Roxton waved acknowledgement. "You may unmoor the ship and take us out of here… Luke, a word."

Wondering, Luke stood up. His mother reached out to him. He shook his head imperceptibly and she withdrew her hand. In the wake of the airship Kapitän and the members of the High Command, Luke followed his godfather out of the room.

"Luke." Roxton hesitated. "You have a head on your shoulders. I see a great deal of your grandfather in you. You're not a milksop – you couldn't have made it here if you were, especially with that ragtag and bobtail crew in tow." Luke thought about the sacrifices Mercedes and her friends had made, but held his tongue. "You can't believe what our government is doing is right," Roxton went on, almost pleading. "Kowtowing to the Irish, the miners and any other bunch of lower-class hooligans who think they can use threats and blackmail to get what they want. Allowing half-naked natives in Egypt and India to get away with murder. Surely you can see that our way is the only way?" Roxton's expression was half mocking, half fearful. "Well, Luke? I'm offering you the chance to join us. To become a part of all this. Think of it! A new world – purified, reborn, remade. What do you say? Will you join us?"

Luke regarded his godfather steadily. "Uncle John," he said at last, "not so long as I live and breathe."

Roxton sagged. "Very well," he said quietly. "So be it." He drew a pistol from his pocket and pointed it at

Luke. "Then I'm afraid you must share the fate of your mother and your friends."

The airship's engines were roaring into life as they reentered the lounge. Three guards remained. The cabin shuddered as the engines revved. Then they settled to a steady throb. Through the lounge's observation windows, Luke saw the ground crew release the mooring ropes and scamper for the tower. A slight movement of the floor beneath their feet indicated that the giant vessel was now tethered to the tower only by the main mooring cable in its nose.

Roxton turned to Malone and the guards. "Our guests will be leaving us shortly," he said woodenly. "They have seen and heard too much to be allowed to survive. Wait until we have passed over the edge of the plateau, then assist them to...disembark."

Malone looked from Roxton to his son, to Harriet, to Luke, and back to Roxton. Then he said, "No."

Roxton stared at him in disbelief. "What did you say?"

"I believe you heard me, John."

Roxton flushed. "That's an order!"

"I've obeyed you in the past, but that was before you threatened my son. I'm afraid I've decided not to take orders from you any more."

Roxton moved fast, but Luke was faster. As Roxton

fired his pistol, Luke knocked his arm aside. The bullet missed Malone and ruined the brocade of a tastefully upholstered chair. Malone, meanwhile, had elbowed the nearest guard in the solar plexus and snatched his gun. A burst of automatic fire from this sent Roxton and the remaining guards scurrying for cover.

"Come on!" Malone stood in the doorway, firing short bursts at any of their enemies who showed themselves. Nick grabbed Mercedes's hand and they hurried past him, heads down. Luke and his mother followed suit.

Malone stepped through the door and slammed it shut behind him so that it was locked, fast. He shoved Luke and the others into an unoccupied passenger cabin. "Wait here!" he hissed.

The ground crew came pouring along the corridor, heading for their stations. Malone grabbed one, thrust the gun into his arms and pointed to the doorway of the passenger lounge, whose trapped occupants were now hammering and yelling on the other side with gusto. "Let no one through that door," he rasped. "The prisoners have broken free. They are armed. I'm going to tell the captain."

The man nodded nervously – from the amount of noise it seemed the prisoners had not only broken free but were in an ugly mood – and raised his gun to cover the door. Behind his back, Malone beckoned, and Luke and the others slipped out of the cabin to join him. They raced along the corridor toward the airship's nose. A burst of firing from behind spurred them on.

The embarkation ramp had been drawn up by the time they reached it. Cursing, Malone operated the winch that wound it down. He gave a cry of relief when he saw that the airship had not yet slipped its mooring. "Nick," he panted as he worked. "I'm sorry. I never wanted any of this. I thought I was acting for the best, for your mother's sake. Forgive me."

The ramp landed with a thud on the platform at the top of the tower. Nick looked his father straight in the eye for a frozen moment. Then he nodded, once. "I'll try, Da."

"That'll have to be good enough for now." Malone gave his son a swift embrace. Then he pushed him roughly onto the ramp. "Go, all of you."

Nick and Mercedes hurried down the ramp. Luke followed – but turned when he realized that his mother was no longer with him.

She was arguing with Malone at the top of the ramp. "What do you mean, you're staying?"

"Harriet, there's no time to argue! I have to finish this. I can't let them get away with those diamonds..."

A shot rang out. Malone let out a gasp and grabbed at his waist. Harriet Challenger screamed and threw her arms around him as he fell. Nick shouted, "Da!"

At the same moment, the line tethering the airship to the mast was released. The ramp tipped, flinging Luke off. He snatched at the handrail of the landing platform as he fell, and with an arm-wrenching shock, held on.

The airship lifted slowly away from the tower. Helped by Nick and Mercedes, Luke hauled himself onto the platform and gazed at the departing Zeppelin in utter dismay.

On board that ship were the diamonds that could bring about the bloodiest war the world had ever seen. So were the enemies that planned to start that war.

So was his mother.

24 DUEL

The loose end of a mooring rope sailed past the platform. Without hesitation, Luke launched himself at it.

"Luke!" Nick and Mercedes threw themselves toward Luke, but too late. Their fingers clutched empty air.

Luke grabbed at the rope. The thick hemp line slipped through his fingers, and he slid down it. But then the rope divided into separate strands, arranged so that several of the ground crew could haul on it at the same time. Luke's clutching fingers caught at these with the strength of desperation and he wrapped his legs around the rope. He stopped sliding and started to climb.

Nick watched all this in anguish. "What can we do?"

"Nothing," said Mercedes briskly. "Not unless we can find a way to fly."

Nick fought to bring his reeling mind to order. "Guns!" he said. "Rifles – if the guards have left some, we can shoot holes in that thing. If we can do enough damage, they'll have to land for repairs."

Mercedes's eyes gleamed. "The guards the allosaurus killed must have had guns. Maybe the others didn't have time to find them all. Come on!" She led the way, clattering down the rickety wooden stairs.

Several hundred feet above, Luke's life was suddenly getting easier. The rope he was climbing was moving. The depleted crew must have started to winch it in. All he had to do was hold on. Luke stopped climbing to conserve his strength.

The crewman who was detailed to retrieve the rope was astonished to see it come through the hatch with a passenger. His astonishment was brief: Luke swung his legs up to give the crewman a kick on the jaw that ended his interest in the matter.

Luke headed along a walkway, with the hydrogen-filled gas cells swaying and whispering above him, in search of his mother.

Harriet Challenger cradled Edward Malone in her arms and stared into the eyes of Lord John Roxton. "Well, John?" she said. "You've about done for Ned. What are you waiting for? Hadn't you better finish me, too?"

Roxton leveled his gun until she was looking straight down the muzzle. Then he lowered it. "I don't kill for fun, Harriet. Do what you can for him." He turned on his heel and walked away.

Harriet watched him for a moment. Then she tore the sleeves from her shirt and rolled them into an improvised pad to hold against Edward Malone's wound.

"Harriet." Malone's voice was pain-filled, his face the color of ash. "Help me to the control room. I have to stop them."

"You're going nowhere. You're hurt..."

Malone shook his head. "I'm afraid it's a bit late for devoted nursing. Luke and Nick are safe. It's up to us now. This ship must never leave the plateau."

Had Malone known it, Luke was far from safe. He had found his way back to the passenger lounge and was gazing at the crate of diamonds.

Could he dump it overboard, through one of the observation windows? It had taken four men to bring it in here, there was no way he could lift it himself. He could carry handfuls of diamonds and throw them out like incredibly expensive confetti – but that would take time he was sure he didn't have. Reluctantly, he gave up the idea. He had to find his mother. But this was a big ship, she could be anywhere...

"I must say, Luke, you do turn up in the most unexpected places."

Lord John Roxton had entered the room.

"Here's one!" Nick shoved aside the body of a guard who had fallen to lie across his rifle. He snatched up the weapon and examined it. There was an ammunition clip in the magazine. He scrabbled at the pouch on the guard's belt in search of more.

"I've found another!" Mercedes scrambled from the remains of the ruined watchtower triumphantly brandishing a rifle.

Nick eyed it dubiously. "Have you ever fired one of these things?"

With professional coolness, Mercedes worked the bolt of her rifle to slide a round into the firing chamber. "Yes."

"All right, then." Nick straightened holding several clips of ammunition, half of which he handed to Mercedes. He stared after the departing airship. "There's the target. Blaze away!"

In the control gondola beneath the Zeppelin's keel, Kapitän Vogts raised an eyebrow at the muffled hiss of a bullet tearing through the gas cell above his head. He gave an angry exclamation as another bullet tore a hole in the wall behind him. "Hold your course," he ordered the helmsman in German.

His First Officer gave him a sidelong glance. "Evasive action, sir?"

Vogts shook his head. "No need. We'll be out of range in a minute." The Kapitän had been an airship commander in the Great War. He knew how much damage could be inflicted by fire from ground troops. He also knew that such fire was only effective if concentrated and prolonged. His ship could take far more punishment than one or two rifles could inflict.

Then, from the corridor above the gondola, rose a shout of, "*Feuer! Es brennt hier oben!*"

Fire was the greatest enemy of an airship captain. Snapping an order to the helmsman to hold his course, Vogts followed his first officer, navigator and radio operator up the stairs and into the airship's hull.

Vogts gazed around wildly. *"Wo ist das Feuer?"*

"Here it is!" Harriet Challenger stepped out of hiding with a fire extinguisher, which she sprayed into the faces of the officers. They staggered back, clawing at their eyes. At the same moment, Edward Malone dropped through the hatchway from which they had just emerged and closed it behind him.

Having emptied the extinguisher, Harriet turned and ran. The cursing officers wiped foam from their bloodshot eyes and turned to the hatch. Half blinded, they scrabbled at the opening mechanism.

To no avail. Malone had jammed the handle on the underside with a length of aluminum tubing. Another length of tubing, swung with all his fading strength, put paid to the startled helmsman, and Malone had control of the airship. With one hand pressing the pad to his wound, he spun the wheel with the other. Jerkily, ponderously, the airship came around.

Nick stared at the Zeppelin in disbelief. "It's turning back! Why's it doing that?"

Mercedes was already taking aim. "Who cares? Fire!"

* * *

In the passenger lounge, the sudden turn threw Roxton off balance. He lost his grip on the pistol, which bounced onto a chair seat and flew out through an open observation window.

Luke, who had fallen onto a sofa, picked himself up and advanced on his godfather. Roxton unhurriedly regained his feet, smiling. With the same lack of urgency, he crossed to the wall of display weapons and selected a pair of Schläger dueling swords. He examined one carefully and tossed it, hilt-first, to Luke.

"I hear you're pretty nifty with these things," he said cheerfully, shrugging off his jacket. "Let's see how good you are." He swept his blade up in salute and took up a dueling stance, sword extended, right foot forward, left leg braced, left hand on his waist. "*En garde.*"

Luke wondered whether the reckless courage he had admired in his godfather had really always been no more than empty bravado. "You're crazy."

Roxton sighed. "I've lost my gun, you see, and you've caused quite enough damage already. So the only question now is, how would you prefer to die? Talking? Or fighting?"

Luke glared at his opponent, but returned the salute. For a moment, they held their poses in a tableau. Then Roxton lunged. Luke parried in tierce, dropping his hand and flicking his sword to the right. Blades clashed and the duel began.

In the control gondola, Malone aimed the nose of the airship directly at the mine pit and throttled back the engines. The Zeppelin slid majestically forward. The rattling of the blocked hatchway redoubled and Malone could hear raised voices beyond it, a veritable babel of German, Italian, Russian and Japanese as the High Command arrived, demanding to know why the ship had turned and what was going on.

Malone's vision was fading as blood poured from his wound. He shook his head to clear it. He glanced at the clock set into the instrument panel to his left. Vogts had given ten minutes as the time the mine was due to explode. More than nine minutes had elapsed since then. The time was nearly up.

Harriet burst into the passenger lounge to find Roxton and her son dueling hammer and tongs. Lunge, parry, thrust: stamp, riposte, lunge again. The blades flashed, hissing through the air. They were quite evenly matched: Roxton was wily, but old. Luke was inexperienced, but possessed lightning reflexes and the vigor of youth.

Tables and chairs lay overturned around the combatants as they circled the chest of diamonds. Luke was bleeding at the cheek, where a cut from Roxton's sword point had sliced his flesh. A spreading stain on Roxton's shirt indicated where a slash from Luke's blade had hit home.

Harriet was beside herself. "Stop that! Stop it at once!" Finding herself ignored, she cast around for some means of separating the combatants. Spotting the bundle of dynamite, discarded and forgotten in the speed of events since Malone's defection, she picked it up and groped in her pockets for matches.

It was the hiss of the fuse as Harriet lit it that broke the concentration of the duelists. They stepped back from each other and turned to stare at Harriet, who held the dynamite aloft like the Statue of Liberty.

"Now," she said triumphantly, "will you be sensible?"

"Mother..." Luke dropped his sword and held his hands out in a pacifying gesture. "Mother...*put that down.*"

Malone leaned against the wheel and cut the engines. There was silence apart from the rip of bullets, as Nick and Mercedes kept up their fire, and the frantic hammering of the airship officers on the other side of the sealed hatch. The gondola was directly over the mineshaft.

The last of Malone's strength ebbed. His vision blurred again and there before him, just outside the control room window, was a figure – a woman, clothed in white, glowing, ethereal – his wife, Nick's mother. She was not as he remembered her during her last illness – pinched, drawn and old – instead she was young again, happy, vibrant. Smiling, she reached out to him.

With his last breath, Malone whispered, "Enid…"

The mine exploded.

A superheated column of gas, flame and smoke erupted from the pit that Luke had so aptly named "Hell-mouth." It drove directly at the gondola, smashing it to pieces in an instant. The officers and the High Command, still trying vainly to break through the hatch, perished on the spot. The force of the blast flung the Zeppelin high in the air, and broke its back. Canvas flapped and girders swung uselessly from the ruined fore-section. In the corridors, screaming crewmen beat at the flames that licked their clothing.

But the force of blast had been upward and, by some miracle, the ship's gas cells had not ignited. At the mercy of the wind, the crippled Zeppelin began to drift toward the center of the plateau.

* * *

The explosion had thrown Nick and Mercedes to the ground. They staggered to their feet and saw the airship hanging above them like a broken toy.

"Where are they going now...?" Nick broke off as Mercedes signaled that she couldn't hear him. He could barely hear himself: the noise of the explosion had left them both temporarily deaf.

Nick had no idea what was happening on the ship, but he was sure that, if there were any survivors from the wreck – who might yet include Luke, Harriet and his da – they would need help. He gestured to Mercedes. "This way!"

The passenger lounge was not in the direct path of the mine explosion, but the lurch as it struck the ship threw the occupants off their feet. Harriet lost her grip on the dynamite: it flew from her hand and landed in the open chest, nestling among the diamonds. The lid of the chest overbalanced and closed with a slam.

"No!" Roxton leaped forward, pawing at the clasp. The only effect this had was to snap it shut. Cursing, Roxton fumbled with the lid.

Luke did not wait to see the outcome. Grabbing his mother by the hand, he dragged her from the room and set off at full pelt down the corridor.

Roxton succeeded in undoing the clasp and opening the chest, just in time to see the fuse wink out as it reached the blasting cap. His eyes widened.

The dynamite exploded. Diamonds shot in all directions, a deadly fountain of glittering shrapnel. The blast drove a gem the size of a child's fist from the pile with unstoppable force. It smashed through Roxton's ribcage, aimed directly at his heart. The shock wave from the explosion flung the old adventurer's torn and twisted body into the blood-red banner. Its snake-and-spear emblem folded over Roxton's body like a shroud.

The explosion was the Zeppelin's death blow. The blast ignited the gas cell above the passenger lounge. Flaming gas roared, turning the mid-section of the airship into an inferno. Within moments, the gas cells on each side went up. Above the darkened plateau, a new sun appeared in the sky.

Luke and Harriet came to the point where the airship's keel was broken. Gaping holes stretched to either side. At their feet, the corridor sloped down at an angle so steep it was almost vertical.

Luke grabbed his mother's wrist. Harriet was appalled. "We can't go down there!"

Another gas cell exploded behind them. "Well, we can't go back," yelled Luke. "Jump!"

They slid down the floor of the corridor. Ahead of

them was the jagged hole where the control gondola had been. Luke tried frantically to grab at girders and handrail supports as they flew past; his heels drummed in a desperate attempt to backpedal. But it was useless. He and Harriet flew out of the gaping wound in the airship's belly, tumbled through the air...and a split second later, plunged into water with a tremendous splash. The airship had drifted over the lake.

Luke kicked for the surface and trod water. His mother's head emerged, gasping, a few feet away. Both watched as the Zeppelin touched down in the lake and began to sink, the water hissing as it quenched the flames.

Luke turned for the shore. "Come on," he gasped, "swim for it. Quick!"

"Don't panic," snapped his mother. "We're both good swimmers. We won't drown."

"Maybe not," Luke shot back. "But there's a liopleurodon somewhere in here and I don't want to meet it!"

25 FAREWELL

July 1933

Harriet Challenger sat on a hill overlooking the Lost World with a sketchbook on her knee, a tray of pastels beside her and a pencil in her hand. Luke's mother had the happy knack of living in the present. Terrible things had happened, but she had thrust them to the back of her mind. Just at the moment, she was entirely focused on her work and gloriously happy.

Before her, the central lake of the plateau glimmered in the morning sun. A family of triceratops lapped at the sparkling water. Far out in the lake, a plesiosaur's long neck reared, wavered for a moment, and disappeared with barely a ripple. In the shallows to her left, the skeletal remains of the Zeppelin stood gaunt and incongruous, a modern fossil thrown back upon the antediluvian past.

Other than herself and Luke, there had been no survivors of the wreck. Only two of the crewmen had made it to the lakeshore alive. Despite everything Harriet had tried to do for them, both had died before morning. Luke and Nick had searched the remains of the airship for any trace of Malone and Roxton, but the conflagration had been so great that their search had produced only fragments of bone, charred and unidentifiable. The conclusion was inescapable: every human being aboard the airship had been consumed by the fire that had destroyed it.

On the plains beyond the lake, herds of diplodocus and stegosaurus roamed. The forest of the allosaurus was quiet. Since the captive iguanodons had been released, the giant predator had contented itself with stalking its traditional prey, and had not ventured anywhere near the mine compound. Pterosaurs still flew over the scene of the Sons of Destiny's labors, but the fallout from the mine explosion had seemingly put them off reclaiming their lost territory and they had apparently established a new rookery elsewhere. Oddly (in Harriet's view) Luke and his friends had not been interested in discovering its location.

She completed the outline of a grazing stegosaurus and began to fill it in with pastel, different shades of green for the body, yellow, red and vivid orange for the double row of plates along its back.

The sound of approaching footsteps was not enough to break her concentration. Luke stood gazing at his mother's artistic efforts for a moment, then sat down beside her. He said, "The Indians are going to return to their village, over by the caves." His mother nodded absently, and Luke continued, "They're salvaging whatever they can use from here, so it will probably take some time, but they're determined to go."

His mother laid down her pastels with a sigh. "I've seen you and Nick down by that wreck..." She waved vaguely toward the remains of the airship. "You should be more careful," she went on severely. "Those dugout canoes the Indians lent you don't look very safe, and that liopleurodon will still be around."

"Don't worry," Luke told her. "It's shallow over there, and anyway, Mercedes keeps a good lookout. We're just salvaging a few bits and pieces for a little project Nick and I have in mind."

"How is Nick?"

"Coping. I suppose he'd already lost his father once.

Maybe it's a little easier the second time."

His mother nodded. "Mercedes is good for him. A fine girl. A good head on her shoulders."

"And a good seat," added Luke before he could stop himself.

His mother gave him a startled look. "I beg your pardon?"

"On a dinosaur, I mean." Luke hurriedly changed the subject. "The Arara men will be leaving soon, too. They're planning to go down the way we came up, and make for the place where we left the canoes. Our guides should still be there. Some of them will go with the canoes, or wait for their people to send more canoes upriver. They say we can go with them if we want to."

Harriet thought longingly of the collection she would have to leave behind. "Do we want to go?" she said wistfully. "It's so lovely here, now that all those horrible men have gone."

"Rosa and Heitor have decided to stay," Luke told her.

"Have they?"

"There's nothing for them in Manaus. They can help the plateau Indians rebuild their village and show them how to use some of the gear the Sons of Destiny left behind at the mine. There's a pretty well-stocked dispensary, for one thing, and Rosa knows how to use it. She worked in a hospital for a while."

"It seems a shame they have to use anything John and his cronies left behind."

"I don't think we should get too sentimental over the life they had before the Sons of Destiny came," said Luke. "It wasn't much of a picnic, from Grandpa's account." He took his grandfather's notebook from his pocket and ran a finger over the battered cover. This little book had brought him here, into an adventure the old man could never have guessed at. Maybe, Luke thought, he should write a journal of their adventures when he got home. He smiled inwardly at the idea and slipped the notebook away. "Anyway," he concluded, "the outside world is bound to find the Indians sooner or later. Better that they should be ready."

"I suppose so." His mother gazed over the plateau with troubled eyes.

"We have to go," Luke told her gently. "Father will be frantic by now, I dare say. He does care about you, you know." He thought it better not to mention the other compelling reason for getting back to England as quickly as possible: his father and the British government would need to know what he had discovered. And though the Sons of Destiny had been thwarted, he very much doubted they were finished. They would rise again and when they did, the world would be prepared – and so would he.

"Yes, yes, you've made your point." Harriet Challenger ran her long fingers through her hair. "But what are we to do? Go with the Arara? Or wait for Andrew to send help?"

"Well now," said Luke casually, "Nick and I have been thinking about that..."

A few days later, two strange-looking devices shot over the edge of the plateau and soared above the forest. They banked to fly along the towering cliffs scattering pterosaurs, which wheeled away from them with shrill cries of alarm. They rose in the updraft where the wind met the cliff, and the thermals rising from the baking rocks.

The gliders looked – and were – distinctly homemade. They consisted of bamboo and aluminum spars looted from the downed airship, lashed together with twine woven by the plateau Indians. Their sails were formed from the wing membranes of the pterosaurs that Luke and his friends had shot down. Each carried one pilot – Luke and Nick – and one passenger – Harriet and Mercedes.

Harriet was in raptures. "Oh, this is wonderful. I can

see everything from up here! Look at that anklyosaurus…"

"Will you stop wiggling, Mother? How can you expect me to fly if you keep thrashing around like a demented eel…?"

Mercedes stared fixedly at the solid ground, so far below them. "You did say you've done this before?"

"Ah, it's been a while now," Nick replied cheerfully. "But it's like riding a bicycle, they say: you never forget how… Here we go!" He followed Luke into a shallow dive, gaining speed. "Wheeeeeeeeeeeeee!"

"Aiiiiiiiiiiiiieeeeeeeeeeeeeee!"

They flew over the Indian village, where huts were already being rethatched and put back in order. The tiny figures of Rosa and Heitor waved, and Harriet (the only one of the four with her hands free and her eyes open) waved back. They flew over the edge of the plateau and the strangler fig, with its new rope bridge across from the cave, where the Arara had already gathered in preparation for their long walk home. They flew over the upper reaches of the river and the Brazilian army unit that had been sent by the reluctant British government as a result of Andrew Challenger's frantic demands. The perspiring soldiers, looking up to see a gigantic flying reptile with the wingspan of an airplane, swore and crossed themselves.

Then, leaving the Lost World far behind, with the sun high above and the breeze in their faces, they flew along the great river as it wound its way through the shimmering emerald forest on its long journey to the sea.

ABOUT THE AUTHORS

STEVE BARLOW was born in Cheshire in northwest England, and worked at various times as a teacher, actor, stage manager and puppeteer. Steve now lives in Somerset, in southwest England. He likes walking, sailing, reading, listening to music and shouting at politicians on the television.

STEVE SKIDMORE was born in Birstall, England, and trained as a teacher of Drama, English and Film Studies, before teaming up with Steve Barlow to become a full-time author. He lives in Leicester, England, and is a great rugby fan.

The two Steves have had over one hundred and twenty books published. Their website is www.the2steves.net.

Look for Luke Challenger's next
death-defying adventure

RETURN TO
20,000
LEAGUES
UNDER THE SEA

Luke learns that Captain Nemo's renowned
submarine, the *Nautilus*, is lying wrecked at the
bottom of the Indian Ocean. The submarine's engine
holds the key to atomic power – a secret the Sons of
Destiny are desperate to get their hands on. Can Luke
brave the terrifying creatures of the deep to save the
world from his evil adversaries' devious plans?

RETURN TO
20,000
LEAGUES
UNDER THE SEA

A LUKE CHALLENGER ADVENTURE

STEVE BARLOW + STEVE SKIDMORE

And join Luke Challenge for a
third, unforgettable quest

RETURN TO
KING SOLOMON'S
MINES

Luke's been expelled from school and sent to Africa
to keep him out of trouble - but trouble has a habit of
following Luke wherever he goes. Now the terrifying
Sons of Destiny are there, searching for a spear of
invincible power, hidden in the fabled King Solomon's
Mines. And if Luke doesn't stop them, world
domination will be theirs...

RETURN TO
KING SOLOMON'S MINES

A LUKE CHALLENGER ADVENTURE

STEVE BARLOW + STEVE SKIDMORE